the secret
between us

BOOKS BY KATE HEWITT

STANDALONE NOVELS
A Mother's Goodbye
The Secrets We Keep
Not My Daughter
No Time to Say Goodbye
A Hope for Emily
Into the Darkest Day
When You Were Mine
The Girl from Berlin
The Edelweiss Sisters
Beyond the Olive Grove
My Daughter's Mistake
The Child I Never Had
The Angel of Vienna
When We Were Innocent
That Night at the Beach
The Mother's Secret
In the Blink of an Eye
All I Ever Wanted

FAR HORIZONS TRILOGY
The Heart Goes On
Her Rebel Heart
This Fragile Heart

AMHERST ISLAND SERIES

The Orphan's Island
Dreams of the Island
Return to the Island
The Island We Left Behind
An Island Far from Home
The Last Orphan

THE GOSWELL QUARTET

The Wife's Promise
The Daughter's Garden
The Bride's Sister
The Widow's Secret

THE INN ON BLUEBELL LANE SERIES

The Inn on Bluebell Lane
Christmas at the Inn on Bluebell Lane

THE EMERALD SISTERS SERIES

The Girl on the Boat
The Girl with a Secret
The Girl Who Risked It All
The Girl Who Never Gave Up

The Other Mother
And Then He Fell
Rainy Day Sisters
Now and Then Friends
A Mother like Mine

the secret between us

KATE HEWITT

bookouture

Published by Bookouture in 2025

An imprint of Storyfire Ltd.
Carmelite House
50 Victoria Embankment
London EC4Y 0DZ

www.bookouture.com

The authorised representative in the EEA is Hachette Ireland
8 Castlecourt Centre
Dublin 15 D15 XTP3
Ireland
(email: info@hbgi.ie)

Copyright © Kate Hewitt, 2025

Kate Hewitt has asserted her right to be identified as the author of this work.

All rights reserved. No part of this publication may be reproduced, stored in any retrieval system, or transmitted, in any form or by any means, electronic, mechanical, photocopying, recording or otherwise, without the prior written permission of the publishers.

ISBN: 978-1-83525-402-8
eBook ISBN: 978-1-83525-401-1

This book is a work of fiction. Names, characters, businesses, organizations, places and events other than those clearly in the public domain, are either the product of the author's imagination or are used fictitiously. Any resemblance to actual persons, living or dead, events or locales is entirely coincidental.

*To the lovely moms at The Geneva School.
Thank you for making my years in New York City so wonderful!
In particular, thanks to Rebekah, Amy, Tiffany, Mary, Bethany,
and Nnenna, who welcomed me so wonderfully.*

PROLOGUE

I stand at the door, gazing through the little pane of glass at the person lying in the hospital bed, so still, so seemingly lifeless, their chest barely rising with each breath. Grief and anxiety claw at my own chest, because even after everything that has happened, I am stunned that we arrived at this place. That someone got so seriously hurt... again.

And I am forced to wonder, *was it my fault?* Could I have done things differently? Each choice I made seemed small, sometimes thoughtless. I never imagined there would be consequences like these. And now someone's life hangs in the balance, and I can't help but wonder if I could have done anything differently so we never would have reached this point.

But it's too late for second thoughts. Too pointless to have regrets.

The woman sitting by the bed with her head bowed lifts her head and then turns to stare straight at me. For a second, we simply look at each other, acknowledging all that has happened. All the grief and sorrow and anger and hurt.

She holds my gaze for a second longer, and then, taking a deep breath, I open the door.

ONE
ELISE

Five months earlier

"Have you seen the new girl?"

Claire's voice holds a hint of malice-laced laughter as she nods toward the woman standing across Central Park's Sheep Meadow, where The Garden School is having its annual preschool picnic.

I don't look up from the picnic basket I am carefully unpacking—organic hummus, cut-up carrot sticks and julienned red peppers, lusciously ripe strawberries still on the stem. I know who she's talking about, of course. There's only one "new girl", and it's not Kyra Tierney, who tomorrow will be joining Class Three. It's her mother.

"I mean," Claire continues, dropping her voice, although it still carries, "*what* is she wearing?"

I take out a container of wholegrain couscous and sundried tomato salad before reluctantly lifting my gaze to the woman in question. Harriet Tierney, mom to Kyra, new to the school as well as to New York City. I know because I learned her details when I packed her welcome bag last week—a TGS water bottle, pen, planner, insulated lunch bag and T-shirt. Our school does a brisk trade in branded merch. The school secretary, Marla, gave me the lowdown.

"They just moved from Texas, I think," Marla had said, conspiratorially. "Single mom, or so it *seems*, but the dad's listed on the form."

I had glanced at said form as she said this—Harriet Tierney and Allan Downs, listed at the same address in Astoria, Queens. Marla's eyebrows were raised speculatively as she waited for me to weigh in.

"Hmm," was all I said, because unlike Claire and a lot of the other mothers at The Garden School, I am not one to gossip. If you don't dish the dirt on someone else, you can at least hope they might return the favor.

Now I narrow my eyes as I catch sight of Harriet—because already I know it has to be Harriet—standing across the picnic blanket-scattered meadow. Most of the mothers present are wearing the accepted mom uniform of expensive separates in neutral shades—tunic tops and capris, linen maxi skirts with peasant blouses or tailored tanks, the occasional boho dress. I'm wearing a Cara Cara shirt dress in cream eyelet, understated and feminine, expensive without being ridiculously so. I've already had several compliments on it, to which I murmured my thanks.

Harriet, however, is not wearing our unofficial uniform. Everything about her, from her dyed-red hair in two messy Princess Leia-like bunches on top of her head to the baggy bright purple overalls in wrinkled linen she is wearing over a cropped tank top that shows several inches of pale waist, is different and, frankly, out of place in this crowd.

Admittedly, on paper, The Garden School *should* attract parents like Harriet. Only thirty years old, run out of a brownstone in Gramercy Park that was bequeathed by its eccentric female founder, it's a school that espouses "progressive, child-centered learning" and offers a pedagogical buffet of Montessori, Waldorf and Charlotte Mason, with a splash of gentle parenting thrown in. Basically, whatever moneyed Manhattan parents decide is currently *de rigueur*, not to be too cynical about it.

You would think, with that kind of educational philosophy, we'd have our fair share of hippies, or at least hippie *wannabes*, Manhattan style. It would be understandable to assume that the average TGS parent is open-minded and maybe even a little rebellious, willing to break the mold, or at least just crack it.

But that assumption would be wrong.

The truth is, The Garden School really has only one kind of parent—those who applied to the city's elite and hyper-competitive private schools and whose children didn't get in. For them, TGS is the unwelcome backup, whose philosophy they disdain yet pretend to endorse, because when it's your only option for your child, what else can you do?

Admittedly, there are a *handful* of true believers, usually the parents whose kids are a little quirky or fragile, and who feel like a "gentler" school will be the answer to their child's issues.

I'm neither of these kinds of parents. I'm too pragmatic to pin all my hopes on a school as a way to change my child, and I have no intention of sending my sons to one of the elite schools that turn boys into pompous Wall Street windbags—not until ninth grade, anyway. It's a compromise my husband Michael and I have reached; TGS till seventh grade, and then to his alma mater, a sporty boarding school in Connecticut.

"Well?" Claire asks, impatient for me to dish some dirt, although she should know me better than that. I never trash-talk anyone.

"She's got a fun, funky style," I say diplomatically, without any innuendo or snark. "I like it."

Claire lets out a huff of disbelief. "She looks like a bag lady. How old do you think she is? Forty?"

I glance at Harriet again, standing on the edge of the meadow, her chin tilted upward and her arms folded as she watches everyone with a slight smirk on her face, like she thinks we're all ridiculous. And maybe we are, at least a little bit. I'm self-aware enough to realize there's more than a whiff of pretentiousness about this whole scene. Amanda Jenkins, whose daughter is in Class Six, has a *cashmere* picnic blanket spread across the trash-strewn grass. This is Central Park, after all, and you can't cross a stretch of lawn without encountering at least one broken bottle. I had to keep Lewis from kicking a crumpled beer can across the meadow as soon as we arrived.

"Thirty-five, maybe," I tell Claire, although it's hard to gauge Harriet Tierney's age from a hundred yards away. Her fashion style is certainly on the younger side, and it holds its own unique appeal. I wouldn't call her pretty, necessarily, but something about her is attractive, appealing. The thought makes my stomach swoop with nerves. "Who knows?" I ask Claire, my tone implying *who cares*? I don't want to make an enemy of the woman simply because she wears purple overalls.

But as I watch her, I'm not sure I want to be her friend, either, based on the way she's surveying the scene with such narrowed eyes, like she's above us all. She has a tattoo, I notice, that runs along her bare shoulders and down her arms. It looks like some kind of vine, twining across her shoulder blades.

"I heard she's an *artist*," Claire says, the same way you might say *sex worker*. Of all my friends at TGS—and I use that term loosely—Claire is by far the prissiest.

I give a soft laugh. "Well, she sounds interesting to me." Not really, if I'm honest, but I'm trying to be nice.

"Oh come on, Elise." Claire sounds a little annoyed now. "I know you're too perfect to say anything really mean, but *look* at her. She's trying so hard to be cool, it's actually offensive."

As I glance again at Harriet Tierney, I silently acknowledge that Claire might have a point. There is something about her, even from all the way across the meadow, that feels brash and in your face, like she's thumbing her nose or even sticking up her middle finger to all of us. There's a tension to her, maybe even an anger, as she stands so apart, like she doesn't want to be here, which *is* annoying because she obviously chose to come.

"Where's Kyra?" I ask Claire, looking around for Harriet's daughter. I saw her from a distance back in the spring, when she came for her admissions testing. I recall a small, fine-boned little girl, with lots of dark hair and big chocolate-brown eyes. A sweetheart.

Claire shrugs, indifferent. "I don't know."

I move my gaze around the meadow, past clusters of parents spread out on picnic blankets and camp chairs, some who are sneakily passing around Chardonnay decanted into Nalgene water bottles, despite the no-alcohol policy in the park. The headmistress, Eleanor Weil, is standing nearby, dressed for work in tailored trousers and a pearl-pink blouse, a sweater thrown over her shoulders even though it's nearing ninety degrees. She's talking to the chair of the board of directors, who clearly came from work and is sweating through his shirt, his suit jacket hooked on one finger and slung across his shoulder.

Some Class Two boys are playing soccer badly nearby, and a couple of girls are attempting hopscotch, although without any chalk or markers. Other kids are careening around without a care, and a handful are sitting quietly by their parents, munching on their organic snacks. My son Lewis is running around with some of the other Class Three boys, and his twin Luke is sitting next to me on the picnic blanket, immersed in his manga. I don't see Kyra anywhere.

"Whose Kyra's buddy in Class Three?" I ask, and Claire looks at me, completely blank. She's not even on the Parent Teacher Association, so she wouldn't know these things, nor would she care. As chair of the PTA for the last two years, I should—and do. I frown, biting my lip as I think through the six other girls in Class Three. "Chloe," I finally say triumphantly, and Claire just shakes her head.

I start looking around for Chloe, but her mother Kim is an ER doctor who works insane hours, and I don't see her anywhere. She might not even be here. I glance down at Luke, and nudge him gently with my foot.

"Luke, honey, why don't you find Kyra? The new girl? I think she'd like a friend."

My son blinks slowly up at me from behind his coke-bottle glasses, saying nothing, but I know what he's thinking—that he's enjoying his comic, and he doesn't want to go find a girl. But I also know he'll do it—for me.

"Lukie," I say softly, and nudge him again.

With a sigh, he clambers up and looks around the meadow, blinking slowly.

I feel Claire's silence like a palpable thing; so often people feel the need to *comment* about Luke. How kind or sensitive or intelligent he is, which sounds like a compliment, but the subtext is always *weird*.

Luke and Lewis are fraternal twins, born at thirty-six weeks. Lewis came out bawling at a healthy five and a half pounds, while Luke emerged blue, barely breathing, and just scraping three pounds. There was no medical reason for the difference in their appearances; the OB, one of the best in the city, could only tell us with a shrug that "sometimes that's just the way it is with twins."

The result has been that Luke has myriad minor health issues, lots of doctor appointments, and is small, shy, and yes, a little quirky. Lewis, however, is the spitting image of his father—dark-haired, brawny, charming, and athletic. And fiercely protective of his twin, which is sweet, as well as a relief. I don't think I could have coped if Lewis looked down on Luke the way so many other people do, all while pretending to marvel at how *lovely* a boy he is.

Right now, I can *feel* Claire hold her tongue as Luke cautiously ventures out into the meadow to look for Kyra.

"He's so sweet," she finally bursts out, like she just couldn't keep herself from it, and I murmur something unintelligible in reply. Her son Brand is much like Lewis, although not as accomplished, and I say that without any bias or pride. I'm not particularly enthused that Lewis made the Yorkville travel flag football team at only eight years old. After all, considering all the coaching he received, it would have been worrying if he hadn't.

I watch Luke's hesitant progress across the meadow, as he diligently looks for a girl I'm pretty sure he's not interested in getting to know. I lift my eyes, still scanning the meadow for Kyra, but my gaze snags on her mother instead.

Harriet is standing in the same place, but now she's not surveying the meadow with that superior smirk on her face. She's smiling, her whole demeanor transformed into lightness, her face lit up so she looks beautiful, in an offbeat kind of way. As I watch, she throws her head back and laughs, a tendril of too-red hair falling against her cheek. The man standing next to her takes a step closer, lowering his head to murmur something into her ear. She smiles and shakes her head.

Claire hasn't caught sight of them, and so I look away quickly, as if I never saw them at all, busying myself with all the picnic items I've brought that nobody has yet touched…

Because the thing I've clocked that I don't want Claire—or anyone else—to know, is that the man chatting so intimately with the *new girl* is my husband.

TWO

HARRIET

"What did you say your name was?"

I didn't, but I say it now with a teasing smile. "Harriet," I reply as the dad, handsome in a manicured, moneyed sort of way, sticks out a self-assured hand.

"Michael Dunnett." He says his name like I should know who he is.

"Harriet Tierney," I reply, giving my name the same deliberate import, like he should know who *I* am, although of course he doesn't.

For a second, as he takes my hand, he looks confused by my tone, but then he laughs and gives it as firm a shake as I would expect, flashing a full set of straight, white teeth. He is very attractive, like a Disney prince—a full head of thick, dark hair, slightly longer than the average city businessman, big brown eyes fringed with lashes any woman would covet. He also clearly goes to the gym on a regular basis, judging from the ridges of muscles I can see beneath his white button-down shirt.

This is a guy who is completely certain of his appeal, as well as his place in the world, and that quality is equally attractive and repellent to me, which probably says more about me than him, but right now I am choosing to be amused.

"Tierney..." he remarks, rocking back on his heels, clearly going through a mental rolodex. "You must be new?"

"Yes, my daughter Kyra is joining this year. She'll be in Class Three."

He widens his gaze in an almost comical double take. "My twin sons are in Class Three," he says, like it's the biggest coincidence ever, which I find kind of funny since we are both at a picnic for a relatively small private school.

"What are the odds," I remark dryly, and again I get see faint confusion cross his face, followed by the boom of laughter.

Michael Dunnett has been chatting to me for the last five minutes, in a way that is both effortlessly charming and the tiniest bit annoying. First he pretended to be a sportscaster to the soccer game a few six-year-olds were bumbling through, and it was as funny as it was barbed, making pointed comments about some of the kids that almost made me snicker. Then he riffed about the city's public transportation, also kind of amusing, but I have a feeling that the last time this guy took the subway could be measured in years, not months.

Still, I appreciate his effort to be friendly, especially since not one person has so much as said hello since I arrived for "The Garden School's Annual Pre-School Picnic!"—exclamation point included on the school calendar. Why Allan insisted Kyra attend this overprivileged place, I really don't know; PS166 Elementary in Queens would have suited her fine. I agreed to let her come to this school because at this point I can't deny Allan, the father of my only child, anything. That's why I'm in New York City in the first place.

"So where were you before?" Michael Dunnett asks, jangling the keys in his pocket. "Public school?" he guesses before I can answer, his diffident tone suggesting that by choosing TGS, I—or perhaps Kyra—have been rescued from a fate potentially worse than death.

"We moved here from Austin," I reply. "But yes, Kyra was in a public school."

"Austin?" he repeats in surprise. "In Texas?"

No, in New Jersey, I think, but I keep myself from saying something sarcastic and just smile and nod.

"So you moved here for work?" he surmises. "Or your husband's?"

Okay, this is starting to feel nosy, as well as just a little bit presumptuous. Since when does someone I've barely met assume I have a *husband*?

"Kind of," I tell him with a slightly cool smile that I hope communicates that I don't want to talk about this anymore. "I'm an artist, so I can work anywhere, but Kyra's father lives here in the city."

The way I say "Kyra's father" makes his eyes widen, and then he tilts his head back to give me an assessing look, dark lashes lowered. He is a good-looking guy, and he knows it. "An artist, huh?" he asks, his tone a little skeptical.

I smile blandly back. "Yep."

"What kind?"

"Pottery, mainly." I keep my tone casual, without so much as a hint of pride, because I really don't want someone like Michael Dunnett thinking I think I'm a big deal. I'm not, after all. I sell stuff on Etsy, so it's not like I have my own gallery. I don't even have a pottery wheel, anymore. I'd been renting one in Austin, but I don't have the same setup here. "And some watercolors," I add.

"And Kyra's father...?" Michael asks, and now he has moved from being friendly to nosy, and on to downright rude.

"Allan. He's not here tonight." Allan was hoping to come, but he backed out at the last minute, as I knew he would. I can't feel angry about it, though, and I'm not about to explain any part of my current living arrangements to this guy. My tone has turned decidedly cool, and Michael notices.

"Sorry," Michael says, hanging his head in a deliberately abashed way that I suspect he thinks is charming, and, I have to admit, it is. "I'm being nosy," he adds, before he peeks up at me to gauge my reaction.

I smile and say nothing, and a gleam comes into his eyes that I recognize. I've officially become a *challenge*. I ignore the flicker of pleasure this gives me and focus on remaining aloof.

Michael Dunnett lifts his head, shifts back a little, widening his stance. "So what do you think of the city?" he asks, with another jangle of his keys.

"I've lived here before," I tell him, "A long time ago. But I've always appreciated the buzz."

"Where are you living now?"

"Astoria."

His eyes widen a fraction, and I feel like I might as well have said Mars.

"I've always liked Queens," he tells me, and I almost laugh. I wonder if he's ever even been to Queens, except when driving through it. "Great Greek food," he adds, and now I really do have to try not to roll my eyes.

I'm being a little mean about this guy, I know I am. Unfortunately, my default setting tends to be somewhat snarky, although I do try to temper it with humor. It's a defense mechanism, born from years of living on my own and having to fend off all kinds of people, from do-gooding moms at the playground who inform me in strident tones that *Kyra said a naughty word*, to landlords who like to be a little too handsy, to everyone in between who eyes me askance because I'm a single mom who likes to look and be a little different.

I've come across guys like Michael Dunnett—entitled while

insisting they're enlightened—plenty of times before. I waitressed at a swanky cocktail bar in Chicago for nine months and guys like him were a dime a dozen, raising their hands from their whisky shots in an *I'm innocent* gesture as they tell me how they marched for #MeToo.

Still, Michael Dunnett is a fellow parent, and I told Allan I would try—with The Garden School, with this new life in New York, with Kyra having a dad for the first time in her life. Right now, it all feels like a lot of effort, but I am going to do my best to make a life here both for me and my daughter, however I can.

"We like the area," I tell him diplomatically. "Where do you live?"

He grimaces, like he knows he's being predictable. "Upper East Side. Seventy-Second and Fifth."

One of the most expensive addresses in the entire city.

I nod, smile. "Great." There seems to be nothing more to say.

I scan the meadow for Kyra, who was quietly accepting, if not particularly enthused, about coming, as she tends to be about so many things. Her placid nature is simultaneously a blessing and a worry; when I can raise a giggle from her, or even a smile, I feel a sense of both triumph and relief.

Now I see her on the edge of the meadow by some trees, listening to a small, serious-looking boy with dark hair and glasses. They seem to be having an intense discussion, or at least he is. Kyra looks as alert but blandly expressionless as ever. Still, I'm glad she's talking to another kid. It definitely wasn't a given.

"That's my son," Michael says, tracking my gaze. "Luke. And Lewis..." He looks around, and then nods, satisfied, as he points to some boys playing Frisbee on the other side of the meadow. "That's my other one," he says with more than a touch of pride, as the tallest boy in the group, tanned and dark-haired like his father, gracefully leaps and catches the Frisbee one-handed. "Named for their grandfathers—Lewis for mine, Luke for my wife's."

I glance back at Luke, so small and thin. He looks closer to six rather than the eight years old he has to be, considering he's going into third grade. The two boys are twins but completely different, and I wonder how that dynamic plays out in the Dunnett family.

"And that's your daughter, I'm guessing?" Michael asks, pointing to Kyra.

I nod. "Yes. That's Kyra."

"She looks like a sweetheart."

I'm not sure how to take this, so I don't say anything.

Michael glances at me, looking amused. "You like to keep your counsel, it seems." It doesn't come out like a jibe, for which I am grateful.

"I've lived on my own a long time," I tell him, a concession. "Sorry. I don't mean to be rude."

He raises his eyebrows. "Single mom?" It's a guess, but there's an interest there too, an avidity that I've heard before.

I force a smile. "Sort of."

"It's complicated?" He chuckles. "Now that sounds like a story."

"It is," I agree, and he chuckles again before holding up his hands, palms facing me, in surrender. "Okay, okay. I get it. No more nosy questions." He lowers his hands, holding one out for me to shake. "Nice to meet you, Ms. Tierney."

Now I feel like a jerk, but also still the tiniest bit annoyed— as well as irritatingly attracted—by his oh-so smooth manner. I take his hand with reluctance, noting the way his fingers close with certainty over mine before he slides his hand back. "Nice to meet you," I say.

Michael nods, considering, and then takes out a business card. "Just in case," he says as he hands it to me, and I can't help but wonder, *in case of what*? But I take it, because it would be rude not to, and I'm a little curious too. I wonder what he does for a living. Investment banker? Hedge fund manager? Something like that.

He starts to turn away, only to stop as a woman walks straight toward us. There is something bizarrely arresting about her—she has a quiet confidence that is understated and elegant, and she's moving across the meadow like she's on a catwalk, but without any look-at-me showiness. For a second, I feel almost blinded by her beauty, until I blink and realize she's actually quite normal-looking—brown hair, hazel eyes, an unremarkable, even-featured face. No supermodel here, but what is compelling is her sense of containment and self-possession. She moves like a ballet dancer, and she holds herself like someone alert and completely in control.

She's expertly and subtly made-up—her natural-look makeup probably took an hour to put on, but I clock the eyeliner, the neutral lip, the expensive mascara. Her chestnut-brown hair falls in perfectly styled waves just past her shoulders, not a hair out of place. Her nails sport a discreet French manicure, and she's wearing a flowing dress in white eyelet that accentuates her tiny waist, her toned arms. How much work does it take to look so perfect? It's probably her full-time job.

I wonder if something of my cynicism shows on my face, because when she smiles at me, her eyes narrow. With a jolt, I realize this woman seems like she doesn't like me, and we haven't even spoken.

"You must be Harriet." Her voice matches everything else about her—quiet, calm, rich, sure.

"Indeed I am," I reply lightly. I have no idea how she knows my name. "And you are—?"

She holds out one manicured hand. "Elise Dunnett."

"My better half," Michael jokes, and slides an arm around his wife's waist. She leans into him briefly, her hand still extended, her unblinking gaze on me never wavering. This feels a little weird, and I'm not sure why. Is she annoyed that Michael was talking to me? He wasn't even flirting, not really. I decide to shrug it off.

"Nice to meet you," I say, and take her hand, which is small and slender and cool. "I'm Harriet Tierney."

"Yes, I know," she says, and then smiles. "Your daughter Kyra is joining Class Three. I made the welcome bag you'll receive tomorrow."

"Thank you," I reply after a startled pause. I didn't even know the school did welcome bags, and it's a little unnerving to have a stranger know stuff about me.

She laughs, a carefully calibrated, tinkling sound. "Every new family gets one, with all the TGS merch. Wear it with pride… or else."

I can't actually tell if she's being serious or not, but then she smiles ruefully, and I decide I might like her, despite her air of glossy perfection.

"Thanks for the heads-up," I say with a laughing grimace, and Elise glances at her husband, a look laden with subtext that undoubtedly comes from a long marriage. I'm not sure what that subtext is, but I feel like she wants this conversation to be over, and so I decide to end it.

"I think I might get some food," I announce, although we didn't bring any. I told Kyra that nobody packs picnics for these things, only to discover everyone had brought an array of gourmet offerings, and I promised her pizza afterward.

"Great," Elise says firmly, and it sounds like goodbye.

I walk away first, with purpose, like I'm going somewhere, although all I'm doing is wandering across the meadow, past clusters of couples and families who are all eating expensive-looking food from glass containers. No Tupperware or plastic wrap for this crowd, clearly, and definitely no pizza.

I glance at Kyra, and I see she's drifted away from Luke, and so I decide now is a good time to go.

"Hey." I speak lightly as I walk up to her and put a hand on her shoulder. "Ready to hit the road?"

She shrugs. "Sure."

"Did you have a nice time?" I ask as we leave the meadow without saying goodbye to anyone. It's my default question, even though I'm pretty sure she didn't. "Did you talk to any of the girls in your class?"

"No." She doesn't sound broken up about the fact.

Sometimes I worry about her, that she's spent too much time with me. She's not like other girls, gravitating toward giggling groups, heads bent together as they gossip about nothing much. Instead, Kyra has watched me battle bills, and a dying parent, and aggressive landlords, and sudden moves necessitated by events I can't explain to an eight-year-old. She's going into third grade, and she's already been in six different schools. I tell myself that that's not necessarily a bad thing, that Kyra has life experience most coddled kids don't get these days before they're eighteen, if then. She's resilient.

But occasionally I worry. I fear I've messed her up more than she can handle. Part of the reason for this move was to give her some stability—a good school, time to get to know her father, a few years at least in the same place, if I can manage it.

"Pizza?" I say now, all chirpy, and she smiles and nods, her brown eyes—so like Allan's—lightening to gold. I love this girl, even if I've messed her up. Have I messed her up even more by bringing her to New York, to get to know her father? It's a question I don't like to ask myself, never mind answer. We're here, and we have to make the best of it... whatever that might look like.

We start walking out of the park, and as we reach the edge, I glance back, scanning the meadow. I don't realize who I'm looking for until I see Michael Dunnett's tall, broad figure in the middle of the meadow; he's talking to another dad. Even though

I'm all the way over on the side, he catches my gaze, raises a hand in salute.

I smile back instinctively, raising my hand, only to freeze when I see Elise watching me with a narrowed gaze.

Quickly I drop my hand and turn around. I keep walking, and I don't look back again.

THREE
ELISE

Neither Michael nor I speak as we head back across the meadow toward the picnic blanket where Luke now sits, morosely munching on some red peppers. I'm not going to ask Michael why he was talking to Harriet Tierney, or what they were laughing about together. I don't really want to know, and he'd brush off such a question, as he always does when I dare to ask, which admittedly is rare. We've learned the art—and importance—of *not* talking about things. It's what makes our marriage work.

Michael saunters along, hands in his pockets, save for when he waves at various parents he knows, calling out a "hey, good to see you" in a jovial tone, almost like he's the host of the picnic, instead of just another parent. It's how he always operates—genial but in control, assured without being obnoxious about it. It's what drew me to him when we first met, at an art gallery showing in the city. I was serving hors d'oeuvres, and he was buying something expensive. I never looked back, never could, even if maybe I should have.

But everything is fine, I tell myself now. Absolutely fine, even if it doesn't feel like it... and I know that's because of me.

I take a quick, steadying breath, let it out silently, and smile at my son.

"Hey, Lukie." My voice is warm, sure. "How about some couscous salad?" I reach for the glass container and a paper plate. "It's your favorite." It isn't, but I know he won't object.

A tension is bracketing my shoulder blades, lodging itself in a knot at the base of my neck. *This is not a big deal*, I tell myself. So Michael chatted with the new mom at school. So she threw her head back and laughed and he stepped closer. So we've been here before, many times.

I will not let it be a big deal.

I fill a plate of food for Luke and then one for Lewis, even though he's still out playing Frisbee with some boys in his class. Then I fill Michael's plate and hand it to him; he's mid-chat with another dad nearby, but he gives me a quick smile of thanks as he takes the food.

I reach for my own plate and serve myself a precise tablespoon of couscous salad, two red peppers, two carrots, a teaspoon of hummus, and a single strawberry. I see Luke watching me and I smile.

"Yummy?" I ask, and he nods, even though he hasn't touched his food.

A few minutes later, Lewis comes over, throwing himself down on the blanket, nearly knocking over the salad.

"Here you go, honey," I say, and hand him his plate. He crunches into a carrot as Michael finally sits down and joins us.

"This all looks super delicious," he says warmly, his gaze lingering on mine. "Thanks, honey."

I smile and nod; I know his appreciation is genuine, and it is a needed balm. For a few seconds, I simply let myself enjoy the moment—my little family, all together in the sunshine.

Out of the corner of my eye, I catch a flash of purple. Harriet and Kyra are leaving the picnic. I see her lift her hand in a wave, and with a jolt, I realize she is waving at Michael…

and he is waving back. I stare at her for another second, until she drops her hand, and then I smile at Luke, determined to forget I saw that telling little exchange.

The boys pick at their food, leaving all their salad and most of their vegetables, before Lewis goes tearing off to join the boys and Luke reaches for his manga again. Michael strolls around, chatting with various parents, and while I know I should probably make the rounds too, right now I just want to sit and enjoy the silence and the sunshine.

It doesn't last long.

"So, what did you think of her?" Claire joins me, holding a paper cup full of what I'm pretty sure is white wine.

"Harriet?" I'm not going to pretend not to know who she is talking about. "I didn't talk to her very much."

"Michael did, though," Claire remarks coyly, and I stiffen.

"He was just making chitchat," I say with a shrug. I glance at her, smiling, my eyebrows raised. "She's just another mom, Claire. Who cares?"

"She's the only new parent in Class Three," Claire points out. "And we're losing three kids in that class already."

"I know." One boy is going to St Andrew's, one of the most competitive private boys' schools in the city; the parents made a sizeable donation to the school last year. Another boy is going to public school, and one of the girls is moving out to Connecticut.

"There will only be fourteen in the class," Claire continues. "That's pretty small."

It is, and I know that the school is concerned about numbers. Twenty in each year is the ideal, and there's not a single class right now that has that many. Progressive private education is a small world.

"It's good that Kyra's joining us, then," I say. I may be the chair of the PTA, but making sure The Garden School stays solvent is not my responsibility. I have enough to worry about as it is, and in any case, I don't think Claire cares all that much, either. It's just her way of justifying gossiping about Harriet Tierney.

My gaze drifts to Michael. He's chatting with Helene Dubois, who is stick-thin and elegant, dressed all in black. She moved here from Paris two years ago with her husband Jean-Paul, who works for the UN, and they have a daughter in Class Four.

"I think we'd better get going," I tell Claire. I raise my voice to a cheery note. "It's a school day tomorrow, after all!"

Claire's gaze has followed mine, to Michael and Helene. "How do Frenchwomen stay so skinny?" she murmurs, more in wonder than envy. Claire is pretty thin herself.

I don't bother replying as I start to pack away our picnic.

Claire watches me, finishing her wine, before she stumbles up to standing. "All right, then," she says. "I'll see you tomorrow."

"See you tomorrow," I murmur dutifully.

It's only a few blocks from the sheep meadow to our apartment on Seventy-Second and Fifth, and so we walk home as a family, the last of the afternoon sunlight turning everything golden. Lewis bounds ahead, leaping on park benches, clambering over rocks, while Luke trots next to me, silent, with Michael sauntering alongside. A couple of times, I notice he slides his phone out of his pocket to check it, but it's probably just work. He had a big surgery this morning, and he always likes to know how his patients are doing post-op.

Central Park on a mellow September evening is so very pleasant, the air drowsy and warm, the sunlight filtering through the trees onto the cobbled walkway, the rumble of traffic on Fifth Avenue comfortably muted. I try to enjoy the moment, to let myself rest in it, but the tension remains at the base of my neck, a knot I can never dislodge.

"That was fun," Michael says to no one in particular as we turn out of the park onto Seventy-Second.

"Yes, it was," I agree.

And that's all we say until we've reached our apartment, and the doorman, Raul, greets Lewis and Luke in his usual cheerful way.

"Why, hello gentlemen! So nice to see you. How was your day?"

Lewis buzzes by him with a yelped 'Fine,' but Luke stops and gazes at him seriously.

"We went to a picnic in Central Park," he tells Raul, his tone still serious. "I had strawberries."

Raul chuckles and ruffles Luke's hair. "That sounds delicious, little man."

Luke nods, looking as grave as ever. "They were."

I smile at Raul as I shepherd Luke along. Lewis is already by the elevator, jabbing the button more than he needs to, and Michael claps a hand on the doorman's shoulder before we walk back to the elevator. Sometimes, in moments like this, I feel as if I am standing outside myself, watching everyone play their parts and thinking, *what a lovely family this is.*

We're so convincing.

As I step into our apartment, I breathe a sigh of relief. This is my sanctuary, my safe space, and the one place where I feel in control. I decorated it all myself, in calming neutral tones, although Michael wanted to hire an interior decorator. The entrance hall leads seamlessly into a living room and adjoining dining room, both with picture windows overlooking Fifth Avenue, heavy damask drapes pulled back from the view of the street and the park.

Lewis squeezes past me to run to the playroom off the living room, no doubt reaching for one of the PlayStation controllers. Luke curls up in the big taupe leather armchair in the living room with his manga, while Michael disappears into his study, promising only to be there "a few secs," and I lug the picnic basket back to the kitchen.

A lot of the mothers at The Garden School have help. Some have a lot of help—housekeeper, nanny, as well as a full-time assistant whose main job seems to be scheduling playdates and doctor appointments—while others manage to get by with a part-time nanny or a couple hours of cleaning a week and are seen as both superwomen and martyrs for going without. But I don't have any help.

Michael has offered, and sometimes even insisted, that I hire someone, a cook or a cleaner or a nanny to make life "just a little easier," but the truth is I don't want anyone else in my space, watching me and remarking on my precise ways. It took nine years and five failed IVF attempts before I became pregnant with Lewis and Luke at the age of forty-one. Why would I go through all that painful effort just to fob them off on a nanny? As for cooking and cleaning... I like things to be done a certain way. I don't need some stranger sauntering around my apartment, moving photos or reorganizing my kitchen drawers just because she can, when I have everything exactly how I like it.

Besides all that, I find it calming to put things away, setting my little world to careful rights. I stack the glass containers in the fridge, carefully fold up the cloth napkins I brought that no one used. I'm just wiping out the plastic-lined picnic basket with sure, smooth strokes when Michael comes into the kitchen, a full twenty minutes after we got home.

"So, back to the grind tomorrow," he remarks conversationally as he takes a bottle of Sancerre out of the wine fridge and brandishes it toward me for my approval. "You think the boys are excited?"

I give a gracious nod of acceptance toward the wine. "I hope so." Last week, when we were heading home from our annual two weeks in Cape Cod, sandy and suntanned, Lewis groaned theatrically about having to go back to school, but I think—or at least I hope—he secretly enjoys it, and I know Luke does.

Michael takes out glasses and pours us both wine. "And are you going to be as busy as ever with the PTA?" he asks as he hands me a glass.

"You know the December gala is always a lot of work." I've been its main organizer for the last two years. It's practically a full-time job for the whole first semester, with weekly meetings, endless administration, and plenty of planning. I have a committee of five or six other mothers, but they need to be told what to do and jollied along. Without me, it simply wouldn't happen, and that's not an understatement.

Michael nods, accepting. I think he likes me being involved and important at the school, but I don't think he really takes the gala seriously, even if we usually spend about ten grand on the silent auction, bidding for things we really don't need or want—a chef's catered dinner for eight, a photo shoot, a skiing weekend in Stowe. Last year, we bid two thousand dollars on a sailing trip on the Hudson that expired before we ever thought to use it.

"Well, don't burn yourself out," he tells me, leaning in to kiss my cheek.

I breathe in the evergreen and citrus scent of his cologne—Tom Ford's Costa Azzurra, I buy him a bottle for Christmas every year—and then say, as casually as I can, "So, what is Harriet Tierney like? You guys seemed like you were having quite the laugh back at the picnic." I take a sip of wine to dilute any potential intensity or—worse—accusation in my voice, raising my eyebrows expectantly.

Michael leans back against the counter, his eyes narrowing as he takes a sip of his wine. I hold my breath, wondering if I wasn't convincing enough in my offhand remark. Then he shrugs, looking unbothered. "I made a few lame jokes that I don't think she found very funny," he says, shaking his head as he gives me a rueful smile. "Frankly, I think she was barely tolerating me."

I smile, relieved. It's exactly the kind of thing I wanted him to say, even if I'm not sure I entirely believe it. But I'm still glad he said it.

Michael puts down his glass. "Shall I get the boys in the shower?" Between dinner and bedtime, the evenings Michael is home, is always "daddy time." He took over bath duties when they were three, and now it's become something of a ritual. After he supervises their showers, he roughhouses with them in the playroom, and reads them a couple of adventure stories he loved as a kid. They adore it all, and I appreciate the break.

"Sure," I say, and turn away. "I'll finish up here."

There's nothing to finish up, but I wipe the counters for a second time as Michael heads into the hallway and I hear him whistle.

"All right, you two tigers, time for a wash!" he sings out, and then there are shrieks and squeals as he undoubtedly starts tickling them.

I smile, feeling better for the first time since I saw Michael talking to Harriet, her head thrown back in laughter. I was being paranoid, I tell myself. It's such an easy trap for me to fall into when I know all too well what signs to look for.

I reach for my wine and take a sip, just as I hear a buzz from the counter where Michael left his phone. Almost reluctantly, I turn it over so I can read the message that has flashed up on the home screen. It's from a number I don't recognize, and I can only read the first few words of the text.

Hi Michael, this is Harriet Tierney. It was so...

I stare at the message, wishing I could swipe to read the rest, but I don't know Michael's password and he doesn't know mine. Not as a matter of secrecy, but rather as a sign of our mutual trust. "We can have parts of our lives that are private," Michael has always proclaimed, "and still trust each other." Which made sense because he's a surgeon, and, of course, he deals with confidential things every day. And, in any case, I have private parts of my life, too. But right now I wish I had his password, so I could see what Harriet Tierney is texting to my husband.

Why does she even have his private number, and why is she texting him the same evening that they met, barely an hour later?

It's not a question I want to have to ask, but I already know I will do whatever it takes to find out the answer—and protect my marriage.

FOUR

HARRIET

As Kyra and I head down to Fifty-Ninth Street to take the N train across the river, I feel the tension ease from between my shoulder blades. I hadn't even realized how tense I was until I'd left the picnic. The snooty parents, the smug air of privilege, and, most of all, the weird dynamic between Michael and his wife, really put me on edge. I can't even say why they make me uneasy, but I am determined to steer clear of them as best as I can.

When we emerge from the subway in Queens, Kyra and I walk the rest of the way to Allan's apartment on Thirty-Fourth Street and Thirtieth Avenue, stopping by Mario's, the hole-in-the-wall pizza place on the corner, for Kyra to get her promised slice of pepperoni.

As I let myself into the apartment, I fight against the feeling that this is not my home, and worse, this is not my *life*. We arrived in Queens a week ago, but everything still feels unsettlingly strange, although I tell myself we just need a little more time. Before this week, neither I nor Kyra had seen Allan in seven years, not since I was passing through New York, and he agreed to meet us for lunch.

Kyra was a baby at the time, and Allan had no idea what to do with her. I'd plopped her in her highchair and given her a handful of Cheerios to eat, and he'd looked mystified by it all, fascinated but also horrified by the very presence of an infant, drooling and in diapers, so messy and loud. He didn't engage with her at all, except to ask questions as if she was some sort of scientific specimen—*does she cry very much? Can she form words?* I'd answered dutifully, a little humorously, and at one point I'd joked that maybe he'd like to hold her. Allan had drawn back, stammering something about how he wouldn't know how. When I'd told him I'd been joking, he'd looked relieved rather than offended.

And yet now we're living with him, so he can get to know the daughter he never asked for, and Kyra can get to know him. I second-guessed myself a thousand times, wondering if this was the right decision. If it would be too hard for Kyra, or if Allan's best intention would peter out after a few days. So far, the verdict is still out; while he does try with her, it's half-hearted at best, and for the last week they've interacted with each other like polite strangers.

Still, I know I need to give it time, for Allan's sake as well as our daughter's.

Allan's apartment is the upper half of a tiny duplex—it has a cramped front hall, two small bedrooms, a narrow kitchen, and a living room that looks over the street. Kyra and I share the second bedroom; it barely fits two twins and a dresser, but we're both used to sharing small spaces.

The places I've lived in over the years have never been anything close to grand or even spacious, but they've been *mine*. It feels weird to now share someone else's home, to step around their belongings, to make room in the medicine cupboard for my own toothbrush. I feel like a cross between a guest and a lodger, and it's uncomfortable, but I tell myself it will get better.

Kyra heads to the kitchen to eat her pizza at the little table for two by the window, and I walk slowly into the living room to check on Allan.

It's an airy room, with a long, sash window letting in plenty of light. There's an upright piano against one wall, and an old sofa against the other. The bookcases are full of tattered paperbacks and sheet music is piled on an old armchair by the window.

Allan is lying on the sofa, a book open face-down on his chest, his glasses pushed up onto his forehead. His eyes flutter open as he sees me, and he smiles.

"How was it?"

I open my mouth to say something somewhat snarky about a picnic where people had cashmere blankets and designer clothes, but then I change my mind. "It was..." I can't make myself say *fun*, even though I know that's what Allan wants to hear. "All right."

He smiles faintly, a knowing look in his tired brown eyes. "That's not what you really think, Hats." He's the only person who has ever called me Hats, and when he started back with it after seven years of not seeing each other, it felt disconcerting, as well as weirdly welcoming, reminding me that we still share something—Kyra—even if it doesn't always feel like we do.

"You know me too well," I quip, so clearly a joke, because the truth is, no matter what we share, Allan doesn't know me at all. We dated non-seriously for six months when I was living in the city, and when I found out I was pregnant and decided, somewhat to my own surprise, that I wanted to keep the baby, Allan was relieved by my reassurance that he didn't need to be involved. He made some fairly half-hearted offers to visit once I moved to California, which never happened, and, to his credit considering he never wanted a child, he wrote a couple of letters; rambling missives about music and philosophy that Kyra might read when she's older. He also sent money, but only sporadically, so I could never depend on it, not that I wanted to.

And then, a month ago, he called, explaining his situation, asking me to move here, offering to pay the tuition for The Garden School so Kyra could have a good education and he could get to know her while he had the chance. Faced with a creeping sense of guilt that I'd denied her a father figure, as well as a sense of responsibility to Allan, not to mention few alternatives at the time, I agreed.

A week later, I'm trying not to spend too much time wondering whether I made the right choice. I made it, and we're here, and now I've got to make it work.

"Have you eaten?" I ask Allan, and he shakes his head, still smiling, his eyes crinkled at the corners. He's only fifty-eight, but he looks older now, his dark hair faded to a wispy gray, his thin face scored with deep lines, although his hazel eyes still light up with the wry humor I remember. Seven years ago, though—at least in my memory—he seemed far more vibrant a presence, a jazz musician who eked out a living playing in piano bars and making the odd recording. A couple of years ago, he received an inheritance from his parents that allows him to keep this apartment and pay for The Garden School, but he's certainly not rich. "I can make you something," I continue. I stoop down to pick up a crumpled blanket from the floor and then fold it, draping it over the back of a chair. "Soup, or a salad?"

"I'm all right..."

"Allan—"

"I'm all right." He speaks more firmly, and then he closes his eyes. He doesn't want me to take care of him, I know, and I don't particularly want to, either, but it's an impulse I find I can't resist, even though it's so unlike me. I've always valued my independence, but I feel like I'm giving it away now.

I leave Allan to his book, or really, his nap, and go into the kitchen to make myself a cup of instant soup, even though I'm not that hungry. Kyra is nibbling her piece of pizza, staring out the window at the view of dumpsters behind the building.

I take a deep breath, let it out. I lived in the city for over a year, back when Allan and I were together. I was thirty-three, teaching pottery classes at a community center in Brooklyn and waiting tables in my spare time; I had a handful of arty friends, a tiny studio apartment in Greenpoint that resembled a closet, and, all things considered, it felt like a pretty good life... until I got pregnant and realized, as rootless as I'd chosen to be, I actually wanted a child and I could not afford to have one in Manhattan, or really, maybe anywhere. So I left the city, moved in with my parents for a few months before I'd saved enough to head to California when Kyra was six months old, and never looked back.

Unfortunately, all these years on, I can't exactly pick up the remnants of my former life in the city and make something of them. I've lost touch with those old friends, as I have with so many people, and, these days, paying jobs in community centers are depressingly rare. Allan insisted he'd pay all our expenses, but I've always made my own money, no matter how little, and I don't want that to change. He can pay for The Garden School tuition because that's his dream, not mine, but I want to pay our own bills for as long as we're here.

And the truth is, I don't know how long that will be. Neither does he, although when we spoke on the phone, he said he hoped he'd be able to see Kyra through The Garden School, which ends after sixth grade.

I turn to Kyra. "You should have a shower," I tell her. "Have you picked out your clothes for tomorrow?" When we first arrived, Allan gave me his credit card and insisted I buy a whole new wardrobe for Kyra. I bought two pairs of jeans and two T-shirts from Target, and felt like that might have been too much, but the truth was, she really did need some new outfits for school.

"Yeah, I already did," she tells me.

"How are you feeling about tomorrow?" I ask seriously, and Kyra shrugs.

"Okay."

"The kids seem nice enough," I offer, although I don't really know. "What about that boy you were talking to, with the glasses? Luke?"

She presses her lips together, glancing down, her focus on peeling a pepperoni off her pizza. "He was okay."

Everything is *okay* to Kyra. Sometimes it unsettles me, how much she takes in her silent stride. I've always wanted any child of mine to develop resilience, but sometimes I do wonder if Kyra has too much of it, or at least *seems* like she does. The truth is, I don't know how she feels about anything, and I'm afraid of what she might be hiding. Eight years old is young to be so private, but at the same time, I don't want to press her too much, and so this time, like so many others, I let it go.

As she heads to the shower, I tidy up the kitchen, check on Allan, who has fallen back asleep, his book still laid open on his chest, and then I sip my cup of soup while scrolling mindlessly on my phone. I feel restless in a way I don't like; I've always considered myself to be a laid-back person, but I like to be busy, to have a plan, a *life*, yet the nature of my arrangement with Allan is that I *can't* have a life. Not that he'd said that, and he'd deny it if I told him, but it's pretty much a given, considering his situation.

After a second, I swipe my phone to get on Google and then type in Michael Dunnett, I'm not even sure why. Maybe because he's the only person I've talked to since moving back here.

A surprising number of links come up, and I start to understand why Michael Dunnett said his name like he expected me to know it. Apparently he's kind of a big deal; he's been on podcasts and interviewed on TV, and he's even done a TED

Talk. I can't figure what makes him such an expert on anything until I click on a link for NYU Langone Health and discover he's a neurosurgeon.

I swipe to read his bio, see the toothy picture of him giving the camera a decidedly direct stare. His biography is full of accolades, detailing his cutting-edge research and pioneering surgery. I swipe a few more times, scanning various praiseworthy paragraphs. I study his photo—the glint in his brown eyes, the warm smile. He really is an attractive man, and even just looking at his photo has something flaring to life inside of me that I quickly quash. I recall how when I'd spoken to him, he'd sounded assured, but not smarmy. If I hadn't felt so tense, being at that picnic, I would have enjoyed talking to him, even upped the banter a little. But then I remember Elise, and I think it was probably a good idea I didn't.

From the bathroom in the hall, I hear the shower go on.

I check on Allan again and see he's still sleeping. Then I go back into the kitchen and take the business card that Michael Dunnett gave me out of my pocket and type in the number. Before I can overthink it, I type out a text:

Hi Michael, this is Harriet Tierney. It was so nice to meet you today. I hope this doesn't come across as strange but would love to chat with you sometime if you're free.

I stare at it for a moment, wondering if it's too forward, too weird. Is he the kind of guy who would have a coffee with a mom he just met, without knowing why she asked? I think he is. I *hope* he is. I press send, and then I slip my phone into my pocket and go to check on Kyra, who's still in the shower.

I don't let myself think too much about Michael Dunnett or the text I sent him for the rest of the evening, and so it doesn't bother me—that much—that there's no reply. If he doesn't want to chat, I tell myself, it's fine. Most likely, it wouldn't have gone anywhere, anyway.

Instead I focus on Kyra, approving her outfit of the Target T-shirt and jeans—The Garden School has no uniform—and making sure her new notebooks and pencil case are in her backpack. I try to talk up The Garden School, but she gives me a look like *who are you kidding*? I'm not sure how much Kyra has enjoyed any of the six elementary schools she's attended. But she didn't seem to hate them, at least, which is something.

After she's gone to bed, I head back to the living room, where Allan is now sitting up, his glasses perched on the end of his beaky nose, reading his book.

"Kyra asleep?" he asks as I sit in the armchair opposite, tucking my legs under me.

"Not yet." I pause. "You could go say goodnight to her, if you wanted."

He nods soberly. "I should."

"That's why we're here, isn't it?" I do my best to keep my voice gentle, although I feel impatient with his dithering. "For you to spend time with her? Get to know her a little more? It's what you said you wanted, Allan, and I want it too."

"I know." He sighs and lays down his book. "I should have realized it would be difficult," he remarks sadly, "to start a relationship with an eight-year-old."

"Not that difficult," I tell him quietly. This isn't the first time in the last week that we've had this kind of conversation, and I want to be patient, but I also know there's only so much time. "She's a pretty easy-going kid, Allan. I'm sure she'd be happy for you to say goodnight."

He nods again and then glances up at the ceiling, his glasses sliding up his nose. "I know. It's just…" His breath comes out in a wavery rush. "I've never been good with kids. I've never been around them…"

"I know." Which was why, eight years ago, I told him he

didn't have to have any responsibility for the baby I was bringing into the world. At least, it was part of the reason why.

I wait, not saying anything more, and after a few moments, Allan rises from the sofa with a creak of joints. He walks slowly to the bedroom, and I listen to the low rumble of his voice; if Kyra is responding to whatever he's saying, her voice is too quiet for me to hear. I stare out the window at the blur of lights from the traffic, waiting, wondering what he's saying, if Kyra appreciates the effort. Also wondering what I'm meant to do tomorrow, or the day after, or the day after *that*, once Kyra is in school. The weeks stretch ahead of me, seeming empty and endless. How can I fill them when my life here is so precarious?

A minute or two later, Allan comes back into the living room. "Well, that went about as well as I expected," he says ruefully, and then sits down on the sofa and picks up his book.

"It will get better," I tell him, and he nods, his gaze still on his book. I realize he's hurt by Kyra's seeming rebuff, and I don't know what to do about it. "You just need to keep trying," I tell him, keeping my voice gentle, and again he nods.

Neither of us speak again until we're saying goodnight to go to bed.

The next morning is one of those perfect September days where the city feels clean and bright and full of possibility. It rained in the night, leaving the sidewalks freshly washed and damp, and there's a slight breeze that takes away any city smell of trash.

The Garden School starts at eight, and Kyra and I leave at seven-fifteen to give us plenty of time to get across to Manhattan and then downtown to the brownstone in Gramercy Park where the school is housed, with a modern addition built out back. One thing I do like about the school is how homey it feels. The classrooms are all in what would have been the townhouse's bedrooms, once upon a time, and the dining hall still feels like a dining room, with family-style seating and oil paintings on the walls. The school is small enough—only one hundred and thirteen students—that it doesn't feel overwhelming, although there is a fair crowd of parents—mostly moms, as well as a few nannies—outside the building as Kyra and I walk up to it.

It feels a little bit like a fashion show, with all the mothers decked out either in designer outfits or what looks like very expensive color-coordinated workout gear. Instinctively, I look for Elise, the one mother I met, and I am relieved when I don't see her. There are a few curious glances my way, and I know I stand out in my Doc Martens, patchwork jeans, and ribbed tank top, my hair in a messy bun with plenty of wisps to frame my face because it isn't really long enough to be held back.

I don't mind so much about the speculative looks; in fact, some perverse part of me almost enjoys them. I am not like these women, I never will be, and I'm glad I won't and that they all know it.

"Okay." I stand in front of Kyra by the steps to the school, where the headmistress, whom I've only met once, is graciously welcoming the students in, greeting them all by name. Elise Dunnett was right about the merch—there are a *lot* of TGS backpacks, lunch boxes, and insulated coffee cups that parents are proudly holding. "You ready for this?" I ask my daughter, resting my hands lightly on her shoulders as I smile down at her.

She blinks up at me, silent and accepting, her dark eyes wide in her little heart-shaped face, before she gives a tiny nod.

"Go get 'em," I tell her, squeezing her shoulders gently. "You'll be awesome, Kyra. And I'll pick you up at three? We'll get ice cream, double scoops, and you can tell me all about your day. I can't wait to hear everything."

She nods again, and then, to my surprise, because neither of us have ever been big huggers, she leans into me, wrapping her skinny arms around my waist. I hug her back tightly, kissing her on the top of her head as a sudden rush of love and fear assails me. My little girl is so strong, but have I asked too much of her this time? And she doesn't even know yet how much.

"You're going to be great, sweetheart," I whisper against her hair, and then I step back, unwrapping her arms from my waist, and give her a gentle push toward the stairs. She goes slowly, and my heart aches for her. I want this school to be amazing for her, even if I'm not sure it will be. Still, I hope.

She's only just disappeared inside when I feel a tap on my shoulder, and I tense in surprise, then turn.

Elise Dunnett is standing there, looking as mesmerizingly elegant as ever as she smiles at me, dressed in a pair of ankle-skimming white jeans and a cream silk blouse. A pair of designer-looking sunglasses are perched on her forehead, holding back her waves of chestnut-brown hair.

"Hey, Harriet," she says, her expression friendly but alert, assessing. "I was wondering if I could talk to you for a sec?"

FIVE
ELISE

For a second, Harriet looks like a deer trapped in headlights as she stares at me, eyes wide and lips parted, clearly startled by my approach. All around us, mothers are chatting, laughing, exchanging horror stories or humblebrags about their summer vacations. I ignore their curious, sideways glances as they watch me saying hello to the mom who is just a little too different from the rest of us.

Admittedly, Harriet Tierney does stand out in this crowd. Her clothes are rumpled, her hair an unruly mess, and she isn't wearing a scrap of makeup. I almost envy her ability to be so unconcerned about what other people think, but maybe her lack of effort is its own kind of arrogance and attitude. She doesn't need to conform the way we all do, and that causes me an unsettling pang of something like envy. To be so unconcerned seems to me to be something akin to a superpower, and it's definitely one I don't have.

In any case, Harriet still looks good, in her alternative way. She has something better than basic beauty, I realize. It's more like a natural charisma, and an instinctive appeal. That's something else I don't have; I have to work hard to look so effortless, and even then, I'm not sure I have the same allure as someone like Harriet.

"Um, sure," Harriet says finally, looking reluctant. Is she thinking about how she texted my husband, and wondering if I know about it? Of course, there might be nothing to know. It could have been a completely innocent message. I haven't asked Michael about it, and I'm not going to, because I know it would only irritate or disappoint him, or both. *Elise, what about the trust?* Trust is all well and good, but Harriet Tierney is still someone I need to keep my eye on, and this is how I'm going to do it.

"There's a café around the corner," I tell her, keeping my voice warm. "How about we get coffee? My treat." She looks even more flummoxed, like she really didn't expect this, and I'm not surprised. "As head of the PTA," I say, an explanation meant to mollify her, "I always want to welcome new moms to TGS."

"*Oh.*" I don't miss the flicker of relief in her eyes that this isn't personal. It's just my job, or so she now believes... nothing to do with that text she sent, naturally. "Okay," she says, still sounding reluctant. "But I kind of need to get back soon, so..."

"Sure, twenty minutes," I reply easily, and I usher her away from the crowd of parents by the school steps. "There's so much to get on top of, once they're back at school," I remark in a commiserating tone as we walk down the street. "How was Kyra going in? Excited, nervous?" I cock my head, all sympathy. "A little bit of both, probably, right?"

"I don't really know," Harriet replies after a second's pause. "She's kind of a closed book. It's hard to tell with her how she's feeling, but at least she went in, right?" She smiles, and I make sure to smile back.

"Oh, I'm sure she'll be fine. Mrs. Ryan, the Class Three teacher, is wonderful, so warm and friendly. She's got three kids of her own, and she's sensible, too. All the kids here love her.

You'll probably be hearing all about her when you pick Kyra up."

"Maybe," Harriet replies, sounding unconvinced, and I wonder if she'll even ask her daughter about her day. She seems like one of those laissez-faire parents who insist they're teaching their child resilience when what it really is, is neglect. That might seem a little harsh, but while I am determined to become her friend, it doesn't mean I have to like her.

"I thought girls told everything to their mothers," I remark, shooting her a laughing look. "I've always been afraid I'm missing out, with boys. Now, *they* hardly tell you anything."

"Only if you want to gender stereotype," Harriet replies, and I can't tell if she's joking or not. She shrugs, looking away. "I guess every child is different."

I can *feel* how uneasy she is, how much she doesn't like walking along with me. We don't talk until we've reached Bellissimo, the café that is the after-drop-off hangout of the moms who aren't hurrying to work. We left the school a little early though, while everyone was still chatting, and so we're the first TGS parents there.

I reach for my purse. "What can I get you?"

"Oh, uh, an oat milk latte, please. Thanks."

"Great." I order her latte and an espresso for me. Then we take our drinks to a table in the back, and an expectant silence ensues. Harriet is clearly bracing herself for some kind of nosy inquisition, meanwhile I'm trying to figure her out.

Yesterday at the picnic, she held herself apart from everyone else, as if she was judging us, but today she seems uneasy, even nervous. The brash confidence I sensed from her before is absent, or at least hidden. It makes me feel like she must be hiding something else, and I need to find out what it is.

"So you just moved here from Austin," I say as we settle into our seats. "New York must feel pretty different."

She takes a sip of her coffee. "I've lived here before."

"Oh?" I raise my eyebrows as I reach for my cup. "When?"

"About eight years ago, when I was pregnant with Kyra. I met her father here, we dated for a few months." She gives me a sideways glance, clearly curious to see how I react to that little nugget of information.

"Are you guys still together?" I ask, making sure my tone gives nothing away.

"No, we're just friends. Living together, though, so Kyra can get to know her dad for a little while."

"That sounds great." I can tell she's expecting some kind of judgment on her living situation from me, and so I just widen my smile. "So, you had Kyra in New York?" I surmise, and she nods. "I had my boys at Langone. Where did you deliver?"

Her expressionless stare bores into mine. "I had a home birth."

I don't miss a beat. "Wow, that's so impressive. I thought about going more natural," I confide, "but with twins it's already high-risk, so..."

"Yeah, well, I didn't actually *choose* to have a home birth." She tries to speak wryly, but it comes out a touch hostile. "I just didn't have any health insurance, so a hospital stay was out of the question." A shrug, defiant, a little angry, like it's my fault she was broke.

"I'm sorry, that sounds tough." I make a face, cock my head. I'm play-acting, and I think Harriet probably knows it, which I'm sure makes her dislike or at least mistrust me. I tell myself I don't care, but then I remember I'm trying to be her friend. It's just so hard when I'm pretty sure she—along with far too many other women—has a thing for my husband. "Everything went okay, though, with the birth?" I ask. "No complications?"

"Not really." She sighs, seeming restless. "Anyway, it was a long time ago."

I take another sip of coffee, keeping my voice casual. "So

why did you come back after all these years? Was it just so Kyra could get to know her dad?"

She tenses, like I've asked a too-personal question. "That was certainly a big part of it."

I am starting to understand what Michael meant, that he felt as if she just tolerated him. That's definitely the feeling I'm getting, but if she really felt that way about my husband, why did she send him a semi-gushing text just an hour later?

It was so...

I've thought of a dozen different ways she might have finished that sentence, and I don't like any of them.

"What about you, Elise?" Harriet asks, her tone sounding a little steely. "How did you and Michael meet?"

I keep my expression neutral but friendly. So, she's going to turn the tables. Fine. "At an art show," I tell her, leaning forward like I'm sharing a confidence. "I was volunteering at the gallery, and he was buying some very expensive, very modern art." I remember the white backdrop with red splat marks on it that sold for fifteen thousand dollars. It's in his study, and it looks like someone bled out on canvas. I find it weirdly gruesome, but I remind myself that it brought us together.

Harriet nods, smiling a little. "That sounds like a classic meet-cute, at least for a certain demographic."

And what demographic, I wonder, *is that?* I ignore any potential barb as I smile blandly back. "As I recall, he did try some chat-up line about the art, but I was too busy making sure everyone had their fill of caviar and crackers." I give a light laugh as Harriet simply stares at me. "He didn't ask me out until the end of the evening," I finish, "but after that, we never looked back."

"How sweet," Harriet remarks tonelessly. She clearly has a chip on her shoulder about people with money, or maybe just about me, married to the man she flirted with yesterday. I decide we've had enough chitchat.

"Well, of course, the school wants to support your transition in any way possible," I tell her, launching into my formal role. "Kyra's been assigned a buddy in class, Chloe Lee. Her mom, Kim, is *your* buddy, and you should have gotten an email from her, introducing herself and asking if you had any questions about the school, or life in the city, really, whatever you might want to know that will be helpful to your transition."

Harriet shakes her head. "I didn't get any emails."

Most likely, Kim hasn't gotten to it yet. She probably wasn't the best parent to pick as a buddy, since she's so busy, but that was the school's call. "Okay, well let me chase that up for you," I tell Harriet easily. "I'm sure Kim will email you soon," I add before I lean forward, dropping my voice conspiratorially. "But what I really wanted to talk to you about was the school's December gala. It's an annual event the PTA puts on, to raise money for scholarships for the underprivileged."

I pause in case she wants to say something since she seems to have opinions about money and privilege, but she stays silent.

"Being on the committee is a great way to get to know people," I continue. "We're a fun little group. We have a pretty short meeting after drop-off every Friday in the run-up to the gala, and the introductory meeting is tomorrow night, at my apartment." I dangle this like the bait I'm pretty sure it is. I don't think Harriet Tierney is the type to want to volunteer for a committee like this, or *any* committee, but will she want to come to my house? Just in case she's on the fence, I add, with a little laugh, "My husband Michael plays bartender, and we make it fun with a few cocktails. It's usually a great evening, and we get a lot of planning done. And, of course, coming to the meeting doesn't necessarily mean you have to be *on* the committee, although, of course, we'd welcome your help."

"Oh," Harriet says into the silence, once I've stopped speaking. She sounds slightly dazed, as well as distinctly unenthused. "Well, I'm not really sure that I'm the kind of—"

"I heard you're an artist," I continue for my second push. "What kind of art?"

She blinks and then answers slowly, "Pottery mainly, but also watercolors."

"That's so cool." I give her an admiring look. "Part of the gala is a silent auction. We'd love to feature your artwork, if you're interested."

She stares at me, still looking like she's not buying what I'm selling. Maybe I've come on too strong. "But you haven't even *seen* my artwork," she points out reasonably. "It could suck."

I laugh, like she's said something funny. "Well, do you have a website, or a card? I'll check it out."

She hesitates, and then says, "I have a website. HarrietTierneyArt.com." She spells it out, including capital letters. I nod without writing it down.

"Wonderful." I sit back and sip my coffee. "I'll definitely have a look at it."

Harriet stares at me like I'm a puzzle she can't figure out, and I give her a little smile in return. I'm guessing she either thinks I'm oblivious or scheming, and at this point I don't really care which it is, as long as she comes tomorrow night. I want to keep my eye on her, and nip in the bud any ideas she has about my husband.

Because one thing I've learned over the years is that Michael backs off any woman I become aware of. We never speak of it; I don't think either of us would dare. It works better if I give hints and he takes them. And so, tomorrow night, he'll figure it out and then he'll leave Harriet Tierney alone.

I hope.

"So," I say. "Do you want to come tomorrow night? No pressure, but I really think it will be fun."

Another hesitation; she looks like she really wants to refuse, like she's *going* to, but then, to my relief, she relents. "Okay, sure," she says, like it's a concession to me, and then she seems to realize how that might come across as rude, and she manages a small smile. "Thank you for thinking of me."

"Of course." I feel relieved, as well as a little worried. Am I crazy, inviting this woman to my house, toward my *husband*? And yet I know from experience that it's always better to have an eye on a woman Michael finds attractive, or, God forbid, *interesting*. Interesting is much worse, much more dangerous, which is why I'm acting so fast.

"So, you said you had to get back?" I ask as I reach for my purse. "Are you working on something? Some... art?"

"I've just got things to do." She tries for a laugh, but doesn't quite manage it. "You know how it is when you move."

"There are always a million boxes to unpack," I agree. "How's it going? You live in Astoria, as I recall?"

"Yes." Her eyes narrow in something like suspicion, and I give her a blithe look as I explain. "I saw your address when I did your welcome bag. Did you get it this morning, by the way?"

"No, I didn't."

I nod in swift understanding. "You need to go to the new parents' coffee morning. Did you hear about that?" Kim should have emailed her about it, but oh well. TGS runs on parent volunteers, and many aren't as diligent or dedicated as I am. "They give them out there."

She tilts her head. "Well, I came for coffee with you."

I give a theatrical wince. "Oh, I'm sorry, I really should have thought of that." I glance at my watch with a thoughtful frown. "You could still make the last twenty minutes or so if you left now."

"I'm good," she says as she pushes up from the table with an apologetic grimace. "I'm really sorry to leave like this, but I do need to get back."

I smile sunnily. "Of course, no problem. And I'll see you tomorrow night?" She nods, and I fling out a hand to keep her from going. "Do you mind giving me your phone number? Then I can text you my address."

Once again she hesitates, and I feel like shaking her by the shoulders. *You can text my husband, but you can't give me your number?* I keep my smile in place, and after another second's pause, she tells me her number and I put it into my phone.

"Thanks, Harriet," I tell her in the warm tone I've used all morning. It feels exhausting. "See you tomorrow. And I hope Kyra has a *great* first day today."

"Thanks," she says, and for a second, she looks regretful, like she wishes she'd been friendlier.

I almost think she's going to say something, but then she just gives a little shake of her head and walks out of the café quickly, without looking back.

I watch her go. I am not going to let Harriet Tierney, the wannabe hippie who thinks she's so above us all, become dangerous.

SIX

HARRIET

I leave the café feeling unsettled, as well as a little guilty.

Maybe I should have been friendlier, but just about the last thing I expected was for Elise Dunnett to ask me out to coffee and then invite me onto some stupid *committee*. As if I would ever do that, and yet it seems like I agreed, at least for the introductory meeting—and cocktails courtesy of Michael, who still hasn't texted me back. Did he not *want* me to call him? He certainly seemed like he did when he gave me his card. I suppose I'll see him tomorrow night, so I can talk to him then, although I would have preferred to do so in a more private setting.

I can't shake the feeling that I was getting a very weird vibe from Elise, though. Her friendliness definitely didn't seem genuine, and I can't decide if it was because she's just one of those people who is fake with everyone, or that she really doesn't like me. Did Michael tell her I texted him? I can't imagine that happening, and even if he did, it's not like I'd texted anything inappropriate. I'm a new parent, interested in getting to know other parents. Is that such a big deal? Still, Elise seemed like she had a bone to pick with me. But if she felt threatened, surely she wouldn't have invited me to her home? I really can't figure her out.

I wasn't lying when I told her I needed to get back, though. It's now past eighty-thirty and I've been gone for an hour and a half. By the time I get back to Astoria, it will be over two hours. I don't want to leave Allan for too long.

As I let myself into the apartment, I hear a few sultry bars of jazz and I smile, because if Allan is playing the piano, that means it's probably a good day.

"I recognize that," I tell him as I come into the living room. He's sitting at the piano, dressed in an untucked blue button-down shirt, the sleeves rolled up past his bony wrists, and very faded, baggy jeans. He grins at me, his hands resting on the keys, and for a second I remember just how much we liked each other, back what feels like a million years ago. How much fun we had, and how lovely he was.

"Artist?" he asks.

I roll my eyes good-naturedly. "Nina Simone."

"Song?"

I pretend to think, tapping my chin, enjoying the moment. "'I Put a Spell on You.'"

He leans back on the piano stool, looking satisfied. "You remember," he says, a statement of fact.

It was a song we danced to, back in the day, long and slow, after I'd listened to his set and the piano bar started to close up shop around us, stools on top of the bar, the air smelling of old beer and stale cigarette smoke. It had been surprisingly and intensely romantic.

"Of course I remember, Allan," I say gently. It remains a poignant memory, bittersweet now with the passage of years. "I won't ever forget."

I walk past him, into the living room, and face the window,

unsettled by remembering how we danced, and how even now I feel a pang of longing for what once was.

I stare out the window for a little while longer and then I say, "You haven't asked about Kyra."

He gives a little sigh. "I'm sorry. I should have. How was she, going into school?"

"I don't really know, to be honest." I turn to face him, smiling wryly. "Maybe you could come with me when I pick her up, ask what kind of day she's had? I told her we'd get ice cream. It could be fun." He looks torn, like he wants to refuse and knows he shouldn't, and I shake my head slowly. "Isn't that why we're here, Allan? At least *part* of the reason why we're here?"

For a second, annoyance sparks in his eyes. "That's the *entire* reason you're here, Harriet," he tells me firmly, an end to the discussion we haven't yet had. "And yes, I'll come with you to pick up Kyra."

I nod, knowing I should feel satisfied, but there's so much more I could—and should—say. I know Allan insisted we had time, that things would stay stable for months, but I'm nervous. I'm worried about what I've let Kyra in for. And my nature is to make things happen, even when it's not within my power.

"How are you feeling today?" I ask, and it's clearly the wrong question because he gives me a pointed look as he rises from the piano.

"I'm fine," he says shortly, and walks out of the room.

The rest of the day passes slowly. I lug our laundry to the laundromat three blocks away and sit in a plastic chair, staring into space, while I wait for the cycle to finish. Then I wait for another forty minutes for the clothes to dry, before I lug them all back to put them away.

Allan is back to playing the piano, a comforting sound, and I make us ham and cheese sandwiches for lunch, which he picks at, before I clear the dishes and brew some coffee. He suggests we play a game of Scrabble, which we used to do back in the day, and glad for the distraction, I get out the old, battered box. One day in and I'm already going a little stir-crazy, although I'm afraid... I might look back on a day like this with sentimental nostalgia.

"Just like an old married couple," he tells me with a teasing smile as he painstakingly arranges his letters on the rack and I feel a sudden rush of pity and sorrow, because we are not an old married couple. Our relationship was casual and convenient for us both, for as long as it lasted. Allan had made it clear that he wasn't interested in anything serious and permanent, and I hadn't been either, because I'd never wanted that kind of life, to be tied down to a place or a man.

Eight years on, none of that has changed, even if Allan's perspective has, and yet, for a second, I wish things were different, that *we* were, and that is an unsettling feeling.

"Hats?" Allan asks gently, as I stare down at my tiles. "What are you thinking?"

"Nothing important," I tell him. I am not about to go into my own complicated emotions when I don't even want to feel them myself. I tell myself I'm not interested in revisiting, much less rewriting, our history. That's not why I came back, even if I've felt a few unsettling pangs. "Who goes first?" I ask instead, pitching my voice bright.

"We have to pick a letter from the bag, remember?" He reaches for the bag, and I hand it to him. "I shouldn't have said that," he says quietly as he roots around inside it for a tile. "I know we aren't an old married couple." Before I can reply, he adds, "I really appreciate you moving back here. I hope you know how much."

"I do," I say at last, and although there's so much I could say, I can't make myself say it. I don't know what the future looks like for Allan, for me, for Kyra, and in moments like this I seriously wonder whether I made the right choice, for my daughter's sake. I tell myself—again—that it's too late for doubts, but they still swirl in my stomach as I pick my own tile out of the bag before dropping it onto the table. "You go first," I tell him, trying to smile.

Life really throws you some funky curveballs sometimes, I reflect as we head out together an hour later to get Kyra from school, Allan walking slowly beside me.

For most of my adulthood, I've made choices that safeguarded my independence, made sure I could always be a free agent, moving where and whenever I wanted, blazing trails and, if I'm honest, being kind of careless of who or what I left in my wake, because freedom was so essential to me. Admittedly, on the surface, at least, having a baby *wasn't* one of those independent choices, but I wouldn't exchange Kyra for any amount of freedom. And Kyra, it has to be said, has never really slowed me down.

And yet, despite all that, I am now living with a man at his behest, doing his laundry and tidying up after him, just like my mother once did. I never wanted to be like her, tied to a small, suburban life raising two children—my older sister moved to British Columbia fifteen years ago, and never looked back—and cooking and cleaning for a man who seemed like he could barely stand to say hello to her. Although maybe that's not fair; my dad was your classic blue-collar guy, gruff but not unkind, very occasionally affectionate, and I have no reason to believe my parents' marriage wasn't solid.

But once upon a time my mother dreamed of being an artist. The only art I ever saw her make was funny little sketches for me and my sister's birthday cards. They were so clever and funny, always featuring a mischievous little squirrel and his misadventures, and I don't think I thought to save a single card, something that fills me with regret now.

And while my mother never talked about her art, after she'd died two years ago, I was going through a filing cabinet and saw she'd kept a single slip of paper in a yellowed manila folder—her acceptance to art school in Chicago, dated a year before my older sister was born. It shook me to the core, that letter, as well as the fact that my mother had never spoken about it, not once. What other dreams had she sacrificed, so my dad could have his meatloaf and mashed potatoes on the table every night at six?

That was never the kind of life I wanted. I might not know what my dreams are, but at least I haven't sacrificed them the way my mother did. That's been the guiding principle of my life, and yet here I am, tied to a kitchen and an apartment that isn't even my own. But, I remind myself, it's worth it for Kyra's sake… I hope.

I glance at Allan, who is looking particularly dapper; he's paired his button-down shirt and baggy jeans with a jacket in maroon corduroy and an old, slightly moth-eaten fedora. Really, I haven't sacrificed anything to be here with him, except the option of being somewhere else. I tell myself that, but I still struggle not to feel trapped, and I have to remind myself that I chose this not just to help Allan, but my daughter. To give her a relationship with her father and the sort of stability I've never been able to offer her before.

We receive our fair share of curious glances as we wait with the other parents at the base of the brownstone's steps for each class to be released. I look around for Elise, more to avoid her than anything else, but I don't see her in the melee of chatty moms and bustling nannies, along with the occasional dad, still in his work suit and checking his phone.

"I don't think I've ever asked, but how did you hear about The Garden School, anyway?" I ask Allan.

He shrugs, smiling. "Google, where else?"

"*Google?*" I repeat disbelievingly. Somehow I'd assumed that Allan had some connection to this school, even if just a friend of a friend or something like that. A bigger reason than it came up first on a search engine, anyway.

"They have a very nice website," he tells me, "And I like their progressive ethos. And I wanted to give something to Kyra that would last."

The Garden School's tuition is forty-five grand a year. If Allan had given that money to Kyra instead, I think it would have lasted a tad longer than the education she's going to get for who knows how long. I don't say any of this, though, because Allan's offer was generous—and he was adamant about it. Besides that, I was not in a position to refuse. My temporary teaching job had ended, and I was struggling to pay the rent on my studio apartment in Austin. As much as I might question the wisdom of accepting it, Allan's offer came at a good time... for all three of us.

The doors to the school open, and the first few kindergarteners come out, clinging to their teacher's hands and blinking like moles, so shy and uncertain. Parents snap photos and coo delightedly as they sweep their children into their arms and then down the sidewalk. Then it's Class One, looking just that little bit older, and Class Two, clearly old hands at this whole school thing, swaggering down the steps like they own the world. Parents continue to peel off, and children's giddy laughter echoes through the street. It's a classically heartwarming scene, heightened by the golden tones of the sunlight streaming through the leaves of the trees that arch above.

I glance at Allan, who is looking interested but also somewhat bemused by everything, as this is surely something he's never experienced before. He's also looking a little tired, his thin shoulders rounded and starting to slump, and I feel a surge of affectionate protectiveness for him. I put my hand on his arm and am about to tell him we can take a taxi back, but before I can, Kyra comes out of the school, and his whole expression transforms as he beams at her in sudden delight.

"*Kyra!*" he calls, and she swivels, searching for whoever called her name, clearly surprised when she sees it is Allan. She walks toward us, her backpack slung over her shoulder, her hair falling out of the neat ponytail I put it in this morning so a few dark brown strands—the same color as Allan's once upon a time —frame her face.

"Hey, kiddo," Allan greets her, giving her ponytail a gentle tug. "How was your big day?"

She smiles up at him, shyly pleased. "It was really good. I like my teacher, Mrs. Ryan. She's so nice."

"Good teachers make all the difference," Allan proclaims solemnly. "What do you say we celebrate with ice cream?"

"Okay." Kyra's smile deepens as she flushes with pleasure, and I watch, more than a little gobsmacked, as they fall into step with one another, heading down the street. In the week since we've been in New York, Allan has had no more than a handful of stilted conversations with our daughter. He's clearly making more of an effort now, and I realize I forgot just how charming he can be, in that offbeat, whimsical way, when he chooses to. And Kyra clearly had a good day, which is great.

And yet... as pleased as I am about all that, and I *am*, I can't quite suppress the unsettling little flicker of jealousy I feel as Kyra and Allan walk in lockstep together, leaving me behind. I hurry to catch them up, and as I walk away from The Garden School, I feel someone's gaze on me, and turn around.

Elise Dunnett is standing by the school steps, ignoring her own children as she stares straight at me, her expression thoughtful, assessing... and decidedly unfriendly in a way that chills me. When I meet her gaze, she doesn't look away, and it feels like a challenge.

Whatever the reason she invited me to join her stupid committee, it wasn't, I realize afresh, because she wanted to be my friend. Far from it.

Because right now, with the way she's staring at me, it feels like I'm already her enemy.

SEVEN
ELISE

My father had his first affair when I was five. At least I think that was the first one; I can't be sure. It was the first one I learned about, at any rate.

I discovered it accidentally, when I was playing at a friend's house, and I overheard her mother talking on the phone in her bedroom, her voice low and laced with laughter. My friend suggested we eavesdrop on the line and, giggling, we snuck into the kitchen and, holding our breaths, picked up the phone to listen in. When I realized the other voice on the line was my father's, I let out a startled and hopeful, *"Daddy?"*

My five-year-old brain couldn't make sense of it. Why would my father, a lawyer who worked in Philadelphia, be talking to my friend's mother, a stay-at-home mom who lived an hour outside the city? How did they even know each other? My father was a busy man; he never did the school run, never knew the other parents, never even cared about any of that. At five, I think I understood that, even if I couldn't articulate it.

I don't remember how my father—or my friend's mother— handled that surprised, childish *"Daddy?"* Somehow they fobbed me off, because I didn't think too much of it afterward, although I was surprised when my father picked me up from the playdate, rather than my mother, who usually did all the driving to doctors' appointments and playdates, ballet and tap, the endless to and fro of family life.

When he picked me up, my father was all jocular joviality at the door, calling me princess and sweeping me up in his arms. I remember the scratchy wool of his overcoat, the leathery smell of his cologne. His cheek was cold from the outside as he pressed it to mine. It was only when we were driving home that he mentioned the call; by that time, I'd already forgotten about it.

"Listen, princess," he had said, giving me a sideways glance. "That telephone call you overheard?" I remember he wagged a finger at me, playfully scolding, his eyes sparkling although I saw a certain sternness about the set of his mouth. "Naughty little princess, eavesdropping on people's conversations!" I had dropped my gaze, ashamed, and he had continued, "Don't worry, darling, I'm not angry. But let's not mention it to Mommy, all right? Because Mrs. Danielson and I were planning her birthday surprise, and I wouldn't want you to spoil it."

"What birthday surprise?" I had asked eagerly, and my father shook his head.

"That's for me to know and you to find out! And Mommy, too, of course, but not today." A pause before his expression had turned serious in a way that made me feel grownup, but also a little afraid. "All right?"

I had nodded meekly, not trusting myself to speak, desperate not to disappoint my beloved father. We never spoke of it again, and there was no birthday surprise, none that I remember, anyway. It wasn't until much later, maybe when I was twelve or so, that I connected the many dots. Because, of course, that wasn't the only time my father asked me not to *spoil a surprise*. My childhood was littered with moments like that one with the phone call, too many to remember, not that I want to. But I've kept every single one of his secrets all these years.

I don't know why I'm thinking about all that now as I get ready for the gala meeting. I've spent most of the day cleaning the dining and living rooms, polishing and dusting, filling them with fresh flowers and arranging wasabi and candied almonds in little dishes, even though hardly anyone eats at these things. I've lined up the liquor bottles on our drinks tray, with the ingredients of several fun cocktails written out in careful calligraphy, for Michael to mix. He'll breeze in here ten minutes before the start of the meeting and be the man of the hour, shaking the cocktail mixer like it's a maraca and charming the socks—and who knows what else—off every flattered mother in the place.

I press my lips together as I carefully snip a curling, brown leaf off a white rose in the bouquet I bought from the florist on Fifth Avenue. *That's* why I'm thinking about my father, and that phone call I overheard when I was five. Because Michael reminds me so much of him, and at times I still feel like that hopeful, frightened five-year-old girl, confused about what is really going on, wanting to keep the secret, and yet afraid to know the truth.

Luke and Lewis have been fed and bathed and are already in their pajamas, their hair damp, cheeks pink and scrubbed, both of them sprawled in the playroom. They seem to have settled well into Class Three, which is a blessing. Mrs. Ryan really is a lovely teacher, who I think might *get* Luke, and I know I never need to worry about Lewis. He collects friends like a planet pulling its many moons into its orbit; half the boys in the class trail after him eagerly, while the girls adore him from afar. He's just like Michael that way, but the lovely thing about Lewis is that he doesn't know it—*yet*. I intend to keep it that way for as long as I can.

I dread the day when that masculine arrogance hits hard,

with the accompanying knowing grin, the gleam in the eye, the casual saunter. My father possessed them all and so does Michael, but he manages to pull off humility like the award-winning act it is for someone so innately confident. Still, I appreciate the effort.

I peek my head into the playroom before I go to get changed, smiling at the sight of my boys sharing a beanbag and poring over a *Guinness Book of World Records* together.

"That is *so* gross," Lewis chortles delightedly, pointing to a photo on the page, while Luke just smiles and nods. My heart expands with the kind of love that feels like fear, because I'm so afraid of disrupting this moment, of letting this fragile happiness slip away from me. Neither of them sees me, and I decide to leave them to it.

In my bedroom, I study the three different outfits I laid out on the bed earlier, considering which image I want to project tonight. The safest option is the tailored trousers in taupe silk, paired with a gauzy, *slightly* see-through tank top in ivory. Understated, with a hint of sexy, and in the neutral palette I usually prefer.

The next outfit is a little more fun, a sweeping maxi dress in mauve, cinched at the waist so it doesn't look like a purple sack, with some intricate, sparkly beadwork on the hem and sleeves and matching mauve slingbacks. It's a party dress without being too outrageous, but I'm worried the grayish tint to the purple might wash me out. I want—I *need*—to look good tonight. And not just good, but fabulous.

Which brings me to the third outfit, which is one I've never worn before. I bought it on a reckless whim a couple of years ago, when I was seized by a sudden urge to be someone different. Michael had been away at a conference in San Francisco, and he'd only texted once, which sent me into a tailspin of doubt and paranoia—sometimes it's hard to know which is which. It's a fire-engine-red pantsuit with flared legs and a halter neck that hugs my top half without dipping too low. Paired with Louboutin red stiletto sandals that I've also never worn, it would be quite the daring look for me, and one I don't normally go for. I much prefer understated outfits, elegant without shouting about it. But tonight...

I finger the red pantsuit, tempted. I want to be the kind of woman who wears an outfit like this with unapologetic defiance, a *screw you* to every sneering doubter. *A woman*, I think suddenly, *like Harriet*.

But if I wear it, people will certainly remark on it. There will be compliments, but also a curiosity about why I decided to wear something so sensational to what is essentially a school meeting. Although, to be fair, all the women tonight will be thinking hard about what they want to wear. Michael's bartending for them, after all. But this isn't my usual style, and people will clock it and wonder why.

And what, I wonder, will *Harriet* wear? Already, I can picture her in some sloppy combo, like what she wore to the school run yesterday—patchwork jeans and a tank top that showed her sweat patches, both of which she wore with a careless confidence that is, I fear, more attractive than my carefully curated ensembles. I imagine her rocking up to my apartment in a similar outfit, looking careless, even slovenly, and then me opening the door in my fabulous red pantsuit. In that scenario, I already know I am the one who will look—and feel—ridiculous, and worse, pathetic. Trying too hard is far more revealing than not trying enough.

My mind made up, I put the dress and the pantsuit back in my closet. I slip on the taupe trousers and the gauzy top, and I even put on a lace camisole underneath so it's not at all outrageous. This is the kind of simple and sophisticated ensemble everyone will expect me to wear; it will get some compliments, but they will be—mostly—genuine, and everyone will forget about it later.

But what will Harriet Tierney think? I tell myself I don't care, but the truth is I don't *want* to care, but I do. I want her to look at me in all my curated, couture beigeness and feel impressed by and envious of how effortlessly sophisticated I look, without even having to try. I want her to see me and realize there's no way a man like Michael Dunnett will be interested in a woman like her, all scrappy and disheveled, when he has a woman like *me* on his arm and in his bed. It's as basic— and immature—as that.

In truth, the only reason I'm inviting Harriet into my home is so I can watch her, and so Michael can *see* me watching her. I need to assess and evaluate the situation... and then decide if there's anything more I should do about it. I've been here before, many times. Harriet Tierney may think she's special, but she's not. And my outfit tonight is all part of showing her why.

I get dressed, and then I tidy up the bedroom, straightening the cream duvet, plumping the satin pillows, my equanimity restored with each comforting little action. I do my hair and makeup, taking my time with each, staring hard at my reflection —the neutral lip, the subtle eye, the hair in carefully carelesslooking waves. I press my fingertip to the faint line bisecting my forehead; does it look deeper than it did yesterday? I do my best to smooth it out.

In my ears, I'm wearing the diamond teardrops that Michael bought me for our tenth anniversary, and the diamondencrusted Rolex on my wrist that was a "push present" for the twins. I spray my classic scent, Penhaligon's Bluebell, closing my eyes as I luxuriate in a second spritz.

Satisfied, I turn away and head to the playroom to tell Luke and Lewis, who are still looking at the Guinness book together, that they need to brush their teeth before getting into bed.

Once out in the living room, I put on some low jazz music and then organize my notes for the gala, color-coded in their monogrammed leather binder. I spray some air freshener around and move one vase of flowers to a better vantage point. I check the glasses lined up by the drinks tray and align them more neatly, frowning in concentration. I want everything to be perfect, to seem effortlessly so. No one knows how hard I work, not even Michael, and I want to keep it that way.

At seven-fifteen, the boys are in bed reading and Michael breezes in, still in his suit from work. He didn't have surgery today, but he had some consultations and was speaking to some other surgeons at some consortium or other, which always energizes him. His face brightens as he catches sight of me, and then he slips his arm around my waist for a quick kiss.

"You smell amazing," he murmurs against my neck. "When are these women all coming, again?"

"In about ten minutes," I reply, laughing as I pull away.

"Not enough time for us…?" he asks, making a playful face as he reaches for me once more, and still smiling, I shake my head and go to adjust another bouquet. Michael heaves a dramatic sigh and then heads into our bedroom to change, just as the doorbell rings. I'd already told Tony, the other doorman, to expect visitors and send them straight up.

I take a deep breath, smooth my hair, and then head to the door. It's Rachel, a younger mom in her early thirties who is always eager to help. Her son, Josh, is in Class One.

We exchange greetings and air kisses just as the next mom arrives—Taylor, who has a daughter in Class Eight. TGS only goes up to eighth grade, so she's on her way out. I'm surprised she's here, really; most Class Eight moms have given up on the school run long ago, never mind volunteering for the gala or anything else. Then it's Joanna, who is new, with a daughter in kindergarten. She's clearly made an effort for tonight, straightening her hair, putting on makeup and a floaty top and bright white jeans. She looks nervous and also very young; I don't think she's much past thirty.

At forty-nine, I am starting to feel ancient, and I think again about that line on my forehead. Maybe it is time for another trip to the beautician for some "medical aesthetics." I wonder—again—how old Harriet is. I don't recall her face looking all that lined. There is a freshness to her that doesn't have to do with her funky clothes.

And then Harriet is there, stepping out of the elevators, dressed just as I predicted in one of her usual boho—or is it hobo?—outfits, this time a batik-print skirt whose ragged hem brushes the floor, clunky Doc Martens, and a white cropped T-shirt that reveals a good inch of pale stomach, complete with belly button ring. Compared to everyone else in their mom clothes, she looks young and rebellious and entirely out of place, that vivid vine tattoo twining across her shoulders, her dyed red hair in frizzy waves around her face.

For a second, at the sight of her, there is a startled pause. Then I swoop forward, grabbing hold of her arms, air-kissing her on both cheeks. "Harriet!" I exclaim. "I'm *so* glad you made it."

I don't *mean* to squeeze her arms that tightly, but I must have because when I step back, I realize my nails have made sharp little crescent moons in her pale skin. She rubs one while grimacing ruefully before she raises her head and gives me such a coolly appraising look that I feel completely jolted. It's a look that says, as clearly as if she shouted it, that she knows my game and she's already playing it. She holds my stare as her lips curve in a small, knowing smile that tells me not only that, but she'll beat me at it.

I'm still processing that when Michael strolls into the front hall. He's rolling up the sleeves of his crisp blue button-down shirt when he looks up and his whole face brightens as he catches sight of the little group of women still standing by the door—one in particular.

"*Harriet!*" he exclaims, and my stomach cramps with anxiety as Harriet's smile widens.

EIGHT

HARRIET

I don't know what Elise's problem is, but she clearly has it in for me, underneath that sickly saccharine smile. I think she might have drawn blood when she squeezed my arms. I decide to ignore her in all her couture glory as I turn to Michael with a smile that's warmer than any I've given him before.

"Nice to see you, Michael," I say, while the three other women, none of whom I know, silently goggle at this exchange… or at least that's what it feels like. In reality, one of them murmurs something unintelligible, another tells Elise she looks fabulous, and the third strolls into the apartment like it's her own. Maybe I'm reading too much into everything—Elise's look and the painful squeeze, Michael's welcome, the other women who *feel* hostile, even if they aren't.

Two days into The Garden School, and I'm not sure how to take any of it. Yesterday, Kyra chatted happily to Allan about her first day, how nice Mrs. Ryan is, and how the classroom is so cool—it has a reading area with a sofa and a beanbag and a roof, that they call the porch. There is a pet hamster *and* a clownfish, and each kid gets a turn to take them home on the weekend.

The lunch food was the best she'd ever had, and there was a snack break where they got rice Krispie treats for *free*.

Allan lapped it all up, nodding and smiling, clearly feeling he'd made a good decision in insisting Kyra go to what was—so obviously—the best school in the world. I was trying to feel that way, too, because how could I not? Kyra has never talked so much about a school. She's never seemed so enthusiastic about *anything*. This morning, she was up before I was to get dressed and pack her backpack, and she skipped into school without a backward glance, a marked change from the usual accepting trudge.

I was happy as well as relieved that Kyra was adjusting so well, and it certainly validated my decision to move in with Allan, and yet… I was ashamed to admit it, even to myself, but there was a mean little part of me that resented Kyra's easy adjustment to a world I knew I would never belong to. I feel anxious about being part of this world, even on its periphery, and what about when we have to leave it, which we will, by the very nature of my and Allan's arrangement? Although, according to Allan, that won't be for several years. If things go the way he thinks they will, Kyra will be able to stay at the school through eighth grade, even if right now I can't imagine what that will look or feel like.

Still, despite all those worries, I am doing my best to be glad that Kyra has settled in so well, and more importantly, that she and Allan have started to develop a bond, which was exactly what I wanted.

"It's like a flip has been switched and the light just came on," Allan told me last night, after we'd been to get ice cream, had dinner and she'd gone to bed. "For *both* of us." He'd broken out a bottle of wine to celebrate, and we sipped a decent Pinot Noir, watching the traffic slide by on Fifteenth Street. "I don't know what I was afraid of," he added, like he'd cracked the conundrum of parenting with a double scoop of Rocky Road, and maybe he had.

I couldn't bring myself to say anything remotely snarky, though, especially when Allan leaned over and touched my hand.

"Thank you, Harriet," he said, his voice thrumming with quiet sincerity. "Thank you for moving here to be with me. Thank you for letting me have a relationship with Kyra when I was a complete absentee father for eight years." He shook his head with rueful regret. "If only I'd known..."

"Sometimes it takes time to know," I replied, a philosophical truth reduced to pithiness. "The point is, we're here now. And so are you." And that was definitely a good thing.

"Yes." He nodded in heartfelt agreement, and I felt compelled to continue.

"Allan..." Already he had started to tense. "It doesn't have to be this way," I told him quietly. "I'm here, I can help, if you could just—"

"*No.*" His voice was soft but final. "This has been a good day, Hats. Let's not ruin it."

I shook my head slowly. "When are you going to tell Kyra?"

According to Allan, he had plenty of time, but I was still worried. When you were satisfied with the status quo, days could slip into weeks and then months without anything changing.

He stared out the window, his lips pressed together, his fingers trembling before he clenched the stem of his wineglass. "I'm just starting to get to know her," he said. "Give me time."

But I don't know how much time we have, which is why I'm here tonight, enduring the speculative and slightly sneering looks of these women—as well as Elise's overt hostility. Michael might not have answered my text, but I still need to talk to him.

As a group, we move into the living room, and while the other women all chat like long-lost friends, I follow Michael to the drinks table. The Dunnetts' apartment is exactly what I'd expected—enormous, on the tenth floor, with views of Fifth Avenue and the leafy enclave of Central Park beyond. Everything is carefully decorated in shades of cream—the artwork matches the furniture, which matches the carpet, with the occasional offbeat piece thrown in to keep it from seeming too much like an upscale IKEA.

It's the kind of place that has uplighting for the artwork and a statement piece for the dining room table, which looks like it was carved out of a single piece of mahogany. Everything screams tastefully expensive, with mere hints of personality.

"So what would you like to try?" Michael asks as he hands me a little menu written out in calligraphy that I bet Elise did herself. He's shrugged off his suit jacket and rolled up the sleeves of his crisp blue shirt, and I have to admit he looks incredibly attractive. He must be well into his forties, but the smile lines by his eyes suit him, as do the streaks of silver by his temples. "The cranberry cosmo," he asks, "the Vesper martini, or the South Seas sling?"

I'm more of a Bud Light and cheap wine kind of girl, but I study the menu like it matters. I'm feeling weirdly nervous that Michael hasn't mentioned the text I sent him. All I did was ask to chat, but his friendly cocktail schtick makes me feel like he's forgotten about it, or maybe even that he's gaslighting me. Maybe the fact that I texted is embarrassing to him, which makes it even more embarrassing to me. I already know I don't want to be the one to mention it first.

"I'll have the cranberry cosmo," I finally say, putting down the little menu, and he starts reaching for bottles. I glance behind me, and although Elise is chatting to another, younger mom, I still feel her hostile gaze tracking my every move. All right, so she thinks I'm flirting with her husband. Well, maybe I will, at least by her absurd standards. My arms are still hurting.

I take a step closer to Michael.

"So did you pay for medical school by bartending?" I ask, smiling, and he smiles back, shaking his head in time with the cocktail shaker, which he handles with an assured and over-the-top flourish.

"Nope, I'm much more boring than that. Dear old Dad paid for it all."

"Some people get all the luck." I speak without rancor, matching his whimsical tone.

"I know it can certainly feel that way," he replies seriously. "But trust me, I don't take my privilege for granted."

Says every person ever who doesn't appreciate just how privileged they are, I think wryly. "Well, that certainly makes me feel a lot better about being saddled with fifty grand of debt," I quip, and he laughs, a genuine shout of amusement that has Elise's head whipping around.

I feel like telling her to chill out, or at least show her there's nothing to worry about by walking away from the husband she's so fiercely protective of, but some contrary part of me decides to do the opposite. Maybe it's because Michael's easy charm actually works, but I'm enjoying talking to him. And so I take a step closer instead, and from the corner of my eye, I see Elise's face tighten.

Why am I doing this? I wonder, as I cock my head and smile at Michael. I'm not flirting, not exactly, but I know it's annoying Elise and I usually don't try to upset people. But something about her gets under my skin. I might dislike her now, but she disliked me first.

"Here you go," Michael says, handing me the cranberry cosmo garnished with a twist of orange. He glances over my head to the other women. "Who's next, ladies?"

I move off, sipping my cocktail, which admittedly tastes delicious, trying not to feel stung by how quickly he moved on to the next woman. That's the nature of charming guys, I remind myself, but I wish he'd mentioned my text.

The other women drift toward the drinks area, which leaves me in an unexpected face-off with Elise.

"I wasn't sure you'd be able to make it," she remarks, cocking her head to one side as she studies me. Her face is flawless, the makeup subtle and expertly applied, her hair in perfect chocolate-brown waves that rest on her shoulders.

"Oh?" I raise my eyebrows in both curiosity and challenge. "Why not?"

Her lips twitch in something like a smile as she shrugs, her gauzy tank top starting to slide off one toned shoulder. I thought about dressing up for tonight, but I could never pull off anything close to the kind of look these women have, and the truth is, I don't want to. Still, some part of me wishes I didn't feel quite so sloppy right now.

"Oh, I don't know," Elise replies thoughtfully. "You just didn't seem very interested when we spoke before. I thought maybe you'd be a no-show."

I'm not interested, I think, but again that contrary part of me rears its ugly head. Why should Elise pigeonhole me, and in such a sneering way?

"Well, I'm usually too busy for this kind of thing," I tell her. "But, lucky for you, I've got some free time on my hands right now, and I'm *so* excited to get involved." And then, matching her little, cat-like smile, I stroll past her and plop onto the sofa. A drop of ruby-red cranberry cosmo spills onto the white silk upholstery, and I try to rub it away with my thumb, but only succeed in smearing it further in, which I do feel bad about, not that Elise would believe that. When I look up, she is watching me, and her eyes are flared like she hates me.

Maybe she does. I wouldn't even blame her all that much. I'm not exactly being the nicest version of myself right now, but these women get my back up, and I already feel vulnerable—with Kyra settling in so much better than I have, with Allan's situation, with the fact that my life has become so tentative and uncertain in so many ways, and not in the happy-go-lucky way that I like. Part of me wants to get up and walk out right now, but I know I won't. I'm still hoping to talk to Michael, after all.

The other women collect their drinks while Michael chats to them in that friendly way of his that is *almost* flirtatious, but not quite. Then he tidies up the drinks tray, disappearing into the kitchen, while Elise, sitting in a throne-like chair by the marble fireplace, takes control of the meeting. She flicks her hair behind her shoulders as she offers everyone a perfunctory smile before launching into a clearly well-rehearsal spiel about the importance of the gala.

I tune out almost as soon as she starts talking. I may have come here tonight, but she was right, I'm not interested in being on this committee, and I couldn't care less about the gala, no matter what I told her. And so as she drones on about sourcing fresh flowers and table decorations and donations for the silent auction, I let my gaze move around the room, looking for clues to the Dunnetts' lives. There aren't any, though; the room is beautifully decorated but without any personal photos or anything that would give me some insight into their marriage or family life.

I tell myself I don't really care, but I am curious as to why Elise seems so threatened by me. Michael and I have barely talked, yet she acts as if she's got some kind of vendetta against me. All through her spiel, I can tell she is pointedly ignoring me, meeting everyone's eye but mine, talking about everyone else's potential contributions while skipping over anything I might bring to this little group, even though she was the one who invited me. She didn't even bother with introductions, although she has to realize I don't know anyone, and she addresses everyone by name... except me. I'm sitting in the middle of the sofa between two other moms, and it's like I don't exist.

It's so juvenile, so middle school, and in other circumstances I'd be amused by such obvious and petty tactics, but I can tell other people have started to notice, and that feels awkward. One of the moms gives me a sympathetic smile, another slides me a sideways glance that is more curious than compassionate. With Elise being so passive-aggressively hostile, they're all clearly wondering what I'm doing here, and frankly, so am I.

And so, halfway through the meeting, I rise from the sofa with a soft murmur of apology and ask if I can use the powder room. Elise's lips compress and her eyes flash with ire before she tells me, in a tone of icy politeness, that it's off the hall.

"Thank you *so* much," I reply, more warmly than I would normally, just to annoy her, and I turn away from the women and their cocktails and their gossip and head to the hall. I open the powder room door and ostentatiously close it again, and then, on silent cat's feet, I move past it to the kitchen, where I'm hoping I'll find Michael.

I hear Elise start up again about the invitations as I turn the corner of the narrow hallway that leads to a butler's pantry, its glass-fronted shelves filled with expensive-looking crystal and porcelain. It opens up into a spacious, airy kitchen, where Michael is leaning against the marble island in the middle of the room, sipping from a tumbler of amber-colored whisky.

His eyes flare wide when he sees me, and then he lowers his glass and smiles.

"Why, hello there," he says.

NINE
ELISE

Graystone Terrace is just outside of Greenwich, Connecticut, a sprawling estate that looks like a cross between a beach house and a castle. Its immaculate, emerald lawns, gracious suites with separate living area and bathroom, and a broad range of activities make it one of the most expensive nursing homes on the east coast.

My father has been living here for the last two years.

I try to visit him once a week, although when things are busy, it doesn't always happen. And things are busy now, as the gala gets underway, but I needed the break from the TGS drama—and the constant worry about Harriet Tierney—and so I drove out this morning, just two days after the meeting at my house, where I'm pretty sure Harriet and Michael got up to something.

She thought she was so clever, opening and closing the bathroom door like I couldn't see her the whole time in the huge hall mirror opposite. And then creeping down to the kitchen, a look of expectant glee on her face. I strained my ears to hear Michael's voice—that low, sexy rumble I know so well. And then I kept talking about invitations and the grade of card stock we should use, as if I wasn't fully aware that a woman I'd invited into my own home was in my kitchen, shamelessly flirting with my husband—or worse.

It's the *worse* that I can't stand, the utter unknowing. I've been here so many times before, and I've never been able to ask Michael outright about any of them, first because I don't want to know, and second, because I couldn't bear it if he lied to me the way my father lied to my mother.

I've been the keeper of secrets for most of my life, first my father's and now my husband's, except Michael doesn't even know I'm keeping them. The truth is, there is no unknowing with Michael. There is just pretending not to know, and learning to live with it.

Now I park in front of the main house and stroll through reception, waving at Lisa, the petite, glossy-haired woman on the front desk. I know everyone who works here by name; I bring them fruit baskets anytime my father has had an "incident," and I tuck generous gift vouchers into their Christmas cards, pressing them into their hands with murmured thanks. It's the kind of stuff my mom should be doing, but as far as I know, she doesn't. We barely speak, quietly coordinating our visits so we don't run into each other, and that works for both of us.

The reception area is decorated like the living room of an English country house, with lots of wood paneling and bookcases filled with leatherbound books that nobody here could possibly read, and as I turn to the right, the double doors suggest I might be entering a library or a study, rather than what it truly is—a locked memory-care unit for twelve residents, all in various stages of dementia.

I press the code, wait for the beep, and then slip inside. Some of the residents are gathered in the Evergreen Room, which looks like a cross between an elegant drawing room and a school cafeteria. No matter how nicely Graystone Terrace tries to decorate, the reality always creeps in, with the wheelchairs, the medicine carts, the smell of antiseptic and air freshener covering a deeper decay that lingers in the air.

My father is in his private suite, sitting in a wingback armchair by the window, dressed immaculately in a three-piece suit, just as he used to wear every day for work. He's seventy-nine, and he was diagnosed with dementia three years ago. My mom managed with him at home for a year, insisting she could do it on her own. I came by anyway, wanting to help, even though she seemed to resent it. But a year ago, his needs became too much for her and it's easier all around now that he's in a nursing home and we can both visit him separately.

"Hey, Dad." I stoop to kiss his wrinkled cheek as he smiles delightedly at me.

"Princess! I was hoping you would come by."

"Were you?" I smile and sit across from him. I'm so thankful he recognizes me still, although the neurologist has warned me that eventually he won't. Michael, as a neurosurgeon himself, has weighed in, too; he has always admired my dad, said he wants to be like him. Since he doesn't know my dad's history of affairs because I never told him, he can't appreciate the irony. "What are you reading?" I ask as I nod toward the heavy tome that lies opened on my dad's lap.

When my mom moved him into Graystone Terrace, he insisted on bringing his entire library of law books, even though by that point he was already struggling to read simple sentences. Now he glances down at it with a slight frown, like he's not sure how it got there. I'm positive he hasn't been reading it, but, as ever, we both participate in a fiction that maintains his dignity.

"Oh, this?" he says dismissively as he closes the book. "Something very dull and dry, I assure you. But I want to hear about you, Princess. How's college?"

I smile, even though something in me sinks at his question.

Every time I visit my father, he freezes me in some time warp—today it's college, last week it was when I was just married, the week before when I was twelve. And every week, I play along, because according to the neurologist, as well as every specialist we've seen or website I've visited, playing along is the kindest and most expedient thing to do with someone who struggles with dementia. It shouldn't feel wrong, even though it does, because I've been lying for my father for almost all of my life, in one way or another.

"College is great, Dad," I tell him. "I'm just thinking about whether to major in art history or English."

"Art history?" He frowns. "You can't go very far with that."

"No," I agree, "but I do love it."

He continues to frown in thoughtful concern for a few seconds, and then his expression clears, and he smiles, looking almost joyful. "Well, if you love it, I say go ahead, darling," he tells me. "Life's too short to be doing something you don't love."

I nod and smile back. When I was nineteen and we had this exact discussion, my father was both furious and disappointed by my choices. He wanted me to do law or pre-med, or at least something reasonable like math or science, with the possibility of a glittering career in a field he approved of. I was his only child, and he pinned a lot of aspirations onto me.

One of the reasons I visit him so regularly is because I can replay all those difficult conversations and give them different endings, with my father so warmly approving of my choices. Dementia Dad is almost an entirely different person to the father I grew up with, and yet I love them both.

That's the other reason I come here so often, when most people in my situation probably wouldn't. I'm sure there are plenty of people who would say I should hate my dad for making me keep his sordid secrets, but the truth is, I don't and I never did. You can't choose the people you love, or why you love them. You can only do whatever you can to try to get them to love you back.

But it *is* nice, and even healing, to be able to bask in his approval now, as he asks me about my art history major, and who my favorite artists are, seeming more engaged and interested than he did when I was nineteen and he was working seventy-hour weeks as a high-powered lawyer.

Plus, it distracts me from thinking about Harriet, or the fact that after the meeting had ended and we were all tidying up our cocktails, she strolled out of the kitchen, completely shameless and unrepentant despite the surprised and scolding looks from some of my friends. She'd missed almost half of our discussion, and spent that time, it appeared, with my husband. Being here with my dad also keeps me from thinking about how after everyone had left, I asked Michael what on *earth* they'd been talking about for so long, keeping my voice light, even laughing, and how he brushed it off, saying Harriet clearly wasn't into the committee and she'd just wanted to chat.

I could tell he was lying; whenever Michael lies, he busies himself with something—rolling down his sleeves, adjusting his watch, playing with his phone. He did all three as we talked about Harriet, and then I stopped asking questions because I felt too sick to hear the answers he gave.

That night, I lay in bed, staring at the ceiling, feeling leaden inside, because I knew where this was going, and I didn't think there was anything I could do to stop it. Maybe I shouldn't have invited Harriet over to our apartment. I thought I'd be the one in control, forcing her to keep away, calling all the shots, which was ridiculous, because that is one thing I *never* have done, even as I try to seem like I do, all the time.

At two in the morning, I got up and went to the kitchen to make myself a cup of herbal tea. At five, Michael stumbled out of bed to get a glass of water and found me there, his shoulders slumping as he caught sight of me by the cabinets, a look of disappointment on his face.

"*Elise.*"

"I couldn't sleep," I said defensively. We'd been here many times before, with Michael waking up to find me elbow-deep in organization.

"And you really needed to do this *now*?" He gestured to the silverware drawer I was emptying out.

I shrugged, refusing to make a big deal of it. "I figured I might as well do something useful."

He shook his head slowly. "How long have you been up?"

"I don't know. An hour?" It had been three hours, and judging from the way he looked at me, almost sorrowfully, I was pretty sure Michael guessed that.

"Come back to bed," he said softly. "Please."

I hesitated, reluctant, even though part of me wanted to hurl myself into his arms, let him lead me back to bed and curl into the comforting warmth of his body. But there was silverware all over the counter, and crumbs in the drawer.

"In a minute," I said, and he sighed before turning around and going back to bed alone.

I ended up not going back at all; by the time I'd finished with the drawers, it was time to get the boys up, anyway, and Michael was in the shower.

I talk to my dad for another hour, first about college majors and art and then, when he gets tired and a little fretful, about the weather, which sometimes feels like the safest subject we can discuss. Afterwards, we take a stroll outside on the manicured lawn, walking slowly along the carefully weeded flowerbeds. It's September, but it still feels like summer, the air balmy.

By one o'clock, my dad's tired and ready for his lunch, so I escort him into the dining room and sit him by himself, although Jennifer and Nancy, two residents of the memory-care unit, immediately join him. Even in his old age, my dad is quite the handsome charmer, with a full head of white hair and those twinkling hazel eyes. Some things, I reflect as I kiss him goodbye, never change.

I drive straight to The Garden School for pickup, parking in a garage around the corner. Lewis and Luke will be thrilled to have a ride home, since we usually walk as far as I can make them before taking the bus. Michael doesn't understand why we don't drive, since we have a car and a dedicated parking space under our building, and sometimes I don't either, except that the bus is such a simple pleasure for children, even if my boys have long since outgrown the novelty of climbing the steps or paying for a ticket.

The sky is a hazy blue, the breeze that tickles me warm and comforting. As I stroll up to the knot of parents gathered in front of the school steps, I look instinctively for Harriet. She's there again with the old guy whom I assume is Kyra's dad. It's no wonder Harriet is interested in my husband, when her child's father could be mistaken for her grandfather. Today he's dressed in a T-shirt, corduroy blazer, and dirty, faded jeans that bag around his hips. Harriet is similarly attired in her usual Doc Martens, the purple overalls from the picnic, and a tank top that shows off her vine tattoos again. She's left her hair loose, and it frizzes out from her face in a bright, artificial red halo. If Michael is interested in her, I tell myself, it has to be just for the novelty. The thought isn't very reassuring.

As I turn my gaze to the opening doors, my heart lurches, because coming out with the rest of Class Three is none other than Lewis and Kyra, *together*. They're not holding hands or anything like that, but it feels as if they might as well be. Their heads are close and they're both giggling. It would be heartwarming, as well as encouraging since Lewis has never been friends with a girl before, if it wasn't Harriet's daughter.

Did Harriet put her up to this? Is she trying to get close to

Michael through our children? I tell myself I'm being paranoid, but as Lewis bowls toward me, still grinning, the first words out of his mouth are, "Can Kyra come over?"

Lewis has never had a girl over for a playdate, not even in preschool. What is going on? The suspicion that Harriet is behind this hardens inside me, and my dislike of her burns even hotter. It's one thing for Harriet Tierney to want my husband, another my *children*.

As I smile at Lewis and murmur something about maybe another day, I glance at Harriet, and find she isn't even looking at me, but it feels deliberate, like she's ignoring me on purpose.

I can't shake the feeling—the fear—that this woman has come into my life and is going to ruin everything I've worked so hard to build and protect. And I will do anything to keep her from succeeding.

TEN

HARRIET

It's Friday morning and I don't want to be here. I wasn't *planning* on being here, except Kyra, in the course of a single week, has somehow inexplicably become best friends with Lewis Dunnett, and when she overheard Allan and I talking about the gala committee last night, she insisted I be part of it.

"Kyra, you know this isn't really my kind of thing," I told her, trying for good-natured exasperation. I'd been amusing Allan with my rather petty description of all the women, but I hadn't meant for Kyra to overhear—or to take it seriously. "Why do you even care, sweetheart?" I asked, smiling to take any sting from the question. "It's just a boring thing for grownups."

"Why can't you just *do* it?" she cried, with more feeling than I'd ever seen from her just about ever. Where was my silently accepting daughter that I worried was too laidback? The emotion I'd always feared was seething beneath the surface seemed to finally be spilling out, causing her face to flush and her voice to rise to a trembling cry as she stamped her foot. "You never do *anything*," she accused as she swiped at her eyes. "Everyone *else's* moms do. They do all the usual mom things that you *never* do. Lewis' mom—"

"I don't want to hear about Lewis' mom," I interjected sharply, and Kyra glared at me, tears sparkling on her lashes.

"You never want to hear about *anything*!" she cried, and ran to our bedroom, slamming the door behind her for good measure.

"Why not stay on the committee?" Allan asked quietly after I'd let her go, deciding she needed to cool off before I explained —again—why I wasn't permanently joining the gala committee. Why I wasn't a gala-committee-joining *person*, which had been okay for both of us until we'd come to The Garden School and Kyra suddenly decided she wanted to be like everyone else, and I should, too. Allan had mentioned their relationship being like a light being switched on, and I was definitely feeling that, although not in a good way.

A little over one week in, and Kyra *loves* The Garden School. She loves her teacher. She loves the reading porch and the art classes and the colorful ocean murals in the hallways, the gym classes where she gets to play soccer with the boys and the fact that the other students are always addressed as *friends* by the teachers, in a way I find a little cloying. Since I clearly don't love The Garden School, at least not with the same intensity, I feel like I've become the enemy.

"It might be nice to be involved," Allan continued gently, his eyebrows raised, "both for Kyra's sake and your own. You could make some friends."

I thought of Elise and the other women at that stupid meeting. They were not going to become my friends. And then I thought of my conversation with Michael, his friendly interest and what it could mean. When we'd been alone in the kitchen, he'd been so much more open, asking me questions, listening to me intently. I'd felt *heard* in a way I hadn't for a long time, and so I'd ended up saying way more than I'd meant to, and he'd even given me a hug. It had all felt wonderfully promising in a way I craved in both body and soul, more for my own sake than was probably right or comfortable.

"Allan, I have other obligations," I told him meaningfully, doing my best to keep my voice gentle. "Other priorities."

"You don't," he replied quietly, and once again, in the blink of an eye, we were at this impasse. It felt like we'd never be able to navigate it, and all because of his stubbornness over something so important, which both aggravates me and breaks my heart. I care about Allan, maybe more than I ever meant to, and I also care about how his choices affect our daughter.

"If you want Kyra to have a relationship with her father," I told him, "Maybe *you* should do something about it."

He closed his eyes, his way of ending a conversation. "Not like that."

Neither of us spoke again for at least ten minutes, and when we did, it was about what we needed to pick up at the grocery store.

When I went to tuck Kyra in a little while later, she refused to speak to me, hunching her shoulders as she rolled over, so her back was facing me.

Gazing at her tucked-up knees and bowed head, it occurred to me then that joining this committee was pretty much the very first thing my little girl had ever asked of me. I'd dragged her here, there and everywhere for her whole life, plopping her into strange schools, making her live in crappy apartments and room shares, always moving on for one reason or another, with the result being that while I held onto my precious freedom, she never got to feel settled. It didn't make sense why she wanted me to join this committee, but I suspected it was because she wanted me to be like all the other moms, and more specifically, like Elise Dunnett, the *ultimate* mom, with her elegant beigewear, her organic snacks and calm smile and perfect hair.

While I couldn't promise my daughter I could be like that, I *could* be on this committee. It was a small enough sacrifice to make, but I'm certainly not expecting any friends from it.

And so here I am, not even two weeks after school has started, walking into the foyer of The Garden School drop-off, already feeling uneasy.

The woman at the reception desk gives me a beady look down her narrow nose. "May I help you?" she sniffs.

I try for a friendly smile, determined to remain undaunted. "I'm here for the gala committee meeting?"

Her gaze sweeps me from head to toe, her lips pinching together. "You are…?"

"Harriet Tierney. My daughter Kyra is in Class Three."

Another sweep of my person and then she gestures to a little machine perched on the desktop. "You can sign in there. All visitors must wear a nametag."

"Thank you," I murmur, feeling chastened, like I did something wrong.

I type in my name and the machine spits out a nametag, and then the woman at the desk informs me that the meeting is in the art room, as if I should know where that is.

I take a breath, summon a smile. "We're new this year," I tell her pleasantly, "so could you point me in the right direction?"

The woman sniffs again and then silently points down the hall that extends from the original building to a glass atrium they've built out back. "The double doors at the end."

"Thank you," I murmur with a little too much sweetness, and then I turn on my heel and head down the hall. I feel a creeping sense of dread as I walk toward the doors.

The end of the meeting at Elise's last week was awkward, to say the least. I came out of the kitchen with Michael just as Elise and her friends were heading toward it with their empty cocktail glasses. Elise regarded me with icy disdain while I tried not to feel guilty. I hadn't done anything *wrong*, after all, although missing half the meeting was, I had to acknowledge, pretty rude. And Elise and her friends looked at Michael and me like we'd just snuck out of a closet with both our shirts untucked and lipstick all over his face.

It wasn't like that, but it's not something I can explain to Elise, not that I'm all that interested in placating her in any way. When I got home from that meeting, I saw I had five crescent-shaped marks on each arm, and they were turning *purple*. The woman clearly has some serious issues. And I'm about to willingly walk into a room with her.

I stand outside the double doors to the art room, steeling myself to enter the fray. I can picture it already—the waft of expensive perfume, the Lululemon gear or whatever designer I don't even know about for the women who are serious about working out, the coffee and bagels they'll have laid out that no one will eat, because *carbs*! It's all so boringly predictable, and I don't want to be part of it, but for Kyra's sake, I will.

Just as I'm about to open the door, a woman who must have been behind me gets there first. She's thin and blonde, perfectly coiffed and draped in a variety of cashmere garments, a pashmina tossed extravagantly over one shoulder. She reaches for the door, throws it open so it nearly bangs in my face, and saunters by in a waft of expensive perfume, utterly oblivious of me. *Good grief*. I want to quit already.

Then I hear Elise's voice. "Grayson!" she says in that warm, rich tone that I now think she turns on like a tap of honey. "So good to see you."

"Oh, are we doing muffins this year?" the woman remarks with a laugh that sounds sharp. "Will anyone actually *eat* them?" She laughs again, even sharper this time.

I can't help but snicker, because I could have practically written their script myself, but unfortunately the door isn't closed, and they hear me. If I was contemplating tiptoeing away —and I'm not sure if I was or not—I can't now.

"Hello...?" Elise calls, just as another mom comes down the

hall. I met her at Elise's, and she looks very young, not much past thirty. She gives me a friendly, uncertain smile.

"Harriet, right? Are you here for the gala meeting...?"

"Yes," I reply, because what else can I say? "Sorry, I forgot your name." I don't think I ever knew it, since Elise didn't do introductions, but I smile like it just slipped my mind.

"Joanna." She brushes her hair out of her eyes. "My daughter Polly is in kindergarten."

"My daughter Kyra is in Class Three," I reply dutifully.

She smiles shyly and points to my Doc Martens. "I love those," she tells me. "I always wished I could rock that kind of look." She gives a self-conscious laugh, and I smile.

"I'm sure you could rock it." Doc Martens aren't all that out there, style-wise. Joanna is wearing what I've come to realize is a very TGS-mom styled outfit of skinny jeans, sandals, and a tank top with lace panels. Hair straightened, subtle makeup perfectly put on.

"Well, I don't know..." she begins, just as Elise throws open the door and stares at us, or really me, in disbelief. She's in another one of her elegantly monochrome outfits, this time flowing, sky-blue linen pants with a tailored top a shade lighter.

"Joanna..." she greets her with a warm smile, before turning to me, all trace of the smile gone. "Harriet." Her voice is flat, and there is a brief look of undisguised displeasure before she manages to mask it with a perfunctory smile.

"Hey, Elise." I try for a smile in return, but she's having none of it, her nostrils flaring as she resumes glaring at me with now undisguised animosity.

Joanna has already walked into the art room, which is lovely and airy, with skylights that let in the sunshine and colorful child-created artwork hanging from clips strung along the walls. In another scenario, I'd enjoy strolling around and looking at everything. Once upon a time, I dreamed about having a studio or classroom like this, and I'm glad Kyra gets to experience it.

Right now, however, I feel too tense to enjoy it for myself. Muffins and coffee are set up on one of the high worktables, and the women from the meeting at Elise's apartment, as well as the newly arrived Grayson, are all standing around, glancing between Elise and me, clearly hoping for something to go down.

I try to sidle past Elise, who is blocking the door, but she takes a menacing step toward me, keeping me out. "Why," she hisses, her voice low, "are you here?"

Even though I've been feeling her animosity for a while, the undiluted hatred in her voice still manages to surprise me with its sheer venom. All right, maybe I flirted with her husband a tiny bit just to annoy her, but it was hardly anything crazy and this level of aggression is... *weird*.

"I'm here for the gala committee meeting," I reply evenly, holding her malevolent stare. "Of course."

She shakes her head, a swift back and forth. "Even though you skipped half of the last meeting, hiding out in the kitchen with my *husband*?" Her voice is a poisonous hiss.

I don't break her furious gaze. "I'm sorry about that, but I wasn't feeling well." I don't feel *too* guilty for the admittedly blatant lie. I don't need to explain myself to Elise, even if Michael is her husband. If anything, he should do the explaining, although, to be fair, I asked him not to say any specifics just yet.

"Yeah, right," she sneers, shaking her head again. She looks like she wants to say something more, or even push me right out the door, but then I see the unwelcome realization dawn in her eyes that we are on the cusp of making a serious scene, and that is something I'm pretty sure Elise Dunnett never wants to do.

For a second, we simply stare at each other, and then she takes a steadying breath, tucks her hair behind her ears, and turns back to the other women.

"All right, ladies," she says in that warm, rich voice I recognize. "Shall we make a start?"

I would admire how quickly she was able to restore her composure, if I didn't dislike her so much.

I glance at the other women, who have avidly been watching this little scene unfold. They might not have heard what Elise said in such a furious whisper, but they definitely got the gist of it. None of them look friendly, except maybe Joanna, although she looks more uncomfortable than anything else. If there's going to be a schism in this little group, I'm pretty sure I'm going to be on one side of it—alone.

And while I might have been tempted to hightail it out of here a few minutes ago, now the contrary part of me comes to the fore again and I find myself sauntering into the room with a warm smile for each and every woman there. Joanna returns it, the two other women whose names I've forgotten look startled, and Grayson and Elise both ignore me. I ignore them too and keep smiling.

I might not have wanted to be here, but, by God, I won't let Elise or any other woman push me out. Not for my own sake, and also not for my daughter's, who wanted me here. Whatever it costs me, for both our sakes, I'm staying.

ELEVEN

ELISE

"Mom, can we have a snack?"

Lewis barrels into the kitchen, full of boy-energy, looking both eager and anxious. Behind him, I see Kyra Tierney's cloud of dark hair and watchful eyes, and I smile at both of them as I usher them further into the kitchen.

"Of course. What would you like?"

Kyra has come over for a playdate after Lewis begged me to have one for several weeks. I kept putting him off, mainly because I didn't want to have anything to do with any Tierney after Harriet gatecrashed the first committee meeting. I didn't mean to lose my temper, but since she snuck away to the kitchen with Michael, I've seen *three* texts on his phone from her. Michael has always been surprisingly careless with his phone, oblivious to what snippets I might see on the lock screen. And while I can't bring myself to ask him why Harriet is texting him, the fact remains that she is.

The snippets I saw didn't give much away, and yet they still revealed plenty. *Thank you so much, you don't know...* was the first. *Tomorrow at ten? Looking...* was the second. And the third, and the most alarming: *See you tonight. I'm so...*

Each one made acid swirl in my stomach, bile rise in my throat, and fear fill my heart.

A few days ago, when Michael was in the shower, I went through the pockets of his suit jacket and found a receipt from Starbucks for an Americano—what he always orders—and an oat milk latte, the same drink Harriet had when I had coffee with her. Along with the texts, it seemed like substantial evidence that they are meeting up regularly.

If I were a braver woman, I would ask Michael directly about why he's meeting her. But I'm not and I don't, because I don't think I could bear to listen to—and pretend to accept—his excuses and lies, and our marriage has always existed in the plane of the unspoken. It works better that way. At least I thought it did, until Harriet crashed into our lives.

Now Lewis and Kyra hop up onto the stools by the breakfast bar while I get out some bran muffins I baked that morning and then start slicing some strawberries to go with them. Kyra tracks my every movement with her dark, liquid gaze, and I offer her a friendly smile. Her friendship with my son is as unexpected as it is unwelcome, although I'm not about to blame a child for the sins of her mother, even if I am still suspicious that Harriet might have had something to do with it all. It would be a lot less awkward all round if Lewis and Kyra *weren't* friends. And, in reality, I have no idea why they are... if not for Harriet's machinations.

According to Lewis, Kyra is good at soccer, beating all the boys when they played at recess, and this made her a queen in my son's eyes. She's also amenable to anything he suggests; they've been playing FIFA on the PlayStation all afternoon, something I'm pretty sure most girls in Class Three would not be willing to do.

If she wasn't Harriet's daughter, I'd be thrilled for Lewis, glad he's made friends with a girl. As it is, I have to keep myself from trying to pump Kyra for information about her mother.

We've had four gala committee meetings so far, and Harriet has been annoyingly vocal at each and every one of them, offering suggestions with that slight smirk on her face that makes me suspect she thinks we're all ridiculous, and she enjoys baiting us with whatever absurdly provocative thing she suggests next. She certainly thinks our ideas—or, really, *my* ideas—are ridiculous.

First it was the invitations. I brought various templates to discuss with everyone, and she dismissed them all.

"Why make it look so *plain*?" she demanded, flicking her fingers at the heavy cream cardstock edged in gilt that we've used for the last two years. "Every fancy invitation has the exact same style, and it's so *boring*. Maybe we should break the mold, go for something different, in the same way TGS is meant to be a different kind of school?" She spoke the words like a challenge, her eyebrows raised, as she glanced around at each of us, daring us to object.

"I think it's more *classic* than plain," I replied, striving to keep my voice level, even light, although, in truth, I felt like throttling her—and not about the stupid cardstock. "People are paying two hundred and fifty dollars for a ticket. They want something elegant. Something they can *trust*."

Harriet's eyes narrowed at my unwitting emphasis, and then she shook her head. "They want something *different*," she stressed, her gaze clashing with mine, her voice rising in a way that made everyone shift in their seats. "Something they can have ownership in, feel a part of." She paused before brightening. "What about having the invitations decorated by the children? Each parent gets one designed by their child? It could be an art project."

I couldn't contain my gasp of horror, and Grayson let out a tinkling laugh.

"I think parents go to this gala to get away from their children," she remarked dryly, and Harriet, unfazed, conceded the point.

"Fair enough, but I still think we should try something different. TGS is supposed to be different from all the other private schools, but with this..." She nodded towards the invitation. "It just looks like their poor cousin."

Biting my lips, I managed to suppress the sharp retort I longed to make. This wasn't the way we conducted our meetings. In the past, I would suggest something, Grayson would second it, and everyone else would murmur their approval. Job done. But not now.

"We could go with a fun theme, make the whole gala around it," Harriet suggested. "Go really crazy and have it be a costume party, even—"

"*No one*," Grayson cut across her, her rich TV-presenter's voice laced with laughter, "wants to wear *costumes*. This is an opportunity for people to look and feel fabulous, not totter around in some ridiculous and uncomfortable getup." She smiled at everyone, as if accepting their adulation; Grayson was a news anchor for a minor cable network, and she showed up at these things mainly so she could pose as the local celebrity. She has never been interested in doing any work, just feeling important, and that was pretty much by her own admission.

"Fair enough," Harriet replied with a breezy smile, still unfazed. "No costumes. But a fun theme? I think that could really work, especially with this crowd."

Did Harriet even know what "this crowd" was? TGS parents were not like her, and I was pretty sure she was aware of that. This crowd wanted what I'd been giving them—a standard, elegant event with good *hors d'oeuvres* and an open bar that they can enjoy and then forget about. Why did she have to be so difficult?

"Well... I suppose it depends on what the theme is," Grayson replied thoughtfully, giving Harriet a quick, smiling flash of her gleaming white veneers.

In that moment, it felt as if the mood of the room had

shifted. My tight control of this little group was slipping away from me, and all because Harriet was so different, a novelty, a *nonentity*. But right then, no one seemed to be able to see how irrelevant she was meant to be. They were fascinated and charmed by her, by her contrary spikiness, and where did that leave me? If I couldn't be the calm, modulated voice of authority and expertise, what was I? And how on earth could these women, my alleged friends, be listening to *Harriet*?

It's only gotten worse since then, with Harriet weighing in on absolutely everything. Some of her suggestions are so blatantly outrageous they don't deserve to be discussed—like having the theme be a Mexican fiesta, complete with *maracas*, *pinatas*, salsa dancers and a taco stand—but the irritating and alarming thing is that instead of being annoyed, everyone is amused and admires her originality. Rachel told her she likes how Harriet thinks out of the box, how *artistic* and *creative* she is. Joanna said she was so *fun*. She seems to have brought a breath of fresh air into the group that I really didn't think we needed.

And every time someone reacts to her suggestion with enthusiasm, she flashes me a quick, smirking look, as if to say: *See? I can do this better than you can, and I'm not even trying.* It's starting to feel like she can be a better me, which is ridiculous, because she's nothing like me. And yet she's usurped my place on the committee. She's taken my place with my *husband*. I'm pretty sure she knows I know about the texting, and the coffee, and I'm afraid to think what else—*see you tonight* echoes in my mind endlessly—and she's rubbing my nose in it all by coming to the committee meetings and then firing all her ideas at us like bullets that shoot down my own suggestions.

Four weeks on, we've finally decided to go with an opera theme, and the invitations, instead of being tasteful and expensive, look like something run off a home printer for a suburban theater group, complete with a pair of opera glasses and a single red rose. The dress code is "old world glamor," whatever that means, and Grayson is going to ask an opera singer friend of hers to sing. It all sounds cheesy and cringeworthy to me, but everyone, including the headmistress, is going for it, claiming that "fun is what we need right now," and Harriet is so smug about it all being her idea.

"So, Kyra," I say now, pitching my voice playful, "are you settling into life in New York? You guys live out in Queens, right?"

Kyra looks up from the bran muffin she's been picking at, blinking at me slowly. "Yes," she says. "We live in Queens."

"And it's you and your mom and your dad?" Inwardly, I cringe at how blatantly I'm fishing for info, but she's eight years old. She won't notice, and I need to know more about Harriet Tierney's life. Is she with that old guy, Allan? Does he know about her meetings with Michael?

Kyra regards me with that quiet intensity that is both impressive and unnerving. "Yes," she says simply, and goes back to her muffin.

"What does your dad do for work?" I ask like I know and just need to be reminded.

Kyra glances up, looking uncertain. "I don't think he works. He's home a lot," she says after a moment. She picks a crumb off the muffin and nibbles it.

I wonder if he's retired. He looks old enough to be. Are he and Harriet together? They obviously live together, but she just moved here from Austin, and when I've seen them at the school run, they've both looked *separate* somehow. All of it makes me uneasy, but I refrain from asking any more questions. The last thing I want is Kyra getting suspicious of me.

Lewis and Kyra head back to the playroom, having eaten all their strawberries and barely touched their bran muffins, and then Luke drifts in, looking forlorn. I ruffle his hair as I smile down at him.

"Hey, Lukie, do you want a snack?" He shrugs and I start slicing more strawberries. "You could play with Kyra and Lewis," I suggest, and he shakes his head.

"I don't like Kyra."

I still in my slicing as I stare at my son, a new unease, along with a curiosity, creeping along my spine. He sounds so *certain*. "You don't?" I keep my voice light. "Why don't you like her?"

Luke just shakes his head, and I know I won't get another word out of him, but it does make me wonder. Why would Luke dislike someone as quiet and seemingly easy-going as Kyra Tierney? He usually likes everyone.

I don't have time to think about it, though, because just as Luke has finished his snack, Michael comes in, early from work, calling out to his boys, so both Lewis and Luke come running. I head out into the hallway just in time to see Kyra drift through and then, quite suddenly, gape at him, so clearly shocked by his presence. Michael smiles at her, his self-assured bonhomie slipping for a second at the look of undisguised vitriol twisting Kyra's features, so unlike anything I've seen from her before.

"Why," she asks, her voice shaking, "were you shouting at my dad?"

I'm processing this question when Michael tries to smile, looking distinctly unnerved. "Kyra, honey..." He lets out a little laugh that wobbles falsely. "I wasn't *shouting*."

"Yes, you were," Kyra insists. "And he was shouting back, and he asked you to leave." Her voice trembles. "I didn't know you were Lewis' *dad*."

My stunned brain is finally catching up. Michael must have gone to Harriet's apartment, and Allan asked him to leave. They were both *shouting*. What was he doing there? Nausea swirls in my stomach and spots dance before my eyes. I've always had my fears, but as much as I worried, I know in this moment that I never considered them true *certainties*. I always told myself I was being paranoid, managed to convince myself there was a chance that I was, because my past history with my father's cheating has skewed my judgment, colored my thinking.

But now the evidence is obvious and overwhelming, pointed out to me by a child.

Michael is having an affair with Harriet Tierney. And I'm just trying to figure out what I am going to do about it when the doorbell rings.

TWELVE
HARRIET

Michael answers the door, surprising me, as I'd been bracing myself for another unpleasant encounter with Elise. I was expecting him to be at work, which would have been easier all around considering how we left things the other night, but I do my best to give him a smile. He smiles back, but it seems unhappy, and I feel a strange squeeze around my heart.

Over the last few weeks, I've come to depend on Michael, just a little bit. I've tried not to, but ever since I cornered him in the kitchen, he's become—not quite a friend, no, but maybe something better, or at least more important. Our coffees have been the highlight of my week. His nightly texts lift my spirits. When he asks me how I am, his gaze so warm and caring, I feel something blossom inside me. In this strange half-life I'm living, Michael is something close to an anchor—the only one I have.

"Hi, Michael—" I begin.

"Harriet." He cuts me off and then stands aside to give me a view of the scene—all three children crowded in the hallway, the boys looking confused and Kyra seeming near tears, which is so unlike her. Elise stands in the doorway to the kitchen, her face pale, her eyes huge, her slender arms wrapped around her waist like she's holding herself together. She seems too dazed to give me her usual cool glare, but I have a feeling she will any second now.

I've walked into the middle of something, and I have no idea what it is.

"Hey," I greet them all lightly as I look around at the unhappy crew. "What's going on?"

Maybe that isn't a question I should have asked, but Elise is the only one who answers. She lifts her gaze to pin me with the glare I was expecting. "That's what I'd love to know," she chokes out, and then whirls around and stalks back into the kitchen.

I glance at Michael, a question in my eyes, and he shakes his head wearily. I have never seen him anything other than completely assured, no matter what the situation, but right now, he looks both exhausted and terribly sad.

I glance at Kyra, who angrily wipes tears from her eyes. Lewis is staring at the ground, and Luke is watching the whole scene with a wary stillness.

"Kyra, honey?" I press gently. "What's up?"

Like Michael, she just shakes her head and then storms past me to get her backpack, fumbling with the straps as she slings it on her shoulder.

"Kyra..." Lewis says, sounding disappointed. "I thought we were playing FIFA?"

Luke slips past him, disappearing into the apartment.

"I have to go," Kyra says flatly, and after a second, Lewis nods disconsolately and follows his brother.

I turn to Michael, who is still looking dejected, his hands plunged into the pockets of his suit pants. "Michael?" I try for a slightly playful note. "Why is everyone looking like someone died?"

"Why don't you talk to Kyra?" he says heavily. "I'll catch up with you later."

And then he walks out of the foyer, leaving me alone with my daughter in the Dunnetts' front hall. I put my hand on her shoulder, to anchor her in place, and I feel her tremble beneath my fingers.

"Kyra..."

She shrugs my hand away. "Let's just go home."

"Okay." I feel bad for leaving without saying goodbye, but they're the ones that abandoned us first, and it's probably better if we just go, so we do.

Neither of us speak until we're on the Fifth Avenue bus heading downtown to Fifty-Ninth Street, where we can get the subway to Queens.

"Kyra?" I ask gently. "You want to talk me through what happened back there?"

She shakes her head, and I sigh.

"I have no idea what's going on. You've got to help me out here, kid."

Kyra glares up at me. "Why was Lewis' dad yelling at *my* dad?" she demands in a low voice that throbs with confusion and hurt.

I stare at her for a second and then I lean back against the hard plastic seat and briefly close my eyes. This is not the time or place for this conversation, and yet I know I can't put it off for much longer. I've been asking Allan to talk to her for weeks, and he always prevaricates, insists he wants a little more time with Kyra, which I understand, but it still frustrates me. We both need to be thinking about what is best for Kyra, not Allan, at least in terms of telling her.

"I thought you were asleep when that happened," I say honestly, and she shakes her head mutinously. I try a different tack. "Why were you so upset today, at the playdate? That happened a few days ago."

"Because I didn't know it was Lewis' *dad*."

"Oh, honey." I put my hand on her head, but she ducks

away. Considering it was Allan and Michael who were shouting, I'm not sure why she's so mad at *me*, but maybe it's simply because I'm here and I'm safe. "I know you aren't going to want to hear this," I say, "but it's complicated."

"Mrs. Dunnett doesn't like me," she says abruptly, and I realize afresh just how *complicated* this whole thing is.

"I think," I tell my daughter, "that it's me she doesn't like."

Kyra frowns suspiciously. "Why not?"

I am not about to go into all of that. "I don't know. Sometimes people just don't like each other. There's not much you can do about it." Wanting to be fair, I add, "I haven't done much to make her like me. I'm kind of different from the other moms." I pause. "I know you don't always like that."

Kyra shakes her head. "This wasn't about that. It felt... *different*."

We've reached Fifty-Ninth Street, and so we can't continue the conversation, which is just as well, because I really don't know what to say. Kyra may seem older than her years, but she's only eight. I can't possibly make her understand the complicated—and, frankly, unhealthy—dynamics of the adults in this situation, and she shouldn't have to try. But I do need to give her some answers.

There's no opportunity to talk on the platform or in the rattling subway car, and we walk home through the mid-October dusky twilight without saying much at all. Five weeks since the start of school, and some things are better than I could have ever expected, while others are definitely much worse.

Allan and Kyra have formed a fledgling relationship that is tender and sweet, and while it unnerved me at first, now I only want to enjoy it... for however long it lasts. Seeing Kyra unfurl like a flower with her father is wonderful, but it's tempered by the knowledge of its fragility. Which makes me think of Michael, and how difficult that conversation where he and

Allan were shouting at each other was. How much I wanted it to help, to *work*, and it didn't.

And that makes me think of Elise, and how I suspect she's assumed all this time that something is going on between Michael and me. That's not necessarily my fault, especially as Michael will presumably be telling her there's nothing between us, but it certainly makes things difficult. And, if I am honest, Elise also hates me because I've disrupted her little fiefdom, the gala committee.

While I never expected to enjoy being a part of that select little group, the truth is, I *have*, and Elise can't stand it. She can't stand that the others have agreed to my suggestions and are looking to *me* for creative advice and ideas. And fine, maybe I've subtly rubbed her nose in it a little. It's hard not to when she is always giving me murderous looks, but I recognize that it is petty of me, and I probably should stop.

But I never wanted Kyra to get involved in any of this drama. As glad I am that she's finally made a friend, I really wish it wasn't Lewis.

We are silent as we climb the stairs to Allan's apartment, and I let us in. Allan has barely spoken to me since Michael came over, although he's still as warm as ever with Kyra. Did I think she wouldn't notice the tension between us? Did I think all the seismic ripples in our adult lives wouldn't be felt by her, *affect* her?

As always, I go to the living room to check on Allan. He's lying on the sofa, slack-jawed in sleep, a little drool trickling out of the corner of his mouth. With his eyes closed and his face in repose, he looks even older than he does awake, with a pasty pallor, his hands, clasped on his chest, skeletally thin, his hair so wispy and turning white. My heart aches for him, but it also throbs with anger. It doesn't have to be this way, and he knows it.

As if sensing my presence, his eyes flicker open. For a

second, he looks confused, and then his expression clears. He has to swallow several times before speaking, each movement painful to witness, and a new development in the last few weeks. Every day, I worry that we won't have as much time as Allan thinks we will.

"What's wrong?" he asks, and I realize I must be glaring down at him.

"You need to tell Kyra," I say quietly. "It's time."

His face crumples a little. "Harriet…"

"She overheard Michael Dunnett when he came by the other night."

Allan's eyes flash and his expression darkens. "That," he says quietly, with dignity, "was not my fault."

"I know that, but…" I trail off, shaking my head. I'm so tired of fighting this battle, for the sake of my daughter. "Allan—"

"Harriet, I've made my decision," he says implacably. "It's a reasonable and informed one. You just need to accept it. So does Dr. Dunnett."

"And you need to accept that wanting a relationship with our daughter affects all your other decisions, including *this* one," I snap, goaded into anger by his sheer stubbornness. I shake my head, caught between fury and despair. "Allan," I ask quietly, "don't you realize you're being selfish?"

He meets my gaze unflinchingly unapologetic. "Is it selfish to not want Kyra to see me like that?" he asks quietly.

I can't be so cruel as to point out that she'll see him *like that* anyway, and undoubtedly sooner than either of us want or hope. "You need to tell her," I say instead, again, and he sighs, just as a voice, trembling and small, sounds from behind me.

"Tell me what?" Kyra asks.

THIRTEEN
ELISE

It is a testament to either my self-control or my stupidity that I do not confront Michael after Harriet and Kyra leave our apartment, slipping out like thieves after that painfully awkward confrontation.

Michael goes into the bedroom to change, and I start making dinner. I don't even bang the pots and pans. By the time he comes in twenty minutes later, I am calmly slicing shiitake mushrooms. Lewis and Luke are doing their homework at the breakfast island, heads bent over their worksheets while I look benevolently on. We are the prototype for the perfect family. Take a picture of us, *please*.

Michael stands in the doorway of the kitchen, observing us all with a slight slump to his shoulders, like it's too much to take in. Like he knows it's fake... but if it looks real, it *can* be real, can't it? I have worked so hard to make this real, and it *is*.

"Glass of wine?" he asks, already going to the mini wine fridge to get a new bottle. We opened one yesterday, but I guess it's already been finished.

I keep slicing. "Sure, thanks, that would be lovely." To my credit, my voice is relaxed.

Out of the corner of my eye, I see Luke look up, watching us avidly. Lewis is frowning down at his homework. Neither of them has asked me anything about what happened back in the hallway, when Kyra flipped out and we just left her and Harriet standing there. Clearly they've learnt from the best, a thought that makes my stomach cramp with dread. I don't want them to grow up like I did, and yet... I already know I'm not strong enough to stop it. The difference, I tell myself, is that I am a loving, present mother in a way mine never was.

Michael takes a corkscrew, opens the wine, and pours two glasses, all with careful, deliberate movements, like he's moving in slow motion. Neither of us speak. When he hands me my glass, I murmur my thanks without looking at him.

We've been here before, of course, too many times. Harriet Tierney may be the most obvious, or at least the most recent, but there have been other women. Helene Dubois, the stick-thin Frenchwoman, for a time, after she first moved and apparently needed *friends*. Miss James, the first-grade teacher, barely out of college, at a parent-teacher event. I can still hear her girlish giggles, the way she batted away Michael's hand as she exclaimed he was *too funny*! Even Grayson Wells, whom I pretend to be friends with, drunk at last year's gala, discovered in an alcove weeping into my husband's arms. Each time, I pretended not to notice. Each time, we got through it, even if the flirting and the murmured words and the low laughter all crawled under my skin, into my brain. Even if I know I will never forget, no matter how much I pretend that I have. We move on.

But now the children are involved, with Lewis and Luke having stood there goggle-eyed while Kyra melted down, and I realize I need to reconsider my tactics. If pretending hurts Lewis and Luke, then maybe I have to finally face the reality of my philandering husband and call him on it... whatever the fallout. The prospect is utterly terrifying.

"Dinner will be ready in about twenty minutes," I tell Michael as I add the mushrooms to the pan. "Risotto."

"Great," Michael murmurs. He's already drifting toward the hall, his back to me. "I'll just check a few things in my study."

I picture him texting Harriet, wanting to get their stories straight, as I stir the mushrooms.

"Mom?" Luke's voice is quiet, coming from behind me.

I turn around. "Yes, honey?"

He blinks at me solemnly. "Are you okay?" he asks, and my heart twists. A child should never have to ask that question of his parent.

"I'm fine, Lukie," I tell him. I reach over to stroke his silky hair, letting it slide through my fingers. "I'm absolutely fine."

For the sake of my children, I have to be.

Incredibly—or not—three weeks go by, and Michael and I don't talk about Harriet once.

I stay almost completely silent in our gala meetings as they continue with their tacky opera theme. Harriet suggests giving every female guest a pair of polyester opera gloves as a party favor. It's like she's planning for a bachelorette party on Staten Island, for heaven's sake, not a two-hundred-and-fifty-dollar ticket event in Manhattan, for parents who expect something elegant and elite. She has no idea about class, and yet, amazingly, the others are going for it. They think it's *fun*. They say it's time to try something different, that life's too short, that we need "new energy." I smile and nod and try not to fume. I am not going to let Harriet Tierney realize just how much she gets to me, even if she already knows. I can at least keep up the pretense, if only to myself.

And so the weeks pass as we send out the invitations, arrange the party favors, receive the silent auction items, including box seats at the Met Opera, courtesy of a friend of Grayson's. Harriet is painting some backdrops for the event, which is being held on the rooftop terrace of the Gramercy Park Hotel, which recently reopened. I had a tour of the refurbished space back in September, and it certainly doesn't need any painted backdrops like we're putting on a school play in the sports hall. I don't say this, however, because everyone else thinks it's *so fun*, doing something different, being a little quirky.

"I know it's all a little kitsch," Grayson tells me one Friday morning in early November, when we get to the art room before everyone else. I've brought coffees for everyone except Harriet, because I couldn't bring myself to be big enough to order her an oat milk latte. Not when I know she's having them with my husband. "But I did feel the old event was getting kind of stale," Grayson continues in her rich, TV-presenter's voice. "People are tired of the same old, same old, aren't they? Gilt edge to everything, tinkling music, champagne? It's so *boring*. I've been to a dozen events like that in the last *month*."

Leave it to Grayson to make this about her and her oh-so hectic social life.

I give a noncommittal shrug. "You might be right."

Grayson laughs, the sound slightly tinged with malice. "She really gets your nose out of joint, doesn't she?" she remarks, and I stiffen at her comment. I thought I had been hiding my reaction to Harriet better than that.

"Who?" I ask, even though we both know it's a dumb question.

Grayson doesn't even bother to clarify. "She's like the anti-you," she muses. "So rebellious, it's a little clichéd. I mean, those *tattoos*. A little much, don't you think? Like she's trying too hard to be alternative."

I don't reply, because I never gossip, but a part of me is

THE SECRET BETWEEN US 107

desperate to descend to Grayson's level and tear apart Harriet Tierney.

"Is that what bothers you?" Grayson continues in her musing way. "*Because* she's so different? I know she's taken over a little bit, but you're still in charge, Elise. You always will be. A two-bit act like Harriet Tierney doesn't have anything on you."

If only my husband agreed, I think, but of course don't say. If Grayson thinks I'm just annoyed about Harriet taking over the committee, fine. I won't disabuse her of that notion.

It's better that than the truth. That Harriet Tierney is involved with my husband.

Early the following week, I drive to Connecticut to visit my father. Crossing the Tappan Zee Bridge over the Hudson River, seeing it sparkle deep blue far beneath me, always releases something in me, a rush of relief that I am leaving my New York City life behind—the tension of all the things left unsaid, the strain of simply being me, the mother who has it all together, whom everyone at The Garden School looks up to, whether they acknowledge it or not.

Grayson really didn't have it right the other day, I realize with a jolt, at least not completely. Part of me is glad Harriet has more or less taken over the gala committee. Yes, it's annoying that it's *her*, but it means I get a break from having to do everything perfectly. Or at least *seem* like I am, which is basically the same thing, just far more exhausting.

The farther I get from the city, the more I relax. I let the worries and fears about my family, my marriage, my *life*, slip away. When I'm with my dad, I get to just be me, a daughter, a child. I know it's not entirely healthy, and that really it's just more pretending, but I still crave his approval and admiration, just the way I did when I was little.

"Princess!" He greets me with the usual delight as I walk

into his suite, only to check myself when I see my mother sitting on a stool near his chair. She looks as primly collected as ever, dressed in a twinset and navy-blue slacks, her hands folded in her lap. I try to recall when I last saw her, and realize it had to have been in the summer, when we went out to her house in Greenwich for a barbecue, the conversation painfully stilted the whole time.

"Mom." I try to inject an enthusiasm into my voice I don't feel as I walk over to kiss her cool cheek. She murmurs an unenthusiastic greeting back.

There is no real reason for my mother and I not to get along. We never had a fight, or a falling out, or anything resembling conflict. And yet, for as long as I can remember, a coolness has existed between us that neither of us have made any effort to thaw. Since my dad got dementia, it became easier for us to visit him in turns so we don't have to see each other. My mom usually visits on Mondays; I visit on Thursdays. Today is Tuesday, so there's no reason for either of us to be here.

"I wasn't expecting you to be here today," I say, trying not to make it sound like the accusation it really is.

She raises her thin, arched eyebrows, her lips pressing together. "Am I not allowed to visit my own husband when I choose?"

I hold back a sigh. "I didn't mean it like that, Mom."

I glance at my father, who is watching our interaction with a look of befuddlement on his face. Another reason I don't visit my dad when my mother is present is because I am worried he'll let something slip. Since his dementia diagnosis, he's said a few things that I would have trouble explaining to my mother. I've kept his secrets for this long; I don't want to have it all be for nothing now.

"Anyway," I say firmly, wanting to move the conversation on. "How are you, Dad?"

"Oh, I'm fine, fine." He nods to the legal pad on his lap.

THE SECRET BETWEEN US

"Just making some notes for my latest case." The pad of paper is blank, but I nod along.

"Sounds like you're pretty busy," I say with a smile.

"Oh, I'm always busy." He smiles back at me. "But not too busy for my princess!"

I feel my mother's tension as she shifts in her seat, recrossing her legs. Maybe that's part of the coolness between us; my father has always adored me. Admittedly, it's been in his own, ultimately self-centered way, but he possesses the kind of charisma that makes you long to be drawn into his orbit, spared a single glance.

Just like Michael.

On my wedding day, my mother, rather acerbically, pointed out this truth.

"I always heard that girls marry their fathers, but I didn't think it was true until I met Michael," she said as she twitched my veil over my shoulder. "He's the spitting image of your father in every way."

"They do look alike," I acknowledged, longing to leave it at that.

"I didn't mean in *looks*," my mother replied flatly. "But as long as you know what you're getting into."

For a single, heart-stopping second, I thought she was referencing my father's affairs. But she couldn't know about them, or least that *I* knew about them, I told myself. Could she? If she had, she would have said something. She would have left him, surely?

Then she continued, "Loving someone who has the whole world at their feet can be exhausting. Frustrating. But as long as you know where you stand, and that they love you back even if it doesn't always feel like it..." She paused. "Well, then you can... manage."

There was too much in that statement for me to untangle, especially when I was moments from walking down the aisle to promise the rest of a life to a man my mother was basically saying would disappoint and even hurt me.

"Mom…" I began, but she quickly bent to kiss my cheek, more, I thought, in an attempt to end the conversation than as a gesture of affection.

"Congratulations, my darling."

Now I glance between my parents, wishing there was a way I could extract myself from this situation. I was up for a casual chat with my dad, a little of his usual cheer, but not managing the passive aggression from my mother. Not after the last few weeks.

"How's Michael?" she asks with a sniff.

"He's fine. Busy, you know, as usual. He's been doing some more teaching in addition to the surgeries, so…" I let that trail off.

"And the boys?" my mother asks after a moment. My mother comes into the city once a month or so and takes the boys out by herself, usually to a restaurant where they have to behave and come back practically twitching with restless anxiety. Neither of us have ever suggested increasing the regularity of those visits.

Michael's parents live in California, and we don't see them nearly as often as we should, as they're so busy with their retirement lives—golf, tennis, European cruises, wine tastings, weekends away, an endless stream of moneyed entertainment.

The result is that my boys don't have much of a grandparent presence in their lives. Before my dad got dementia, he'd come for the weekend and take them to the movies or the park, before spending the evenings drinking whisky with Michael. I miss those days.

"The boys are fine," I say dutifully.

"How's Luke's health?" My mother always asks this question like Luke is the next thing to an invalid, rather than a little boy with a few minor health issues—myopia, hence his thick glasses, asthma, slight hearing loss and mild anxiety. All of them under control.

"He's *fine*," I say firmly, and her eyes flash ire, like I've rebuked her. "Really," I add, softening my tone. "He got a new glasses prescription last month, and he hasn't used his inhaler since September. He had his hearing tested at his well check in August, and the pediatrician still thinks he doesn't need hearing aids."

She sniffs, sighs. "Poor boy."

My hands clench into fists and I smooth them out. I don't think my mother means to be rude, but it's been obvious since the boys were born that she favors Lewis. Lewis, who is made in the mold of both Michael and my father. When we named the twins after our fathers, she was annoyed that Luke was named after mine. She didn't say as much—how could she without being utterly offensive—but I could tell.

"There's no need to feel sorry for Luke," I say as mildly as I can. "He's incredibly smart and happy, and he manages all his health issues without any problems."

"Still," my mother says, like that's a reason. "It has to be hard, especially when he'll always be compared to Lewis."

Anger flashes through me in a hot, white streak. "No one needs to compare Luke to Lewis," I say, even though, since they're twins, it's an understandable assumption to make. "And certainly not *you*."

My mother holds up her hands in a parody of surrender. "Elise, I'm just stating the obvious," she says. "Lewis will have it easy in life, just as Michael does, just as your father did. With Luke as Lewis' twin… it has to be difficult for the boy. I'm *empathizing*."

I don't reply, although a retort springs easily to my lips, that if this is my mother's *empathy*, I don't want it. I've spent a lifetime protecting her feelings by keeping my father's secrets…

although, if I'm honest, I didn't do it for my mother's sake. I did it for mine.

My mother's words rattle around in my brain as I head back into the city a short while later.

I didn't stay for lunch, since my mother made it clear she wanted the time alone with my dad. I was getting a headache anyway, as well as battling that sense of despair I always feel when I interact with my mother. Somehow she makes me feel like I'm doing something wrong, even when I'm simply sitting there silently. I've spent my whole life trying to be good enough, to be perfect, all the while knowing my mother won't even consider me mediocre, and my father, no matter that I'm his darling girl, won't really care.

But I keep thinking about how my mother said Lewis has it easy in life, and Michael too. I've made life easy for my husband, I know. I've smoothed his path in a thousand different ways, not least of all with his relationships with other women. I did it for my own sake, my own sanity, but now I wonder...

In the last three weeks, I know he's kept talking to Harriet. Once I overheard him talking in his study, his voice low and heartfelt.

"I know how difficult it is, Harriet, but *please* trust me..."

I walked away quickly, not wanting to hear any more, my stomach swirling with nausea and dread.

Lewis and Luke have picked up on the tension, I'm sure of it. Luke keeps watching me like he's worried about me, and Lewis has been quieter than usual. His friendship with Kyra seems to have cooled, maybe because of the awkwardness when she yelled at Michael. Lewis didn't ask about it, but he certainly noticed.

In any case, I haven't had her over again, which is a relief. I certainly could do without another run-in with Harriet at pickup. Seeing her at the gala committee every Friday is bad enough; it's hard not to let my frustration slip out, although I am trying my best to treat her like everyone else. In any case, it's clear from her smirk that she looks down on me. I picture her and Michael laughing about me together and it makes me want to scream.

Clearly I'm not holding it together as much I want to be, because even Luke, dear little Luke, has asked me if I'm okay almost every day. He's so anxious, and it tears at me, because he's far too young to carry that kind of worry.

My impulse is to do better, *be* better, for the sake of my children, but as I drive back into the city, I think about my own parents, my mother's sourness, the life she's lived of feeling second best, and that's without even knowing about the affairs, although maybe she suspects, because as a woman scorned, I know how hard it is not to... and I wonder if *I'm* not the one who needs to do better. Be better.

Maybe, for Luke and Lewis' sake as well as my own, it's Michael. And the only way for him to know that is for me to tell him.

Maybe some secrets aren't meant to be kept.

FOURTEEN
HARRIET

In the end, I took pity on Allan. While he stared in abject dismay at Kyra, who had just asked us what we needed to tell her, I filled in the tense silence with a blatant lie.

"Just about this weekend, honey. Allan can't take you to the zoo like we discussed."

Kyra's gaze swung to me suspiciously, and I could tell she didn't believe me. We hadn't even talked about going to the zoo as a definite, just as a possibility if the weather was nice and if Allan was up for it. I thought she was going to argue, but thankfully she didn't, and the moment, like a storm cloud hovering over us, passed.

"Thank you, Harriet," Allan said quietly once Kyra was in her room, having flounced there in a way she never used to.

"This can't go on," I warned him. "I mean it this time, Allan. She needs to know."

He nodded soberly. "I thought it would be easier to tell her once I knew her better, once we liked each other. I should have realized it would only get harder."

As I should have, I thought. All of this would have been far easier before Kyra cared about Allan, but the depth of her feeling and how quickly it happened took me by surprise. From that first day when Allan picked her up from school, Kyra has shown him a warmth and affection that she doesn't always show me anymore.

At night, she sits on the sofa with him while he reads his book and sometimes even rests her head on his shoulder. He's teaching her to play chess, and she holds hands with him as she skips down the sidewalk. It's like she had a dad button that has now been pushed, and it's turned her into a whole new person, a little girl who giggles and snuggles and hugs. It's nice, but it's also weird to watch it all happen so fast.

I wasn't prepared for it, for what it meant, and I'm still trying to recalibrate our lives with this new relationship right smack in the middle of it all. And now we face having some very painful conversations with a little girl who has surely had enough upheaval and uncertainty in her short life.

When Allan was settled back on the sofa, I went into the kitchen and called Michael. I knew I shouldn't have, considering how things had played out back at his apartment, but I needed to talk to him. To know how he felt. And, I confess, I'd become a little bit addicted to hearing his voice, its thrum of kindly certainty steadying me in a way I craved.

"Harriet..." He sounded tired as soon as he answered my call.

"I'm sorry about earlier," I said quickly, rushing in with the explanations, even though I was only just putting the pieces together myself. "Kyra overheard us talking the other night. I thought she'd been asleep, but she must have crept out and seen you."

"I figured," Michael replied wearily. "I suppose we should have expected it." He paused. "Unfortunately, it's created a very awkward situation here. Kyra got really angry, said I was shouting at Allan... and Lewis and Luke had no idea what was going on. They still don't, and I'm not really sure how to explain it to them."

"And Elise?" I asked after a moment. My knuckles ached as I clenched my phone. I pictured her furious look, and my stomach cramped. As much as I didn't like her, I didn't want to be the cause of her misery—or fury. I've told myself I wasn't doing anything wrong, but she doesn't know that. Obviously.

"I don't know what Elise thinks," Michael replied after a moment. "I hardly ever do. But... I must say she certainly seemed surprised when she heard Kyra talking like that."

That wasn't my fault, but I still felt guilty. I was the one who had requested Michael not explain the nature of our relationship, not until Allan had talked to Kyra. And today was yet another missed opportunity for that conversation to happen. "I'm sorry," I said after a moment. "I really do appreciate your help and... and understanding. I'm sorry if it's making things more difficult for you." My voice caught, and I could tell Michael heard it.

"Oh Harriet," he said, his tone softening. "Don't worry about me, or Elise. You have enough to be dealing with. Just focus on your own family."

And so, over the next few weeks, that is what I try to do. I take Kyra to school every day, and I make sure to keep our conversations light and easy. We point out houses we like; we study the ads on the subway and make silly jokes about them. After I drop Kyra off, I hurry back to check on Allan, work on some gala prep, which has ended up taking up a lot more time than I expected, but I've found, to my own surprise, that I enjoy it.

I'm painting some backdrops—a pair of crimson curtains where people can get their picture taken, as well as a small watercolor of Central Park, all smeary purples and greens, for the silent auction. It's fun to have different projects to work on, to feel like I am doing something productive after months of just kicking around since my last job ended in June.

Allan and I spend some time together too, if he feels energetic enough for a walk around the block, a game of Scrabble, a bowl of soup. It's slow and easy, and we chat like old friends in a way that feels both familiar and strange, painful and sweet. I remember how much I liked him—his wry sense of humor, the careful way he has of considering things. We work well together, in a way I never expected. And it tears me apart that this time is going to be so fleeting.

It's now been two months since we moved in with him, and even though he said it could be years before any further symptoms manifested themselves, I'm starting to notice some changes, even though I don't want to. He tires more easily, his hand shakes when he reaches for a Scrabble tile or a spoon, and when he speaks, sometimes a little drool collects at the corner of his mouth before dripping onto his shirt. Small things, but each one hurts, and I wonder if Kyra has noticed them too. This is all going so much faster than I thought it would, and it scares me, because I'm not sure I'm ready to handle any of it, never mind Kyra, who is far too young to be dealing with this.

We really do need to have that conversation, and yet somehow the weeks slip past, the leaves curl and fall from the trees, autumn drifts into winter, and we don't. Maintaining the status quo is always so much easier, and Kyra isn't asking questions. She's still happy enough to go to school, but she's quieter, and her and Lewis' friendship seems to have cooled, and I'm afraid it's because of me. Because of *us*—Elise and Michael, me and Allan, and the complicated dynamics I never intended to create.

In some ways, though, it's nice to have the old Kyra back—quiet and calm, not trying so hard to be a TGS kid, or have me be a TGS mom. Besides, life has gotten even busier as the gala approaches. During the Friday morning meetings, Elise pretty much ignores me, but it's harder for her to do so, when, in late November, we start meeting on Wednesdays too.

Elise is still in charge, and she's the one with the checklists and invoices, the one who calls the hotel and the caterer and the photographer, moves all the chess pieces on the board. Really, it's her show, but I can tell she feels like it's become mine, because I'm the one with the ideas, the one the others instinctively look to for any creative decision. It has to be a bitter pill for her to swallow, and I am not above letting her know I know that, especially when she tries to—subtly, it's true—cut me out.

I've lost track of the number of times she turns to me with a look of faint surprise, like she's forgotten I'm there. Once she brought coffees for everyone—except for me.

"I couldn't remember what you drank," she explained, her eyes rounded in innocence, and I just smiled and said I hadn't wanted coffee anyway.

Then there are all the passive-aggressive comments about my ideas—how the backdrops are "kind of cute," with a wrinkled nose like she really doesn't understand why we need to have them. How I might be confusing the musical *Phantom of the Opera* with *actual* opera... "Have you ever seen real opera, Harriet?" she asks with her eyes extra wide in curiosity. And then there are the comments about my own art—how she hopes someone will bid on my "little watercolor," although people prefer more established artists, don't they? "Such a shame they're not willing to try someone new." And on and on and on. I take it all on the chin, with a flinty smile, but I can't keep a little snark from slipping through on occasion. I'm only human, after all. And after a while, so many digs will draw blood.

Fortunately, the two weeks before the gala are so busy that there's no time to feed our pointless little feud. It's all hands on deck, nearly every day, first cataloguing the auction gifts and wrapping items that were donated, or really dumped, at reception into glorious gift baskets and bags. It turns out I am a dab hand at tying a nice, big, even bow—something I think annoys Elise.

We're in constant competition with each other, and even if it's not a game I chose to play, it's one I can't help but want to win.

By Thanksgiving, when the gala is just over a week away, things are mostly under control—the auction items labeled and displayed, the party favors in little gold cord-handled bags, the opera singer booked, the caterers signed off on the menu and serving. I've even bought a fabulous dress—from a consignment store—for the occasion. Allan is hoping to go, depending on how he feels. He's got a tux in eggplant-colored velvet that is perfect. His downstairs neighbor, Barbara, has offered to babysit Kyra.

It's nice to have Kyra at home for the week of Thanksgiving —we have no other plans but to be quiet by ourselves—but she has definitely started to notice things more, too. How much Allan sleeps. How his hands shake when he reaches for anything. At breakfast, his spoon shook so much as he raised it to his lips that there was nothing on it by the time it reached his mouth.

And then, the night before she goes back to school, we wake up to the terrible, startling sound of Allan sobbing wildly in the middle of the night. I scramble out of bed, while Kyra whimpers in distress, and run to Allan. He's sitting up in bed, his hair wild, his face in a rictus of shocked agony as he sobs like his heart is breaking. Maybe it is.

All I can do is take him into my arms. I haven't hugged him since we moved in, and the feel of him is both familiar and strange. I remember the wiriness of his body, but he's so painfully thin now. He feels frail, fragile, and it turns me tender, an ache of something between love and pity lodging itself under my breastbone.

"Allan…" I murmur, stroking his hair as he continues to sob. "*Allan.*"

I see Kyra's pale face peeking around the doorway, and gently I shake my head at her. She doesn't need to see this. She creeps away as I continue to hold her father, murmuring to him as if he is a child, my heart filled with grief and a strange kind of love that takes me by surprise. Poor, dear Allan.

Eventually, after what feels like far too long, he subsides. Before I can ask him anything, he falls asleep in my arms, his thin body slumping against me, and gently I kiss his forehead.

A deep sorrow sweeps through me as I hold him and nearly drags me under. This is only the very beginning, and it's all going to get so much worse. I thought I was strong enough, but maybe I'm not. And even if I am, Kyra surely isn't. She's too young to witness this. To understand, to *have* to understand.

For the first time, I seriously question the wisdom of coming here at all, of going down this long and painful road together. My reasons seemed so sound at the start, and even now I can't regret the time Kyra has had getting to know her father.

But what does the future hold, and how will either of us cope? I came here for the sake of my daughter, but what if being here hurts her more than I could have ever imagined… but should have?

FIFTEEN
ELISE

I smooth the dress over my hips as I study myself critically in the full-length mirror of my walk-in closet. It's the night of the gala, and I need to look better than I ever have in my life.

The three-thousand-dollar Pamella Roland gown I bought from Bergdorf Goodman helps, at least. It's an obviously couture piece, made of shimmering cream chiffon, with diamanté sequins sewn into the fabric so I glitter when I move. It hugs my figure, dipping to show a hint of cleavage, cinched at the waist, flaring out about my ankles with a thigh-high split that shows a golden slice of leg with every step. Understated, but very sexy. I picture Harriet in whatever second-hand getup she'll come in and I smile. This time, I'm going to win.

It hasn't been easy, these last few weeks. I know Michael talks to her almost every day. It's amazing how arrogance makes people indiscreet; he leaves his study door open, his phone on the hall table, the receipts for coffees crumpled in his pocket. It's like he wants to be found out, or maybe he just wants me to know. Maybe he's so sure I won't say anything, because I never have before.

After I came back from my father's right before Thanksgiving, I was determined to speak to him. I felt almost giddy with the power of it, even though I knew I didn't really have any power. Whatever conversation we had would invariably end with me begging him to stay. I knew that before I said a word, and yet for my children's sake, as well as my own, I was willing to do it.

And then... I didn't. At school pickup, Lewis flew down the steps and barreled into me, his expression thunderous, his eyes shiny with held-back tears. I held his thin shoulders, hugging him to me, shocked because Lewis never cried. He barely emoted at all, except when he scored a soccer goal or we were having chocolate mousse pie for dessert, a rare treat.

"Lewis, honey..." I pulled him to me, ruffling his hair. "What happened?"

He shook his head against my stomach, sniffing loudly, and then said, "Can we just go home?"

I glanced up to look for Luke, who was walking steadily toward me, his expression grimly composed. Should I talk to Mrs. Ryan? I glanced around at the other parents, who were watching this little scene unfold with both sympathy and bemusement. Lewis was charmed; whatever was upsetting him had to be small. The reminder steadied me. I didn't need to talk to his teacher.

It was only when we were walking back to the parking garage, Luke's hand slipping into mine as Lewis marched determinedly ahead, that I learned something about what had happened.

"It's Kyra," Luke confided solemnly, and I turned to look at him.

"*Kyra?*"

"She's not friends with Lewis anymore, and she told him so. Said she didn't want to play with him ever again." Luke stated this matter-of-factly, although I thought I heard a note of satisfaction in his voice that I didn't understand. "He was sad about it."

"Why..." My mouth was dry. "*Why* isn't she friends with Lewis anymore?" I asked, although I already knew. Because Lewis's dad had shouted at Kyra's dad. Because the grownups' complicated lives made their children's lives confused.

"I don't know." Luke shrugged, seeming determinedly unbothered. "She just came into school and told him she wasn't his friend."

"And Lewis was *that* upset?" Part of me knew I should not be pressing Luke for information on his brother, but I was both desperately curious—and nervous. How much had our drama affected our children?

Luke shrugged again, slipping his hand out of mine. "I don't know," he said, and for him it was clearly the end of the conversation.

But it was enough to make me hesitate—and, in truth, I knew I didn't need much of a reason—when it came to confronting Michael. I watched Luke put an arm around his brother's shoulders, and, with my heart squeezing with love, Lewis lean into his brother's half-hug. *This is my family*, I thought fiercely, *and I will do whatever I can to protect them.*

And that, I knew, meant not rocking the boat with Michael.

Now, the night of the gala, I am trying to put all that behind me. After tonight, I will avoid and ignore Harriet Tierney completely. I can pretend she doesn't exist. And pretending, I remind myself, is almost as good as the real thing.

Carefully, I dab at my eyeliner, studying my reflection critically. My makeup is subtle as always, but is it *too* understated? Do I look washed out? It's so hard to maintain the balance between effortless and not trying. But if I change anything—add a crimson lipstick, or a cat-flick eyeliner, people will notice and comment. They'll wonder why, and they'll whisper about how I must be trying to prove something to somebody. I can picture Grayson already, eyeing me up and down with that slightly superior smile on her face. *Oh Elise, you look amazing. I love your new look. So different!*

Just thinking about it makes me wince and I quickly stop, running my thumb along the line bisecting my forehead that is thankfully now much fainter, due to a trip to the salon. Why, I wonder, does everything have to be so *exhausting*?

As I stare at my reflection, I find myself thinking of a vacation we took when I was ten or so. I don't remember why, maybe our usual place in the Hamptons had been already booked, but we ended up in a little cottage on the Finger Lakes, far from the life I already knew too well—private school, ballet and tap classes, etiquette lessons every Saturday, holding a teacup and crossing my ankles. I was on the waiting list for cotillion by the time I was six.

That summer by the Finger Lakes was *magical*. I splashed and swam and read books on the beach. I went for walks by myself and stared up at the blue, blue sky. There were no tennis or pony riding lessons, no swanky dinners where I had to use the right silverware and never speak, no saying hello to slightly drunk strangers who came to talk to my parents about business or golf. It felt like freedom.

If I could travel back in time and live those three months over and over again, I would. I don't know why I'm thinking of them now. They certainly feel very far away from my current reality.

I turn away from my reflection and go to check on Luke and Lewis, who are eating dinner under the smiling eye of Rosita, our Guatemalan babysitter, who is the closest thing I've ever had to a nanny. She's known them both since they were born.

"You look so *beautiful*, Mrs. Dunnett!" she exclaims, her hands clasped to her chest.

"Thank you, Rosita." I smile, doing my best not to smear my lipstick. "Behave, you two, all right." I drop kisses on their foreheads, moving carefully in my designer dress, feeling like I am made of glass, the skirt shimmering as I take little mincing steps. "Bedtime at seven-thirty," I remind Rosita, who smiles and nods.

I've arranged a car to take me to The Gramercy Park Hotel, so I don't have to either deal with parking or wait in the frigid December air for a taxi. I'm getting there a full hour before guests arrive to make sure everything is perfect, even though I was on the terrace all morning, doing the exact same thing. Grayson came for about ten minutes; Harriet didn't come at all. Her ideas might be fun, but she doesn't do the hard graft, that's for sure. I'm not surprised.

As I step into the hotel, a porter's eyes widen, and I feel vindicated. *I look good*. In addition to the dress, I've added all my understated bling—my usual Rolex, with a few diamond bangles, diamond tear-drop earrings and a matching tear-drop pendant. Nothing too garish, but there's no question that they're all real stones. My high heels click across the floor as I give the concierge a quick smile.

"Everything is ready upstairs, Mrs. Dunnett," he informs me, his tone deferential, and I nod.

"Thank you, Luis."

I feel like the lady of the manor, and it bolsters my confidence.

I step through the elevator doors to the rooftop terrace, wincing slightly at the backdrop Harriet has made behind the check-in table—it's nicely done, I'll admit that, but the swirling script promising "A Night at the Opera" still feels very middle school to me. I do my best to ignore it as I check the guestlist—of the seventy-two families at TGS, forty-six are coming. Last year, only forty-two came, so I suppose Harriet can claim a win there; maybe the opera theme does appeal to a certain demographic.

I walk through the empty rooftop terrace, the glassed-in roof letting in the orange-hued, twilit sky. The silent auction items are on a velvet-covered table, with framed descriptions of each item, and a box for sealed bids. The mahogany bar gleams, the champagne flutes are lined up on top, ready to be filled. The string quartet should arrive any minute, along with the opera singer Grayson booked. There's nothing more to do, and so I simply stand there, savoring the moment. Forget Harriet, *I* made this happen.

In my little beaded bag, my phone buzzes. I take it out and see it's from Michael: *Running a little late. Be there by 8.*

The gala starts at seven. He knows how important this evening is to me, to *us*. I asked him to come early, and he agreed.

I take a breath, let it out slowly. I will not let myself be annoyed. I don't have time to, anyway, because the quartet is arriving, and then the opera singer; everyone wanting to know where they should set up. By the time I show them where to go, the rest of the committee members—minus Harriet, surprise, surprise—are arriving, exclaiming over how beautiful everything looks, telling me I'm a star. I lap it up, I admit it. I need this. It might be shameful, but I am unapologetic.

"And that *dress*," Grayson exclaims, her gaze roving every sequin. "That's not something you just had in the back of your closet." She laughs, and I tense. There's a criticism in there somewhere, I know. She probably yanked her Yves Saint Laurent gown from the back of hers.

"Thank you," I murmur, as if she's paid me a compliment.

I turn to see who else is arriving, just as Grayson asks me where Michael is.

"Work, as usual," I reply with a shrug, and her eyebrows rise.

"I thought maybe he was helping with the gala." Her lips curve cat-like, and I realize she must know something that I do not. "Because I saw him downstairs at the bar with Harriet Tierney."

For a second, I can't breathe. My lungs freeze, and so does my expression. Grayson notices, and her smile widens. Why, I wonder, are people so catty? So horrible?

And why is Michael in the bar with Harriet? Why is he lying to me about running late?

After way too long, my sense of self-preservation kicks in. "Oh yes, I forgot about that," I say airily. "They arranged a meeting before the gala, something about showcasing her artwork at his office. You know how Michael likes to help people out." I want to turn away, to blink back the tears that are coming to my eyes, to give myself a moment to scrape my composure together, but I know Grayson will see that as a victory and so I keep her stare, smiling slightly.

She smiles back, a face-off, and then suddenly I can't stand participating in this farce for a single second longer, and so I turn and walk away without a word. It's not my usual MO, and Grayson's probably delighted that she raised a reaction from me, but right now I can't even make myself care. Michael is in the bar downstairs with Harriet. I could go down there, force a confrontation. Finally have all these secrets out in the open.

But I know I won't.

I walk to the bar, where a black-jacketed waiter is filling up the flutes with champagne. Guests are about to arrive, the gala is going to begin. I take a flute of champagne without looking at him and guzzle it down. I've barely eaten today, and so I feel the buzz almost instantly. My head is light, and the tension eases from my shoulders. I put the empty flute back on the tray and walk toward the check-in table.

Joanna is there, sorting through the party bags. "I think we have enough..." she murmurs, sounding anxious and so desperate to please.

"It doesn't matter if we don't," I tell her. "Do people really need a pair of polyester gloves and a plastic set of opera glasses?"

She eyes me uncertainly and I realize I might already be a little drunk.

Quickly, I take a breath, paste on a smile, and reach for a bag. "I was just joking," I tell her. "It'll be fine. I made extra, so there's absolutely no need to worry."

"Okay..."

The first guests are arriving, and I turn to face them, raising my voice, letting it carry. "Welcome to a night at the opera!" I exclaim grandly. "Come and find your seats..."

Soon people are exchanging greetings, shedding coats, oohing and aahing over the decorations. Joanna checks names off the list while I hand out the gift bags and explain about the auction; in addition to the cheap opera favors, each bag contains a pencil and gilt-edged notebook to write notes about the items.

"This is so fun," Claire enthuses as she takes the gloves out of the bag. "Was it your idea?"

"No, it was Harriet Tierney's," I reply, and her eyes widen.

"I forgot she was on the gala committee." She gasps. "How was *that*?"

I've barely seen Claire all fall; she's brought Lewis and Brand to soccer a few times, but otherwise our paths rarely intersect, and while we keep saying we should get together when we cross paths at the school run, I haven't minded. "It was fine," I tell her smoothly, only to realize my mistake when Claire smirks.

"*Fine*?" she repeats, and I know I should have said it was great, or fun, or interesting. "Fine" suggests it was anything but, which is, of course, the truth. "That bad, huh?"

I smile pointedly. "Genuinely fine. Enjoy the evening!" I turn to the next guest.

Half an hour passes of checking people in, everyone exclaiming and effusing, words pouring out of my mouth in a sure, honeyed stream. *Oh yes, check out the week in Tuscany, for sure! The villa is amazing, and it's such a steal. And make sure you try the canapés, especially the lobster with ikura. I know, I know, can you believe it's already almost Christmas?*

I keep an eye on the elevator, waiting for either Michael or Harriet to step through, everything in me tensing every time the doors ping open. But they don't. Seven-thirty passes, and they still haven't arrived. I know Michael said eight, but what on earth are they doing down there together?

Then, at seven-forty, when the arrival of guests has slowed to a trickle, the doors open and Michael steps out—with Harriet. I don't recognize her at first, because she looks so different. She's dyed her fake-red hair midnight-black and smoothed it into gleaming waves like a 1940s Hollywood star. The dress matches the look—fire-engine red velvet, pouring over her figure, with a deep vee and a thigh-high slit, a fake fur tossed over her shoulders, and white silk opera gloves reaching past her elbows. She looks amazing, gloriously over the top in a way I've always been afraid to be, and I immediately feel like a bland, beige potato.

In this moment, I realize that not only have I been striving my whole life to seem perfect, but also to be invisible. And that's how I feel as Michael and Harriet step onto the terrace, with Harriet's partner—if he even is her partner—behind them, wearing a tuxedo in shabby purple velvet.

I stand frozen by the check-in table, shocked that Michael could be so *blatant* with this other woman, but he doesn't even see me. Neither does Harriet. They're caught up in their own little world, *smiling* at each other, both me and Harriet's partner forgotten. Michael's hand on the small of her back, and something in me snaps clean through.

"Welcome to the party," I call over to them, my voice shaking. I realize my hands are shaking too, and I place them flat on the table. "So *good* of you to turn up."

A few people nearby pause in their conversations, glance at me uncertainly. My voice is vibrating with anger, with hurt. I know I should stop, rein it all in and pretend as I always do, but this time I simply can't.

Michael finally sees me, and his expression tenses as he gauges the look on my face. I'm not even sure what it is, but it certainly isn't friendly. Harriet looks guarded, and then she turns to her partner, murmuring something to him I can't catch.

"Elise—" Michael begins.

"No, *really*," I cut him off. "You're only forty minutes late, but who's counting? I suppose it was hard to tear yourselves away from the bar downstairs."

A pained look crosses Michael's face, as if I'm being difficult. As if *I'm* the problem.

I reach for Harriet's gift bag and thrust it at her hard. "I guess you've already got the gloves."

She takes the bag, slips it over one gloved wrist, frowning, her other arm looped through her partner's. "I'm sorry I'm late," she says with dignity. "Something came up."

I let out a laugh, a high, sharp sound, like the crack of a limb. "Oh, right," I say. "*Sure.*"

Harriet's eyes widen, like she can't believe I'm acting this way, and I understand why, because *I* can't believe I'm acting this way. This is not how I operate. This is not who I *am*. And right now everyone is watching me melt down, and there is nothing I can do to stop it.

Abruptly, I stride away from the little group, stalking through the terrace without meeting anyone's eye. My cheeks are burning and my stomach swirls with nausea. I realize I might vomit.

At the bar, I reach blindly for another flute of champagne and toss it down, even though I know that the last thing I need is more alcohol. There are little dishes of candied almonds on the bar—I filled them myself—and I reach for one, practically throwing it into my mouth, knowing I need something to absorb the alcohol.

But I hurl it too viciously and it catches in the back of my throat.

For a second, I think I'm okay. I try to swallow, then double over as the almond sticks and I keep struggling to swallow, hating the fact that I'm now drawing even more attention to myself. People are starting to stare. But, I realize with horror, I can't choke it down.

It's another second before I realize not only can I not choke it down, but I am actually choking. I can't breathe and I am making garbled, gasping sounds, my hands clawing at my throat, my eyes streaming as I struggle for air.

This *can't* be happening. I am both shocked as well as terrified; how can it be possible that I might actually *choke* to death with everyone around me simply standing and watching, doing nothing? I can't see anyone's faces, but I feel their stares. I hear the low ripple of their concerned murmurs, and I think, *Do something. Help me.*

And then someone finally does. I feel arms around me, and then one fist wrapped around another is pressed in and then up toward my ribcage, hard enough to hurt. Someone is giving me the Heimlich, and it isn't until I hear her voice, telling me not to panic, that I realize who it is.

Harriet.

The one person I can't stand to help me.

Instinctively, I start to struggle, trying to wrench my way out of her grasp. *Where is Michael? Why isn't he running to my rescue? Why do I have to suffer this indignity, after everything else?*

"Elise, stop fighting me!" she says in a low voice, her arms still holding me as I struggle and flail. "I'm trying to *help you.*"

I want to tell her I don't need her help, but of course I can't. I can't speak. I can't breathe.

Again she pushes into my ribcage, her body pressed hard

against my back, and I wince, my head going fuzzy and light, my chest aching, my whole middle throbbing.

"Why do you always fight everything?" she demands, her voice a hiss in my ear that only I can hear. "Even this? Honestly, you deserve... You are *so* aggravating!" She thrusts again, and pain blazes through me. *Everything* hurts... and I'm still choking.

Time feels as if it has both slowed down and sped up. I can't see anything but the dazzle of the chandeliers above me, a thousand glittering lights hurting my eyes, and I realize my vision must be tunneling.

I might actually be about to die, and in Harriet Tierney's arms, of all places.

And then, amazingly, Harriet gives me one more savage abdominal thrust and the almond shoots out of my throat. I suck in a huge breath as I start to cough and wheeze, collapsing into her arms before she guides me onto the floor, so I am on my hands and knees.

"Are you okay?" she asks gruffly, sounding annoyed, but I can't speak because I'm coughing so much, and absolutely everyone is staring.

She might have just saved my life, but part of me hates her now more than ever. Did she have to push so hard? I know I have never looked so weak or felt so pathetic as I do right now, on my hands and knees on the floor, my gown rucked up over my legs, dribbling onto the parquet.

Harriet puts a hand on my shoulder and, like a sulky child, I shrug it off. She mutters something under her breath as I wipe my streaming eyes and try to get my breathing under control. People are venturing nearer, with murmurs and whispers.

"Elise... you *scared* me... are you okay?" It's Claire, bending down toward me, but I can't even look at her. I only want Michael. *Where is he?*

"Let me get you a drink of water," Harriet says, and I force myself up to standing, even though my entire body aches like I've done a hundred crunches *and* have the flu. My breath is still coming in gasps, and there is drool on my chin. Somehow I manage to speak, the words dragged from me.

"Please…" I whisper to Harriet, my voice a croak. "Just… get away from me."

I'm not looking at her, but I *feel* her freeze, then recoil. I haven't even thanked her for saving me, but I *can't*. Not now, and maybe not ever. I think of her voice in my ear, telling me I deserve… what? *This?*

And yet right now *I* look like the big jerk, because everyone heard me. A murmur of surprised speculation ripples through the crowd at my ungrateful words. This will feed the school gossip mill for *weeks*.

Then, without a word, Harriet turns on her crimson stiletto heel and walks off, leaving me still gasping, trying to hold onto the last piece of dignity I have.

SIXTEEN

HARRIET

She really is crazy.

I walk away from Elise, adrenaline coursing through me from the whole episode, and trying not to feel furious that after I *saved her life*, her first words were for me to get away from her. Fine, I will.

A few people I don't know try to stop me as I cross the terrace, wanting to know what happened, but I shrug them off. I still feel shaken, and I need to find Allan. He probably shouldn't have come tonight, but he was adamant that he wanted us to be here. Together.

It's hard to believe that just a few moments ago I was so full of hope, buoyant with it. After talking to Michael downstairs in the bar, I finally felt like we had a *future*. After months of battling every step, it felt like possibility was hovering on the horizon. Then Elise had to go and have a hissy fit, before nearly choking to death.

I have struggled not to feel guilty for my part in whatever dysfunctional relationship Michael clearly has with his wife. The last time we had coffee, about a week ago, we ended up talking about Elise. Admittedly, I was the one to bring her up; I asked him if she minded how often we met, and he'd given a funny little grimace.

"I don't know if she does or not," he said with a wince. "I'm not sure she even knows."

"You haven't *told* her?" I asked in surprise. Somehow, despite my insistence on confidentiality, I had thought Michael would have explained *something*. Some stupid part of me felt shamefully pleased that he hadn't. I was his little secret. Something he wanted to keep hidden from *her*.

I knew I shouldn't have been thinking that way, and I was trying not to, but when life was hard and lonely, the longing crept in. Once I'd got to know him, I discovered that Michael was funny and kind and a terrific listener. He has a way of looking at me, his chocolate gaze so warm, his attention so arrested, that when I'm with him I feel as if I am basking in a bright light. When he speaks, his voice is a low thrum of sincerity that hums right through me. If I've been enjoying our coffees more than he has, well, I know it doesn't mean anything and so it can't actually *hurt* anyone, right?

Except maybe it already has.

"Elise's and my marriage works best when we don't talk about serious things," he said last week, the words spoken on a sigh. "Whether that's good or bad, I don't know."

"It doesn't sound particularly good," I ventured cautiously. I was curious about his marriage, too much so, and I admit part of me loved that he was talking to me about it. *Confiding* in me. The uneasy ripple of guilt I felt about that fact I pushed away. I wasn't hurting anyone.

"No, maybe not," he replied. "But Elise... she grew up with very controlling parents. She's not controlling with others," he clarified quickly, "not at *all*, but she... she controls herself." He gave an unhappy little smile. "She actually has fairly severe

OCD," he went on. "I'm not talking about just wanting things to be neat, but her having to spend all night organizing the kitchen drawers. Having to arrange the food on her plate in exact ninety-degree angles. Wear only one color at a time. When she puts the boys to bed, it can take ages, because she twitches every blanket, lines up all the shoes... I try to do it as often as I can, just so they can get to sleep. And it was the same with bathtime... she was scrubbing their skin until it *hurt*. I haven't let her give them a bath in years, if I can help it."

A sigh escaped me, long and low and weary.

"And then she has these weird little rituals she *has* to do, like walk around our bedroom three times every night—" He stopped abruptly, like he'd said too much, but I was fascinated. I had no idea Elise had these hangups. It definitely sounded more than being a little too neat. A *lot* more.

"I'm so sorry," I said, and Michael shook his head.

"I shouldn't have said anything. She wouldn't have wanted... Well..." He let out a breath. "It doesn't matter. The point is, it's better if Elise doesn't know some things, because she'd... obsess over them."

I nodded, the pieces falling into place. Michael's words were wise, but also, I feared, too late. I was pretty sure Elise was already obsessing.

But that's not my fault, I told myself as Michael hugged me goodbye—he was definitely a hugger—and told me to "hang in there." *I'm not doing anything wrong*, I reminded myself as I headed toward the subway.

Now the adrenaline is still churning through me, along with the guilt, as I wander to a quiet corner of the roof terrace, leaving the whispering crowds behind, because what if Elise had *died*?

Everyone was simply standing there staring at her as she started to gasp, thinking, no doubt, that she was having some kind of mental health crisis after the little display she put on when Michael and I arrived. I figured out she was choking only because I've seen it happen before, when I used to be a waitress. There have been a couple times with Allan, too, where I've wondered whether I need to give him some help. I'm glad I sprang into action, but it still all feels like it was way too close.

I take a deep breath and pass a hand over my face. I was looking forward to this evening, but now I feel like it might as well be over. I need to find Allan, and make sure he's okay. But just as I'm about to move on, a hand claps down on my shoulder.

"*Harriet.*" It's Grayson, looking, I think, like she's delighted with all the drama of the evening. "You are the hero of the hour," she proclaims in her showy way, one hand still on my shoulder, the other clasped dramatically to her chest. "Or should I say heroine? You literally *saved* Elise's *life.*"

I try to shrug her hand off, but it's not moving. "I just did what anyone would do in that situation."

"And yet no one else did," Grayson points out. "I think we were all just so *shocked.*" She drops her voice to a husky, just-you-and-me murmur. "But really I think you were especially amazing... you know, *considering.*"

I tense and then take a step away, so she has no choice but to drop her hand from my shoulder. "Considering what?" I ask warily. I'm not sure I want her to explain.

"Well." Grayson gives a throaty laugh. "I mean... you and Michael?" She smiles playfully as her eyebrows lift, or at least as much as they can considering how much Botox she must have had done.

I freeze. "Grayson, there's nothing going on between me and Michael." Even if I've enjoyed our coffees together way too much. Even if getting a text from him is enough to lift my spirits. That's a far cry from an *affair*, which is clearly what Grayson is insinuating.

"Oh come on, Harriet." She gives another laugh, this one

with an edge, and with a jolt, I wonder if she's jealous. "I saw the two of you down at the bar."

I shake my head slowly. "If you saw us, then you also had to have seen my—Kyra's dad. He was with us the whole time."

She cocks her head, her eyes narrowed like she's trying to figure me out. "Nooo... I saw you and Michael, getting cozy at the bar. Kyra's dad wasn't anywhere in the picture." She lets out a huff. "I'm assuming her dad is the old guy who sometimes comes with you to pickup?"

"His name is *Allan*," I tell her stiffly.

"Whoa... okay." She holds up both hands in the age-old gesture of someone who is being obnoxious, but pretending that they're not.

I shake my head again. I am starting to feel panicked, because while I suspected Elise might be feeling threatened by my relationship with Michael, I had no idea the whole school was gossiping about it. That is definitely not something I want. "Grayson, whatever fires you're trying to stoke," I tell her earnestly, "Please don't. My... relationship with Michael is not what you think it is, and Elise almost *died* back there. Let's just... leave it."

Grayson is clearly not someone who likes being told what to do. She draws herself up, flicking her platinum-blond hair behind one fake-tanned shoulder. "I think you're the one who just needs to leave it, Harriet," she snaps. "Leave *him*. You can offer up all the excuses you want, but I saw the two of you at the bar, looking *very* cozy. And, trust me, I know just how *charming* Michael Dunnett can be." Her smile turns brittle as her voice takes on a sharper edge. "He makes you feel like the center of the world—*his* world—but you aren't, so be grateful for the warning." Then, without waiting for a reply, she turns and stalks off.

I stare after her, my mouth agape. Grayson clearly has some personal experience with Michael. Maybe Elise is so suspicious of me because there's history here... a fact which, I am ashamed to realize, causes me a flicker of—entirely inappropriate—jealousy. It's just as well Michael, Allan, and I had that chat this evening, because things are finally going in the right direction, and I don't need to keep texting Michael for support... even if I know I still want to. But right now, I need to find Allan.

I look around the terrace, scanning the various clusters of couples scattered around the space. Everyone seems to have recovered from the drama of Elise's choking episode, including Elise herself, who is standing apart from everyone else with Michael, his arm around her shoulders, her face like a mask.

I make a mental note to avoid them all evening. In fact, I'm tempted to just go home; the pleasure I took in arranging so much of this—although I didn't do nearly as much as Elise—has completely vanished. I just feel tired, as well as anxious, both for Allan, whom I still can't see, and Elise, whom I fear I've treated badly. More badly, even, than I ever realized.

I knew she was anxious about me and Michael, but I let it spin out because I told myself it wasn't my problem. *I* knew I wasn't doing anything wrong, so what did it matter if she didn't? That was for Michael to tell her, not me.

But right now, it doesn't feel that simple.

"Excuse me..." A man approaches me, someone I don't recognize. "Aren't you with the guy in the purple velvet tux?"

That's certainly an easy way to identify Allan. "Yes..." I say, panic fluttering beneath my breastbone as I catch the frown of concern on the man's face.

"Well, I don't know if he's had too much to drink or what, but he's passed out in one of the stalls of the men's bathroom."

"*What!*" I stare at the man in shock while he gives an apologetic grimace.

"I was just about to inform the management... but there's no one else in there, if you want to check."

"Thank you," I mutter, wishing the man had been a *little* more proactive.

How long has Allan been on the floor of the bathroom? Because that's where I find him, sprawled in a stall, his cheek resting on the tile, his arms and legs twitching, his eyes rolling back into his head.

"Allan, oh Allan!" A sob catches in my throat as I kneel on the cold, hard tile and try to take him in my arms. "I'll call 911—"

"No." He blinks me into focus, his voice is a slurred rasp as he tries to grab my arm and ails. "No, no... I'm... fine. Just... weak. Help... help me get up, please."

"Oh, *Allan*." Tears streak my cheeks as I do my best to get him into a seated position, his whole body slumped as he takes a few gasping breaths that tear at his chest. I've never seen him this affected before, and it terrifies me. I knew he was getting worse, but I didn't think it would get this bad so quickly. Right now, that feels like the most dangerous kind of naivete. I *knew* what the stats were. I'd researched it all before I'd agreed to come. And yet still I'd been determined to believe we'd have time. No matter what I've been trying to convince myself, I'm not ready for this, not remotely.

"I'm... so sorry," he gasps out.

"Allan..." My voice chokes. "You don't need to be sorry."

He gives me a look so full of sorrow that I have to hold in another sob.

"Let's go home," I tell him as I put my arms around him. "That's the only place I want to be right now."

He rests his head on my arm and for a second we just sit there, breathing. Being. His painfully drawn breaths start to settle down, which fills me with relief, but it's also so unbearably sad, knowing things will only get worse. Even so, as we sit quietly, there's a strange peace in it, as well, at least in this moment, and I let myself rest in that, brief as it surely will be.

Just a few minutes later, I'm helping Allan to stand when I hear a scream from the terrace, a high-pitched shriek that seems to go on and on and sends the hairs on the back of my neck standing straight up. Allan tenses in my arms, gives me a look of silent concern.

Already I know something terrible has happened.

SEVENTEEN
ELISE

Claire is hovering near me as Harriet stalks off, but I can't look at her. I can't look at anyone, even as I feel all their speculative stares like needles burrowing into my skin. I wipe my chin, feel my hair, which is clearly a disheveled mess. Joanna comes up to me and silently hands me a glass of water, and for that I'm grateful.

"Elise." *Finally* Michael is here, his arms outstretched, a look of concern etched on his features. "People said you were *choking*... what happened?"

"Where were you?" I demand in a low rasp. My voice still sounds funny, and my whole body throbs. I feel like crumpling into a heap, but I force myself to stand erect.

Michael drops his arms, his look of concern morphing into one of uneasy guilt. "I was putting our coats away."

Our coats. Not his and mine, because I hung mine up when I arrived before everyone else, but his and Harriet's. That stupid fake fur.

Suddenly, I can't stand there for a second longer.

"I need to clean myself up," I say abruptly. I thrust my glass of water at Michael and then head for the bathroom on shaky legs, praying no well-meaning friend tries to follow me. I need to be alone.

In the bathroom, I force myself to look at my reflection, and it's about as bad as I thought. Hair like a bird's nest, makeup smeared, with raccoon eyes and lipstick on my cheek. There are specks of spittle on my chin, and I grab a paper towel and wipe them away. I'm still feeling shaky from the whole episode, and my chest and stomach are throbbing with pain. Harriet certainly used enough force when she gave me the Heimlich, I'll say that much.

But worse than any of that, worse than the humiliation of having created such a scene amongst people who I *know* will gossip about it under the flimsy pretext of concern, is Michael's betrayal. It's like a sucker punch and a stab wound all at once, and it leaves me breathless and reeling in a way that has nothing to do with how Harriet manhandled me.

How can I go on pretending after this?

The door to the bathroom opens, and I tense, waiting for the simpering question. *Oh my goodness, Elise, are you okay? I was so scared...*

But instead I see it's Joanna, who simply smiles at me in sympathy and hands me my little beaded bag.

"You left it on the check-in table," she explains quietly. "I thought you might want it now."

The simple kindness is almost enough to undo me. "Thank you," I whisper as I blink back tears.

She hesitates, lingering by the door. "Do you want anything else?" she asks after a moment. "Or just to be left alone?"

I try to smile, but my lips wobble and a shudder escapes me. "I don't even know," I reply, putting my bag down and bracing my hands on the sides of the sink. I wipe my eyes as discreetly as I can. "Is everyone talking about me out there?"

"Some people are," Joanna admits with an honesty I appreciate, no matter how raw I feel right now. "I've only been at

TGS for a couple of months, but I've already seen how gossipy some people here can be." Her tone turns wry, although with a hint of hurt. "The first week I showed up in workout clothes and some woman I don't even know asked me in fake surprise, 'Oh, do you work out?' while glancing at my stomach." She does a parody look of surprised malice, and I can picture it perfectly.

I give her a small, commiserating smile, and she grimaces.

"I know I'm still carrying some baby weight... Sorry." She shakes her head. "I didn't mean to make this about me."

"I guess that's the nature of a small school," I say. I straighten and reach for my bag, taking out my compact, lipstick, mascara, brush.

"I don't know," Joanna says slowly. "I don't think it's just about the smallness. This place seems kind of... *toxic* to me. We might try public school after this year."

"Oh, Joanna." I turn to her, surprised and disappointed, because she seems like a genuinely nice person. "I'm really sorry."

She shrugs. "Hey, we'll save a lot of money. I thought when we signed up, the school would be a kind of community for us. People would be behind the progressive ethos, you know? The gentle, child-centered style of learning, but they all seem secretly bitter about it. It's not the vibe we were looking for."

"Well, pretty much all the parents here wanted to get into the elite, academically competitive schools," I explain, gazing at my reflection as I widen my eyes and carefully brush some mascara on each lash. "I think very few people actually believe in what The Garden School is trying to do, unfortunately." And the ones who do, stay away from all the gossipy functions like this one.

"Which is a shame," Joanna says. "It feels like a few people have poisoned the whole place."

I stare at my reflection, wondering if she is including me in that assessment. I make sure never to gossip, but maybe I'm still part of the problem. I'm certainly living in the TGS fishbowl, concerned with how everyone perceives me.

"Anyway," she says on a sigh. "I'm sorry for what happened back there."

I'm not sure if she's talking about the choking or the scene before, and so I don't reply, but then Joanna clarifies.

"Harriet seems like a decent person," she says quietly. "I... I don't think she'd do anything, you know, sneaky, from what I know of her."

I think Joanna means it kindly, but it's like salt in my gaping wound right now. I don't need someone defending Harriet Tierney to me.

Carefully, I insert the mascara wand back into the tube. "Thank you for your concern," I say a little stiffly, and then I wish I hadn't been so snooty, because Joanna looks hurt. She was, I know, only trying to be kind.

"I hope you feel better," she says quietly, and then she slips out of the bathroom, the door whispering shut behind her.

A weary sigh escapes me. I should have handled that better. I could use a friend—a *real* friend—but I'm not sure I need one who's going to defend Harriet's actions to me.

I spend a few more minutes repairing my makeup and hair, and then I face my reflection squarely, ignoring the pain still throbbing through my middle, willing myself to assemble that glossy shield of perfection that has helped me my whole life. Nothing can touch me, I tell myself, and then I head outside to the fray.

A few different people accost me as soon as I emerge, nails digging into my arm, faces thrust close, and somehow I manage to put them all off, laughing lightly, assuring everyone *I'm absolutely fine, yes, it was scary, so scary, but thank goodness everything ended well, and why don't we all have champagne?*

They seem in equal parts relieved and disappointed; the drama is over, but at least I'm okay.

I can't see Michael anywhere... or Harriet. Could he really be so insensitive as to be with her now? Maybe he's making sure *she's* okay, rather than me. I picture him comforting her, his arm around her shoulders. *Harriet, you're so brave... such quick thinking! Are you okay? As a doctor, I know how handling that kind of emergency can really shake you up...*

I close my eyes. I don't think I can stand this for another moment.

"Elise." I turn, and Michael is there, his arm under my elbow, then sliding around my shoulders, his expression one of tender concern, although I see anxiety in his eyes. Is he worried I'll create another scene? "I was worried about you," he says, pulling me toward him. "Are you feeling better?

"Just repairing the damage," I reply coolly. Even though I crave his closeness, I edge away from him. I don't know how to be with him anymore; our marriage, I realize, depended on the pretense we have both so carefully maintained all this time. What do we do when it's gone, when we have to face who we really are and what we've really done? How do we even talk to each other?

"Elise," Michael says, "I need to tell you—"

"Not here," I say quickly. If he's going to say he's leaving me, I *cannot* hear it in the middle of a crowded room, filled with parents, just after I've had a near-death experience. "Not tonight," I add. "There's been enough drama. And the auction is starting soon." As the head of the PTA, I'm meant to give a little opening speech and introduce the auctioneer. I'm not at all sure if I'm up for it.

"There's no drama," Michael says, his voice tinged with exasperation. "That's what I'm trying to tell you—"

"We *cannot* have this conversation here." I feel the curious stares centered on me like a dozen lasers. A hot flush sweeps through my body, and for a second I feel dizzy.

Michael is shaking his head, looking both aggravated and

troubled, and it feels like my whole life is hinging on this moment. I know I'm not strong enough for it, not right now.

"*Please*, Michael," I whisper.

He cocks his head, looking concerned. "Elise…"

I shake my head, take a few steps away from him, and then suddenly stumble. I fling a hand out, which he catches, but I'm barely aware because the room is spinning and my body is shaking. Worse than that, though, is the pain that has suddenly started radiating through my stomach, all the way up to my shoulders, like someone has stabbed me all over. I gasp, and then suddenly I double over, retching helplessly, the action taking me by surprise.

I have no idea what is going on, only that I am in the grip of something so powerful it feels like I am outside my body and yet at the same time very much in it, transfixed by a pain so severe it nearly blinds me.

Distantly, I feel Michael's arm around me, hear people's concerned cries. I continue to retch, helplessly, over and over again, my vomit now streaked with blood. I'm in too much pain to be afraid, but for the second time tonight I wonder if I am about to die. I have no idea what's going on, but it feels like it will never end.

And then it does—the room spins, and again, for a second, I see only the lights, dazzling high above me. Michael's arm is still around me and he's saying something, I have no idea what, as the pain takes over, like a blanket being pulled over my head.

As I crumple to the blood-spattered ground, I hear someone scream.

EIGHTEEN

HARRIET

By the time we get back to Allan's apartment, he is gray-faced with exhaustion, his arms and legs twitching again, leaning heavily on me all the way up the steps. I am exhausted, too. It's certainly been a night to remember... and not in a good way.

When I stumbled out of the bathroom with Allan, a crowd of people were clustered in a knot, and someone was crying. I couldn't see who or what they were standing around, but somehow I just knew.

I grabbed someone's arm, a stranger. "What happened?"

The woman looked both unhappy and excited, the way people so often do when there's a crisis that doesn't involve them. "Elise Dunnett just... *collapsed*."

"*What*?" I was deeply shocked and yet not surprised at the same time, and meanwhile Allan was practically lolling in my arms. I didn't have the time or ability to stick around and see if Elise was okay. Besides, that wasn't my job. I'd saved her once tonight already.

Somehow, half-staggering, I managed to get Allan to the elevators and downstairs. With all the furore around Elise, no one noticed our ungainly exit. By the time we were crawling into a taxi, the paramedics had arrived. I had no idea if it was just to play it safe or if Elise was really unwell, and at that point I didn't have the headspace to think about it, or, if I'm honest, even care.

And now we're home, and I settle Allan in bed before I find Barbara, our neighbor, in the living room, reading a magazine. As I greet her, Kyra comes out of our bedroom, narrow-eyed with suspicion.

"Why are you home so early?" she demands.

"It's not that early," I say quickly. "After nine. You should be asleep, Kyra." She just shrugs. "The silent auction was starting," I explain, "and we can't afford to bid on anything, so we left."

"Where's Allan?" She hasn't yet moved to calling him "Dad," although I think she wants to.

"He's just in his bedroom. Go back to bed, Kyra, please." I temper my tired voice with a smile. "I'll be in in a minute to say goodnight."

Kyra continues looking at me in suspicion, while Barbara, whom I don't really know, hauls herself up from the armchair. Finally, after a tension-laden few seconds, Kyra disappears in her room.

"Sorry about that," I tell Barbara. "Thanks for watching her."

"She's a sweetheart." It reminds me of what Michael said, back at the picnic, what feels like a million years ago. "Is everything okay?" Barbara asks with a frown, looking concerned. "Allan hasn't seemed like himself lately…"

"He's just tired." Allan hasn't told anyone, not his neighbor, not his daughter. The burden of me knowing feels too heavy to carry right now. "But thanks again." My words sound like more of a goodbye than I meant them to be, but I'm so very tired.

Barbara seems to understand, because she smiles and squeezes my hand, which almost makes me cry. "You've been good for Allan," she tells me. "He was alone for too long. You take care of yourself."

I nod and sniff.

After Barbara goes, I start toward Kyra, but then I check myself, because I can't answer her questions until I've talked to Allan.

His eyes flutter open as I come into the room, and he smiles tiredly, his face still possessing a grayish cast.

"I'm sorry about that," he says, his voice a little slurred.

"It's not your fault." I perch on the edge of the bed. "You pushed it today."

"Yeah." He sighs. "I wish it wasn't that way, but it is."

I rest my hand on his, which is laying atop the blanket. "Allan…"

"I know." He jerks his chin down in a nod. "I need to tell Kyra. I will. Tomorrow."

I can't push him anymore, not when he's like this. "Okay."

He glances up at me, and his hazel eyes are glassy with unshed tears. "Sometimes…" He pauses, his throat working as he struggles to swallow. "Sometimes I feel like I threw my life away."

"Oh, Allan." I don't know what to say. "I imagine everyone feels a little bit like that," I venture after a moment, "especially when they're facing what you are."

"Maybe, but…" He sighs. "Why didn't we stay together?"

That surprises me, and yet I understand where he's coming from. It's easy to put everything in a rosier glow when you're looking backward.

"Because we wanted different things out of life," I remind him gently.

"What did you want, Harriet?" He glances at me searchingly. "What do you want now?"

"I…" I trail off, not knowing how to answer that. What have I ever wanted? Freedom, the agency and ability to make my own choices, to not be beholden to anyone. To not be like my mother, tied to a stove and a vacuum cleaner and a man coming home every night at six, grumpy and hungry.

"You were always so restless," Allan says with a faint smile as his eyes flutter closed again. "Always moving on to the next thing."

That much is certainly true. I'm forty-one years old and I haven't held down a job for more than a year, usually less. I've kept my art going all this time, in a haphazard way, telling myself I can take or leave it. I can take or leave anything—except, of course, Kyra. She's my one anchor, and yet seeing her blossom here, both at the school and with Allan, it makes me wonder if my restless heart has hurt her. If I haven't thrown my own life away, but hers. The thought is unbearable, especially as we are about to hurt her more now than she could ever imagine, although maybe she's guessed, at least the gist. Maybe that's why she seemed so suspicious tonight.

"I don't want to tell her," Allan whispers. "I wish... I wish I'd asked you to stay with me, back when you told me you were pregnant. I wish we'd been a family then, and not just now." His fingers clutch at mine. "I know that's not what you wanted back then. I know that, but..."

"I know," I say softly. "But the important thing is, we're a family *now*."

His fingers tighten around mine as he gazes at me with a naked yearning. "Are we?"

With a rippling sense of surprise, I realize we are. The last few months have been difficult in so many ways, but they've also been sweet... and somehow I've fallen in love with Allan again, gently and quietly, without even realizing it. It's a love that is touched by pity and sorrow, but a love all the same. And so I lean forward and brush my lips across his. I haven't kissed him since before I found I was pregnant. His lips now are papery and dry, and a small sigh escapes him, a sound of sorrow as well as peace.

My heart aches with grief and regret, although I know Allan is right. It wasn't what I wanted back then. It's only that now I wish it was.

I kiss Allan's forehead and then I lean back; he's already falling asleep, and I pull the covers over his bony shoulders. I cup his cheek with my hand and then I get up and walk out of the room to find Kyra.

When I go into our bedroom, I find, somewhat to my relief, that she's curled up on her side, already asleep. Our conversation can wait till tomorrow, even though I am already dreading it.

Gently I stroke her hair, kiss her cheek. My brave girl, facing so much, and even more than she knows.

As quietly as I can, I peel off my evening gown, tossing it in the corner of the room, the last remnant of an evening that did not go at all according to plan. Then I take a quick shower to wash out the hairspray that cemented my hair into dyed-black waves before I pull on some pajamas. It isn't until I'm in the kitchen, drinking a glass of water, that I think to check my phone. There are dozens of messages on the gala committee text chat.

OMG! OMG! Touch-and-go??? Seriously?

That's what they said.

Michael will update the school tomorrow.

My stomach drops. Touch-and-go? Is Elise's *life* in danger? Somehow I hadn't realized it was anything that serious.

Quickly, I scroll through the messages, trying to get the gist of what happened. Apparently, while Allan and I were in the bathroom, Elise collapsed, vomiting blood. She hadn't regained consciousness by the time the paramedics arrived.

Slowly, I lower the phone, my stomach churning. Is it a coincidence that she collapsed after I gave her the Heimlich? Are the two related?

I thought I saved her life... but what if I actually endangered it?

What if I've *killed* her?

NINETEEN
ELISE

I wake slowly, blinking in bright light, feeling as if I am floating outside my body. I can't feel *anything*.

In the distance, I hear the beep of a monitor, and I recognize, dimly, that I must be in a hospital. I still feel completely disconnected from my body; I'm not even sure I can turn my head. I know this should terrify me, but all I can summon is a mild curiosity. For a few seconds, or maybe even minutes or hours, I am simply existing in this free-floating state, and it feels weirdly comforting.

Then reality crashes in. A touch on my hand, Michael's face swimming into my vision. He looks terrible—unshaven, anxious, eyes bloodshot. Briefly, this gives me something almost like a frisson of pleasure, followed by a cold stab of fear. *He must be really worried about me*, I think. This is followed by, *I must be in really bad shape*.

"Elise?"

I can't open my mouth to reply; I feel like I don't even know where my mouth *is*. Am I paralyzed? Am I *dead*? Why can't I move anything?

"Elise... you're awake." The lilt of uncertainty is replaced by assurance as Michael takes on his neurosurgeon's voice. "You're at Langone, in the ICU." He touches my hand again. "You had a gastric perforation, Elise, otherwise known as a stomach rupture." Uncharacteristically, his assured doctor's voice wavers. "We were really worried there, for a couple of hours, but they've done surgery to repair the hole and you're going to be okay."

I blink at him, saying nothing. I still feel completely separate, not just from my body, but from everything. I want to go back to that free-floating state, where the whole world was white and bright and lovely, and I didn't have to make sense of all the words Michael just threw at me.

"Elise..." Michael's voice falters as I close my eyes. "Maybe you just need more sleep," he says.

I sink down into unconsciousness, letting it swallow me whole.

When I wake again, I have no idea how much time has passed. I turn my head—I have come back into my body—and look out the window at the pale blue sky. I feel every part of my body now—my arms and legs leaden, my middle numb yet strangely also throbbing, my head heavy. I try to move my arm, but I can't, and just the barest twitch sets a monitor beeping angrily. I do my best to lift my head and manage maybe a half an inch. I see that I have tubes and bandages all over me.

My heart flutters inside my chest and I feel the first real stirrings of panic. I am truly unwell. It's a strange thought, because I've been healthy for most of my life, beyond the occasional cold and the terrible morning sickness I had with the twins. I have never known what it feels like to be *really* sick, but already I know it's awful. And where is Michael? The room is empty as the wintry sun slants through the window.

Then I hear voices from outside the door, which is ajar. I

strain to make them out—Michael's low rumble, and then a woman's voice. I tense, because I recognize that voice, the stridency of the tone, and I cannot believe she is here.

Harriet.

Harriet has come to the hospital to talk to Michael. Unless I'm hallucinating? I must be, I tell myself. If I'm in the ICU like Michael said, they wouldn't allow non-family members. She couldn't be able to just waltz in here... But does that mean Michael invited her? *Accompanied* her? Is he out there comforting *her* rather than his own *wife*?

"I'm sorry," Michael says, his voice tired but firm. Then he slips inside my room and closes the door. "Elise." I hear relief in his voice, but also a hint of anxiety, and I know why. He's worried I heard him out there with Harriet. "Thank God you're awake," he says as he comes to sit next to me, reaching for my hand. "You've been asleep for nearly forty-eight hours. They moved you out of the ICU early this morning... you're on the mend, sweetheart."

So I'm not in the ICU. Harriet could have been out there, is all I can think.

"Elise... darling." Michael's voice has softened, turning abject. "You're going to be okay, I promise."

Tears are running from my eyes down the sides of my face, soaking my hair as well as the pillowcase. I can't even lift my hands to wipe them away, but at least I have the strength to shake my head.

"Were you..." My voice is a rusty croak. I can't believe this is the first thing I have to say to my husband after waking up from surgery for what surely was a near-death experience. "Were you talking to... to *Harriet* out there?"

"Elise..." The exasperation as well as the apology are both audible underneath the tenderness, and he doesn't need to say anything more. I know that he was. "Let's focus on your recovery," he tells me.

"So you can leave me as soon as I'm better?" The question spurts out of me before I can think better of it. I'm in too vulnerable a state to guard my words, to be as careful as I usually am. I close my eyes. "Why... why don't you just go now, while she's waiting?"

"*Elise*." Michael's voice manages to sound both gentle and strident as he takes my hand. "You've got it completely wrong. There's nothing between Harriet and me, I promise you."

I open my eyes, mainly to judge the truth of what he's saying by the expression on his face. He is gazing at me steadily, his dark eyes wide and clear.

"Why all the coffees then?" I force out. My voice sounds like it's been through a cheese grater. "The texts and the phone calls? Did you think I didn't *notice*?"

"I..." He shakes his head slowly, clearly surprised by my admission. "I guess I didn't," he admits. "Or if you did, that you didn't mind. Or maybe you just didn't want to talk about it." He shrugs helplessly.

"Those are three different things."

"I know." His voice is soft, sad as he gazes down at his hand resting on top of mine. "Please believe me when I say there's nothing going on between me and Harriet."

I start to shake my head against the pillow, but it hurts too much so I stop. "I don't want to talk about this anymore," I say, and then I close my eyes and will myself back to sleep.

Before I drift off, I feel Michael let go of my hand.

When I wake up, I'm alone. I also feel much more present, my mind clearer than it's been before.

It's nighttime, and I have no idea how long it's been since I last woke up and Michael and I spoke. Since he denied having an affair with Harriet, and I didn't know whether to believe him or not. I still don't know what to think.

The door opens, and a nurse comes in, smiling at the sight of me. "Ah, you're awake," she says in the briskly cheerful tone that all nurses seem to have mastered. "Michael's just getting something to eat in the cafeteria. He's been by your bedside almost this whole time. *Very* devoted." She has the admiring and slightly envious tone of someone who has been relentlessly charmed by my husband. "Of course, he knows his way around this hospital," she adds, because this is Langone, and Michael operates here.

"How long have I been in the hospital?" I ask, and she frowns in thought.

"Well, let's see… you came in Friday night and they moved you from the ICU on Monday morning… and now it's Monday night, so… three days?"

Three days? And Michael has been my bedside? As gratified as I should be, I feel only alarm. Who has been with Lewis and Luke this whole time? I move restlessly, as if I would get up from bed, but, of course, I know I can't and all I do is twist my IV tube. The nurse clucks and comes over to fix it.

"Don't worry," she says soothingly. "Everything's fine. You're recovering well. And you have a wonderful husband to support you."

I really do not need to hear about how wonderful my husband is right now. I get that all the time—how lucky I am, to have a man like Michael. I don't know that many people are telling him how lucky he is to have me.

The nurse is just stepping away from my bed when Michael comes in, holding a paper cup of coffee. His face brightens as he sees me, and then immediately his expression turns wary.

"Elise…"

"I'd like to sit up, please." I speak coldly, and the nurse notices. She glances between us in silent curiosity and then uses the remote controller to raise the top half of my bed. I feel better when I'm not lying flat on my back, even if I'm in a hospital gown, with tubes and wires and bandages everywhere, feeling like a broken, old woman.

"I'll check back in a little while," the nurses murmurs and slips out of the room.

Michael eases himself into the chair next to my bed.

"Where are Luke and Lewis?" I ask. "Who's taking care of them?"

"Your mom."

"My *mom*?" I am incredulous. She's never had them overnight before.

"She offered, and Rosita wasn't available. I've been checking in every night with the boys. They're doing okay."

I nod slowly, although I still struggle to imagine my mother managing my home life for three hours, never mind three days.

"How are you feeling?" Michael asks. He's gone back to being tender.

"I don't know." My stomach hurts, a low, throbbing pain that I suspect would be much worse, but I'm probably dosed up to the gills on pain meds. And I'm so *tired*, with a deep exhaustion, both mental and physical, that makes doing anything, even thinking, an impossible challenge. "You said..." I am struggling to remember. "Did you say I had a stomach rupture?"

He nods.

I lean my head back against the pillow. "From Harriet giving me the Heimlich," I surmise slowly.

Michael doesn't answer, and I open my eyes.

"Right?"

"Well... probably," he admits with obvious reluctance. "But if she hadn't, Elise, you would have choked to death."

"How would you know? You weren't even there." Even in my exhaustion, I can't keep the edge from my voice. "You were putting away Harriet's fake fur," I remind him.

He presses his lips together, looking both annoyed and guilty. "Yes, I was," he admits, "but can you please believe me when I tell you nothing was going on between us?"

"Why should I?" I retort, but I sound weary. I'm too tired to have this overdue confrontation now, and yet I make myself keep going in a way I never have let myself before. "Coffee dates, phone calls, texts... *Michael.*" I shake my head slowly. Finally talking about this is, in its own way, a relief. "Why on earth should I believe you?"

"Because I was meeting with Harriet to support her," Michael replies, a throb of feeling to his voice. "It wasn't personal, Elise, honestly." He pauses, seeming to debate whether to tell me anything more and then says, dropping his voice like he's sharing a secret, "This is confidential, but I think, for the sake of our marriage, you need to know. Kyra's father, Allan, has ALS, Elise. That's amyotrophic lateral sclerosis, or Lou Gehrig's disease. The disease that is progressive neurodegenerative," he informs me, even though I already know, "so you eventually lose the ability to walk, talk, even breathe. Most patients with ALS die within two to five years of diagnosis, from respiratory failure. It's frankly an incredibly difficult way to go." He pauses. "Allan has had it for eight months already."

I stare at him, trying to absorb what he just told me. The steady and slightly scolding look on his face suggests that I should be chastened, horrified, and deeply apologetic for all my assumptions, but I'm not. At least that's not all I'm feeling.

Yes, I'm relieved there's a reason. I'm very sorry for Allan, a man I've never spoken to but whom I have sympathy for, of *course*, for having to face something so frighteningly overwhelming and terrible. But beyond all that... all those coffees? All those texts? And Michael couldn't tell me about *any* of it?

"Well?" Michael prompts, and he sounds like he wants an apology. "Do you believe me?"

"That Allan has ALS?" I lean my head back and close my

eyes. I am already feeling too tired to keep this conversation going. "Yes, I believe you about *that*."

But the rest? My tone implies. That Michael isn't involved with Harriet Tierney?

Of that I am not at all convinced.

TWENTY

HARRIET

Saturday passes slowly. I keep checking my phone for updates on Elise, but there's nothing. I have no idea why she collapsed, how unwell she truly is, or, more worryingly, if I had anything to do with it. Meanwhile, I have something else to focus on—telling my daughter the truth about her father's condition. We've left it far too late as it is, and it's never going to get easier.

And so, on Saturday morning, I make pancakes and, while Kyra is pouring maple syrup over hers, Allan tells her the truth.

"Kyra, honey... I have something to tell you." His tone is grave, his eyes drooping at the corners, and Kyra stills, holding the bottle in mid-air so syrup floods her plate. I quickly rescue it, returning it to the table. "There's no easy way to say this," Allan continues, his voice choking. He's already emotional, and he's barely begun. One symptom of ALS is uncontrolled laughing or crying, but this is something different. This is the pain of death, right in the midst of life—pancakes on a sunny Saturday morning, my daughter's sleepy expression suddenly turning alert, the grueling reality we have to face.

"What is it?" she asks, her voice full of uncertainty.

"Kyra, sweetheart..." He swallows several times, each movement convulsive and full of effort. Kyra, I can tell, notices. "I have a disease," Allan tells her. "I've had it for a little while. It's why I get so tired sometimes." He stops, running his sleeve across his eyes, and my heart aches for him, for my little girl, for *us*.

Last night, after I'd said goodbye to Allan, I'd lain in bed and tortured myself by imagining a different life for all of us. One where I had stayed with Allan, where we lived as a little family, right here in Astoria. I kept up my art classes; he did his music. We raised a great kid, and we had fun together. A small, simple, and so very satisfying life, far from the restless searching I ended up doing, without even knowing what I was looking for.

After just a few minutes, I had to stop imagining because it hurt too much. No matter how much I tell myself it wouldn't have worked, that we were different people then, some part of me still wished it had happened. That it could have, that I could have been the person who chose that, who wanted it.

And now this.

"What kind of disease?" Kyra asks in a small voice.

"It's called ALS," Allan says shakily. "Or sometimes Lou Gehrig's disease, because he was a famous baseball player who had it."

She gives a little shake of her head, baffled by the information.

"It means I'll keep getting tired," Allan explains, "and I'll have trouble walking or even speaking or eventually doing anything." He stops, his expression going distant as we all are forced to envision that awful, impending reality. Even now, when I see the evidence of Allan's debilitation right in front of my eyes, it's hard to imagine the future, or maybe it's just I don't want to. None of us do.

"And then what?" Kyra asks into the silence, her voice so terribly small.

"And then…" Allan draws a ragged breath. His face is slack,

his eyes full of despair. "And then..." Another swallow. "And then I'll die," he finishes in a whisper. "I'm so sorry, Kyra. Maybe I should have told you sooner, but I couldn't bear to, when we were just getting to know each other."

He gives her a small, sorrowful smile, while Kyra simply stares at him, like she can't process the words. Like she doesn't know what that means. And yet I know she does, because when she was six we lived with my dad for three months while my mother was dying of cancer. She watched me sit with her, her claw-like hand resting in mine, my mother's breaths becoming slower and slower, each one a gasping rattle. Kyra saw it happen. She remembers, I know she does. She understands death more than a lot of kids her age do.

"But," I say into the silence, trying to inject my voice with an appropriate level of cheerfulness, "Allan can take some medicine that will slow down how the disease progresses. And that will give us all more time together."

Kyra turns to stare at me, her eyes bright with both tears and hope. "You mean he can get better?"

"Not better, no, honey," he says, his voice full of sadness. "Just... a little more time before I get worse."

If he goes back to the neurologist and gets the prescription, as I've been trying to get him to do for months. Before the gala, Michael finally convinced him, or maybe Kyra did. I know it's because of their relationship that Allan is willing to prolong his agony, which is how he's seen taking any medication, and why he's been fighting me about it ever since I moved in.

"So you can't get better?" she asks, and now she almost sounds angry. "*Ever?*"

"Kyra..." Allan's voice is a plea, although what he's asking for, I don't know.

Neither does Kyra, because she just shakes her head. Then she slips off her chair and runs to the bedroom, closing the door behind her with a soft click that somehow feels more devastating than a slam. She hasn't touched her pancakes.

"I don't know how I expected that to go," Allan remarks after a moment, his head bowed. "There's no good way, is there, to give her news like that?"

I shake my head as I stare down at my own uneaten pancakes. I have no appetite. "No," I say quietly, wishing we hadn't had to tell her this, wondering again if I should have ever brought her into this situation. "There isn't."

On Monday, Kyra is still quiet and withdrawn as I take her to school. Allan and I both tried to engage with her over the course of the weekend, but she shut down every conversation before we began. We didn't press, partly because we didn't want to pressure her, and also because we didn't know what to say. What encouragement could we offer? The medication isn't a magic pill, no matter how much Kyra or I or any of us wants to hope. It will just stave off the inevitable, slightly, for a little while. But at least now Allan thinks that's worth doing.

On Saturday night, after Kyra had gone to bed, Allan told me he was going to call the neurologist on Monday morning. "For Kyra," he said heavily, "I have to. I don't want to get her hopes up, never mind my own, but if there's a chance I can have a little more time with her, time like this..." His voice caught as he slumped onto the sofa, and I put my arms around him. Neither of us spoke, and it made me both happy and sad to sit there like that with him, because it reminded me of what we'd missed as well as what we still had to lose. Here we were in the in-between time that felt so poignant and fragile. I was doing my best to hold onto it, to let it be enough... for both of us.

And now, as I approach the entrance of The Garden School, my thoughts return to Elise. There's been no more messaging on the group chat, which makes me think they're probably texting each other privately. I wasn't close enough to anyone to warrant that kind of communication, but I also wonder uneasily if it's because people might blame me for her collapse. I might have saved her from choking, but what if, in doing so, I caused something even worse? And if I'm already half-blaming myself, what are other people doing?

I'm afraid to ask anyone about it all, but as I approach the school, someone rushes up to me, eager to impart either condemnation or sympathy, I'm not sure which.

"Oh, Harriet! How are you? Isn't it *awful*?"

I don't even know this woman, and for a second I simply stare at her, afraid to ask what is so awful. Dear heaven, I hope Elise Dunnett hasn't *died*.

"Yy—yes," I stutter uncertainly. "I mean, I haven't actually heard what..."

"Elise just got out of ICU this morning. She had to have emergency surgery. For the last twenty-four hours, they weren't sure she would *survive*." The unknown woman imparts all these details with the kind of relish that turns my stomach.

"I'm glad she's doing better," I say faintly.

I thought she was being sympathetic until she lays a hand on my arm. "I hope you don't feel guilty," she says in the sort of voice that suggests I should. "No one blames you, of course. You were only trying to help. And she *was* choking."

"Right," I whisper. I feel my face start to burn. Has everyone been talking about me? "Right," I say again, and pull my arm away. "Well... I need to get Kyra in, so..." I take a few stumbling steps away, my mind whirling.

I say goodbye to Kyra in a blur, giving her a hug, because while she doesn't even know about what's happened to Elise, I know she's thinking about Allan.

I don't even know who to think about.

As I walk away from the school, I text Michael. *I heard about Elise. I'm so sorry. Is she ok?*

I slide my phone into my pocket as I stride away, desperate to avoid any more conversation—or gossip.

I meant to go home—I don't want to leave Allan for too long—but on the way to the subway, Michael texts me back. *Thanks. It's been intense. I've basically lived at Langone since Friday, but she's doing better now.*

Langone is only a few blocks away. I need to know how Elise is, and whether she—or Michael—blames me. And so, somehow, against all my better judgment, I end up walking to the hospital on First Avenue where she's recovering. I know I probably shouldn't go, that Michael probably won't want to see me, and Elise certainly won't, but I can't help myself. I need to know what's going on. I need reassurance that Michael, at least, isn't blaming me.

At the entrance to the hospital, I think about texting him again, but I end up just bluffing the receptionist, and asking for the ward Elise Dunnett is staying on, using a chatty tone and enough personal information that she's convinced it's okay to tell me. It's amazing what you can get away with, as long as you have confidence.

The mood on the ward feels somber, a few nurses in rubber-soled shoes walking quietly by, the steady beep of machines a muted backdrop. I hear hushed voices behind half-closed doors, and I stop when I find Elise's, tapping once. Even though I really do know that I shouldn't, I poke my head around it.

"Hello?" I whisper.

Michael jerks up from where he is sitting by Elise's bed. She's barely a bump under the sheet, completely motionless and surrounded by tubes and machines, all of which horrifies me. And Michael is horrified too, by my presence. I can tell by the way his face drains of color, and his jaw goes slack.

"*Harriet...*" He sounds shocked, as well as a little disapproving. "What are you doing here?"

"I just had to see..." I begin feebly. I realize I've made a big mistake. There is no way I should be part of this situation in any shape or form. "I was worried..." I try again.

Michael takes me by the elbow and steers me out of Elise's room, so I feel like a little kid being disciplined. "You shouldn't have come," he says shortly once we're in the hallway. "I'm sorry, Harriet, but this is not the kind of complication I need right now. And Elise doesn't need it either, for that matter."

"Michael..." He's never talked to me like this before.

When we've met for coffee, when I've told him how hard it's been with Allan, how afraid I am, he's always been warm, sympathetic, reassuring. His hand resting on mine. His dark-eyed gaze so steady and kind. Now he seems almost like a different person, and it both hurts and embarrasses me, because if I thought, in some dim corner of my mind, that we had any kind of *connection,* I realize I was very much wrong. I was completely deluded.

"I'm sorry," I say finally. "I was just worried. I thought maybe I'd done something..."

"Administering an abdominal thrust probably did cause the gastric perforation," he confirms shortly in a doctor's voice. "It's a risk of the procedure. But you saved her from choking, so..." He sighs, raking a hand through his hair. "This isn't about *you*, Harriet."

"I know that!" I jerk back as a hot flush rises to my cheeks. "Of course I know that. I was just *concerned*."

"Look." Michael's tone turns weary as he rubs his hand over his face. "I appreciate that you've been going through something and, as a doctor, I've wanted to support you in that. But..." He pauses, seeming to weigh his words. "I think now, really, all that needs to stop. I'm not Allan's doctor or neurologist, and it wouldn't be right if I was. I think... I think we need to just... not meet anymore." I flinch, I can't help it, and he reaches out and catches my hand. "Harriet, I'm sorry. I wanted to be supportive."

"Was that *all* it was?" I whisper and then hate myself for having to ask. Of *course* that's all it was. I knew that all along. "All I mean is," I clarify hastily, wishing I wasn't having to fight back tears, "I thought you were my friend. And I could really use a friend, Michael..." I sound like I'm begging. I *am* begging. I sniff, wipe my eyes. I can't even look at him. I've humiliated myself more than I can bear to think about, simply because I feel so vulnerable right now, in so many ways.

"I *am* your friend, Harriet," Michael says in the tone of someone who is simply trying to be kind. "Of course I am. But Elise... Elise has misread our relationship completely and I can't let that continue. I... I never meant to hurt her." He swallows hard before shaking his head, resolute. "I'm sorry, but I think it's better if we don't meet up anymore. And also... if you stop texting me."

Which makes me sound like I was *stalking* him, when it was pretty much the opposite. "You texted me too!" I flash back before I can help it. He checked in every night. *How's your day been*? I could practically hear the warmth in his voice through the text. I'd reply, he'd ask more questions. I wasn't *nagging* him, the way he's making it sound now. "This wasn't completely one-sided, Michael."

A nurse walks by, glancing at us in disapproving curiosity, and Michael's eyes flash with irritation. We're causing a scene, and I'm making it sound like what I didn't want it to—some kind of sordid affair. He practices here, I recall. People will recognize him, and wonder who I am, what we are whispering about. No wonder he's annoyed.

"I don't know what you thought this was, Harriet," he states coolly, "but I assure you I was only acting in a professional capacity—"

"But you *weren't* a professional!" I cry. "You said that yourself, you're not Allan's doctor—"

"*Harriet.*" He looks properly angry, and I realize I need to stop.

This is going nowhere; if I didn't feel so fragile over Allan's health, if I wasn't so worried about Kyra, and feeling so tired and scared and lonely, questioning just about every decision I ever made... I wouldn't be acting this way. It's not at all like me, it's not how I operate, how I think. Where is my independence, my freedom, now?

Yet somehow I *can't* stop. "I'm just saying," I tell him in a choked voice, "you enjoyed my company. I know you did."

He looks pained as well as pitying, and finally, *finally*, I close my mouth. I wipe my eyes, wishing I had the composure to explain that I feel vulnerable now, that this isn't even about Michael, at least not as much as I'm acting like it is.

"Look," he says quietly, taking a step back from me. "I can recommend other doctors..."

I feel flat now, and I am definitely not going to prolong this painful conversation any longer. "Of course," I reply woodenly. I don't trust myself to say anything else, because God knows I've said enough already. "I'm sorry," I say stiffly.

"I'm sorry, too," Michael says, and his tone is formal. "I like you, Harriet, and I appreciate you have a... a hard row to hoe. But... I need to focus on Elise now."

Which is totally understandable, but it still makes hurt flash through me. "Understood," I tell him, and then I walk away.

"I'm sorry," he says one last time, and, burning with humiliation, and worse, hurt, I force myself to keep walking.

TWENTY-ONE
ELISE

By Wednesday, I am feeling more myself, although I'm still swathed in bandages and sometimes my stomach hurts so much I can barely breathe. My doctor has started weaning me off the opioids, and I can feel the difference. Still, I am determined to get better—and to get out of here.

I walk up and down the corridor, holding onto a Zimmer frame, desperate to get stronger. I take a shower, covering my bandaged stomach in plastic, grateful to wash away the grime of dried sweat and the crusted adhesive of bandages and tape of the IV. I sit in the chair in my room, trying to stay as upright as I can, and look outside at the bleak, wintry cityscape.

Michael has gone back to work, at my suggestion. I can't have him hanging over me all the time, not when I need to consider our future. He may be insistent that he hasn't had an affair with Harriet, but it still feels like there is a gaping hole in the middle of our marriage and I don't know how to move around it.

And I don't have the mental or physical energy to think about it. I have to focus on getting better, so I can return to my life and, more importantly, my children. My mother might be taking care of the boys, but her patience is paper-thin and the thought of her patronizing Luke, calling him sickly or worse, is enough to have me asking when I can be discharged.

"Maybe Friday," my doctor, a smiling woman in her mid-forties, tells me when she stops by on her rounds on Wednesday afternoon. "But you'll have to take it easy for quite a few weeks. Abdominal surgery isn't a walk in the park."

"No," I agree and then find myself asking, "So, do you think the rupture was caused by me being given the Heimlich?" I keep my tone casual, innocent, but I know what I'm really asking: *Is this Harriet's fault?*

"Certainly that sort of pressure to your stomach could cause trauma," the doctor replies carefully, clearly not wanting to assign blame. "Although gastric perforation from an abdominal thrust is fairly unusual. I didn't perform your surgery, so I can't be sure of all the ins and outs of what caused it, but I'm sure they're running tests to rule out anything else."

Like what, I scoff mentally. I'm given the Heimlich and it's just a coincidence that I collapse less than an hour later? I don't think so. Harriet is the reason I'm in here. And yes, she *might* have saved my life, but what if she pressed harder than she needed to? It *felt* like she was pressing pretty hard when I was struggling against her. And what about what she hissed in my ear?

You deserve…

Was some part of her—maybe a subconscious part—looking for a way to punish me? To get revenge? Maybe she didn't even realize she was doing it, but I think she used more force than necessary. I've always known she hasn't liked me. Everyone has known it.

And when Claire visits me the next morning, these nebulous suspicions are further cemented into my psyche.

"You look amazing, all things considered," she tells me, air-kissing my cheek a good three inches away from my face before glancing around the room, looking for somewhere to put down her designer handbag. "I don't want to touch you!" She lets out a nervous laugh. "All those bandages and things."

"It looks worse than it is." I try to smile. I'm glad to see someone other than Michael, but the thinness of my friendship with Claire—who is meant to be one of my closest friends—feels painfully obvious to both of us when it's put to the test like this.

At least she visited, I think, but I'm pretty sure it's for the potential gossip as much as out of concern. And for once I feel like breaking my own rules and giving it to her.

"Have you seen Harriet?" I ask as Claire settles in the chair next to my bed, and her eyes gleam.

"She's been at drop-off and pickup the last few days," she confirms. "Not really talking to anyone, though, but then I can't blame her."

I raise my eyebrows. "Why not?"

Claire gives me a conspiratorial smile. "Well... everyone blames her for what happened to you, of course."

"They do?" This gives me a guilty little dart of satisfaction, I admit. Harriet is finally getting some comeuppance.

"Well, come on," Claire says, rolling her eyes a little. "After... you know..." She pauses, clearly waiting to see to how I react to mention of what happened *before* the choking incident.

"Does everyone think she and Michael have something going on?" I ask bluntly.

I can tell Claire is surprised; neither of us is used to this kind of honesty.

"Well, I mean..." She shrugs, instantly uneasy. "I don't know."

"Do *you*?" I ask, curious now. After years of prevaricating and pretending, I realize I finally want to face the truth. Not just from Michael, but from everyone. How many lies have I been living?

"I don't know..." Claire says again, but she sounds so uncertain.

I straighten in my hospital bed, even though it tugs painfully at my stitches.

"Claire, come on. We're friends, aren't we?" I let those words hang in the air for only a second before I realize I don't want her to answer that honestly right now. "Tell me the truth, please."

Claire shifts uncomfortably. It's so much more enjoyable to gossip about someone, I realize, than to tell them the truth to their face. "I mean, maybe...?" she finally says, each word dragged out of her with reluctance. "But not an *affair* affair, you know. I think probably just more a flirty thing. You know how Michael is."

Yes, I know all too well how he is. He flirts as naturally as he breathes, a relentless charm offensive aimed at absolutely every woman, from Rosita to the lady at the grocery checkout to our children's teachers to the mothers at school. For years, I told myself that didn't mean it meant anything, or went anywhere, and I could almost convince myself that was true. But maybe now I finally have to face facts.

"But with Harriet...?" I press. "Have people been talking about it? *Them*, I mean?"

"Elise." Claire almost sounds impatient, as well as grudgingly sympathetic. "You know how everyone at school is."

I think of Joanna, feeling so disillusioned about the community at TGS. "So they are?" I surmise.

Claire lets out a short sigh. "Of course they are."

I feel as if I am peeling back the curtain on all the perfection, except maybe I'm the only one who couldn't see the truth. Has everyone been talking about me and Michael all these years? I thought I was fooling people, but maybe I was only fooling myself. On some level, I think I knew that all along, but

I convinced myself that it didn't matter. That fooling myself was enough.

I turn to gaze out the window; the sky is the kind of heavy white that promises snow, the city a muted landscape of concrete and brick. It's only a few weeks till Christmas, but it feels impossibly distant, the whole world, my whole life, completely remote from this room, this moment.

"I mean, you must have known that, right?" Claire says into the silence, still sounding uneasy. "People at TGS talk about *everyone*."

"But especially *me*," I reply quietly. I'm the head of the PTA, the mom who always looks flawless, whose husband is so unbearably charming. The person they love to hate, maybe, but it never bothered me before. "Right?" I say, turning to look at her. Claire stays silent. I sigh. "So what are they saying?" I ask. "This time?"

Another silence as Claire shifts in her chair.

"Just, you know, that maybe Harriet went a little too hard on the whole Heimlich thing because she was mad about you outing her. Grayson saw them together in the bar before the gala, you know."

"Yes, I know."

I glance at Claire; she seems slightly disappointed that this isn't a revelation to me. "Well, I don't know how Harriet can be mad at you," she huffs, "when she was being obvious about it all. I mean, meeting up in the bar where we have the school gala? *Ridiculous*."

To both our surprise, I start laughing, softly, because it hurts my stomach.

Claire frowns, her eyes narrowing. "Elise? What's so funny?"

"I don't even know." I wipe my eyes; I'm not sure if they're streaming because I'm laughing so much, or if I'm crying. My stomach throbs with the effort of it all, and I force myself to stop, subsiding on something like a hiccup. "Just this whole... microcosm," I try to explain. "It's all so... petty. So puerile and *stupid*."

"*Well.*" She draws herself up, seeming affronted by my judgment. "We *are* talking about your marriage."

"No, we're not," I tell her, and she blinks, clearly annoyed by what sounds like a scolding. "We're talking about everyone else and how they feed off people's problems and pain." My breath catches in my chest, and I turn back to the window because I suddenly feel as if I could sob—or scream. I don't want to be part of this petty world anymore. I want *out*.

"I appreciate you're going through something," Claire says after a moment, "but you don't have to sound quite so sanctimonious, Elise. I mean, people are *concerned*. And they're on your side. Some people were even saying you should consider suing her."

I turn back to Claire, shocked. "*Sue* her?"

Claire nods solemnly. "For malicious intent. You know the Good Samaritan Law that protects people who help someone out?"

"Yes..." Vaguely.

"Well, you can sue someone for allegedly helping you if you can prove intended malice. Kim Lee was telling me about it."

Kim Lee, Harriet's supposed school buddy, who was meant to email her and probably never did, now selling her down the river with her knowledge of law.

"And what did she say about it?" I ask, curious now, and Claire leans forward, her eyes gleaming once more.

"Harriet could be sued for gross negligence. If you proved malicious intent—and I mean, *obviously* you could—then she'd be liable to pay damages. Your medical costs, at a minimum, plus the emotional damage." She pauses to take a breath. "And, if your lawyer thought you had a case for it, it could become a criminal case. Harriet could face a prison sentence for assault." Claire sounds positively gleeful now, and it turns my stomach.

I already know I don't want Harriet to go to prison. She has a small child, for heaven's sake. And yet… even with our excellent medical insurance, this hospital stay is going to cost a pretty penny. And as for the emotional damage—what about the torment she's knowingly caused me for the last three months? Let alone for my children, my marriage?

"I think you have a case," Claire states, clearly wanting me to weigh in. "And you have plenty of witnesses to what happened."

Yes, practically the whole school, but do I really want to keep the gossip mill churning, trot out every acquaintance I possess to explain how Harriet's been messing around with my husband? The old me wouldn't, not in a million years. Never mind what it might do to Harriet, it would be far too painful for *me*. It would be my absolute worst nightmare, to have all my secrets spilled out in a courtroom to be dissected by all and sundry, strangers and friends alike.

And yet aren't they already?

This new me—the one who is lying in a hospital bed with a broken body and maybe a broken marriage—thinks differently. This new, battle-worn, broken-down me, is tired of pretending to be perfect. That nothing bothers me. That I can't be hurt.

This new me, I realize, wants someone *else* to pay for once.

"I might look into it," I tell Claire, and she can't resist giving me a triumphant grin, like she's convinced me singlehandedly, which maybe she has.

I smile back as the certainty settles into me. Yes, I am definitely going to look into it. For once, I'm not going to be the one picking up the pieces, trying desperately to glue them all back together and pretend nothing's been broken. For once, I'm not going to pay that price.

Harriet is.

TWENTY-TWO

HARRIET

I *feel* the looks as I approach the school pickup. I hear the whispers, too, like a malevolent serpent slithering around me, hissing and spitting.

Something has changed since Monday morning. I've sensed it growing every day when I've dropped off Kyra in the morning, picked her up in the afternoon. I'm not friends with these people, so I don't stay to chat, but the air feels poisoned. Somehow, in this whole thing with Elise, I've become the bad guy.

I do my best not to let it bother me. I don't care about these other mothers, I tell myself. I never liked them anyway, and they probably knew that, which is why they now seem so eager to gather like vultures, to feast on the carrion of what happened at that stupid gala. I have other things to worry about, like getting Allan the medication he needs.

He called his neurologist on Monday, but he had trouble speaking, his voice giving out as he struggled to swallow, and I ended up taking over the call while he looked on miserably. The neurologist can't see us till Friday, which feels like forever when I really want Allan to start on these meds, but I tell myself to be patient. A few days won't matter, even if every second seems precious. How many months did Allan already waste, refusing the medication that could slow his decline? I don't want to waste another moment.

Thursday afternoon is the worst. I stand alone as I wait for the school doors to open, but every so often, someone throws a glance my way before turning back to their friends and furiously whispering. They're so obvious, it's pathetic. I wonder, guiltily, if somehow they've found out that I went to see Michael at the hospital.

The memory of that conversation causes me to cringe in shame and humiliation every time I think of it, which is far too often. How could I have been so *desperate*? It's like I took every principle I had and threw them out the window. My only consolation is I have no intention of texting or even *seeing* Michael ever again, if I can help it.

Last night, I looked up a support group for carers of people with ALS. There's one that meets uptown, at the Lou Gehrig Center at the Neurological Institute of New York. I don't need Michael, I realize. There are plenty of other people who can give me—and Allan—the support we need.

I hunch into my coat as an icy December wind funnels down the street. When are they going to open the doors so I can get Kyra and bust out of here? Then I feel a light touch on my shoulder, and I turn to see Joanna, perhaps the only person here I'd dare to call something close to a friend.

"Hey..." I can't quite make myself smile.

"Hey." Her voice is soft, her smile sympathetic.

Recklessly, I decide to face the gossip head-on. "Am I being super paranoid," I ask with a crooked smile, "or is everyone here talking about me?"

Joanna winces. "Not *everyone*," she says, and I almost laugh.

"Really? About—what? Elise?" With a frisson of fear, I realize that maybe I shouldn't have asked. Maybe they're gossiping about me and Michael, and I really don't want Joanna to have to tell me that. But after what Grayson intimated at the gala...

"People here just like to gossip," Joanna says with a shrug. "It's like an Olympic sport here."

"Tell me about it," I reply feelingly. I glance at the doors of the school, which are still closed. "Joanna..." I hesitate. "Are people... *blaming* me for what happened to Elise? Her stomach rupture?"

Again with the wince. A poker face Joanne does not have. "I don't know..." she demurs.

"Seriously," I say. "Are they?" I can't understand it. Yes, the Heimlich might have caused Elise's stomach rupture. I can't argue with that. But *blaming* me? What else was I supposed to do? Watch her choke to death, along with everyone else who was simply standing there staring as she fought to breathe, clutching at her throat?

"Kind of?" Joanna says, looking uncomfortable. "I mean... I try not to listen to all that."

As kind as she's being, I feel like grabbing her shoulders and shaking her. "But what are they saying?" I demand. "I mean, I saved Elise's life. What was I supposed to do?"

"Well..." Now she looks uncomfortable, like she'd rather have her teeth pulled than tell me whatever is coming next.

"Joanna..."

"They're saying you might have done it... on purpose," she finally confesses in a low-voiced rush. "Hurt her, I mean."

"*What?*" Now I'm the one just standing and staring. "What does that even mean?"

Joanna shifts from foot to foot, throwing a glance toward the school doors like she wishes she could will them to open. "Like, maybe you thrust too hard on purpose? Because you know, you guys have... history."

For a few seconds, I can't speak. Can these mothers, these

strangers who have never even known me, think something so *evil* of me? I glance around and see that many of the moms are studiously *not* looking at me, even though I'm sure their ears are well and truly pricked. I feel sick—sick with anger that they could think something so terrible of me, and sick with shame, like I did something wrong, even though I know I didn't.

Did I?

Are these women really going to make me second-guess myself?

"Sorry..." Joanna murmurs, looking wretched.

"Thanks for telling me."

I turn away from her, feeling numb. I can't talk anymore; I can barely think. If all these women think I was malicious to Elise on purpose, deliberately trying to harm her... what does *she* think? What does Michael?

And how is it going to affect my daughter?

As if on cue, the school doors open and the first children trickle out. Joanna gives me a smile of apology before going to collect her daughter Polly, while I scan the huddled children for Kyra. Then I see her, standing apart from the other children, her face an expressionless mask.

My heart lurches, and I realize I've become accustomed to her new self—the animated little girl who holds my hand and tells me about her day. This Kyra, the one who slopes toward me without a word, is the daughter I remember from before, the one I'm used to, the one I worry about.

"Hey." I ruffle her hair as I try to smile. "How was your day?"

Kyra just shrugs, and we start walking down the street. I know her friendship with Lewis isn't as strong—and that's probably my fault, thanks to the shouting match Michael and Allan had when Allan insisted *he didn't want to take those damned drugs*—but she'd seemed to be settling in well to the class.

Why does it feel like things have changed? Or am I just

being paranoid, because everyone was giving me the cold shoulder while I waited?

"You want to tell me about your day?" I ask lightly and Kyra shakes her head. Unease needles me. "Kyra? Tell me one good thing that happened today."

She glances at me for a moment, her expression veiled, and then she says flatly, "Luke and Lewis left early with their grandmother."

Ouch. "And that was a good thing?" I ask, doing my best to keep my voice light.

Kyra shrugs. "I'm not friends with them anymore."

"Not with Lewis? You guys seemed so close."

She shrugs again, looking away.

I decide there's no point in pressing. We have other stuff to be dealing with.

And so, as I walk away from The Garden School, I let myself feel only relief as I leave that poisoned world behind.

Back at our apartment, Allan is in the living room, waiting for Kyra; he rested for most of the day in order to be present and alert for her.

"Look what I have," he tells her, brandishing a puzzle box. It's a thousand-piece jigsaw of a seventeen-piece orchestra, a little complex for an eight-year-old, but Kyra's face lights up.

"Can we do it together?" she asks hopefully, her heart in her eyes. She so clearly wants to spend every moment she can with her dad.

"Of course," Allan replies with a grin that is crooked because part of his face is now drooping, although we all pretend not to notice.

They set up on the kitchen table while I make dinner, and the scene is so cozily domestic that I feel a rush of gratitude that we can have this at all, even as part of me is shaking my head at myself. *This* is what I resisted for so long... standing at the stove, my family at the table, waiting for me to feed them. At one point, it was anathema to me.

I picture my mom stooped over the gas burner, my dad cracking open a beer. Was it really so bad? Do I have any tangible proof, besides that letter of acceptance to art school, that my mother was unhappy with what she'd chosen?

I feel like I don't know anything anymore. And I decide it doesn't matter, because that was the past and this is the present. All I need to do now is enjoy this time together... and make sure Allan gets his meds. I smile at Kyra and Allan, their heads bent over the scattered pieces of the puzzle.

"First," Allan says, and I try not to notice how slurred his speech sounds, "we need to get all the straight edges, to make the frame. Can you help me find the straight edges, Kyra?"

"Is this one?" Kyra asks eagerly, and Allan beams at her.

"Yes, clever girl. Clever... girl." The words come laboriously, but at least they come. As I turn back to the stove, I find I have to wipe my eyes.

On Friday morning, Allan and I are seated in front of his neurologist, Dr. Bayler, as he gives us news I suspected but still don't want to hear.

"Look, I have to be honest with you," he says. "If you'd started these medications eight or even six months ago, when you first had your diagnosis, I'd be more encouraging."

Not a good start, but I still smile, waiting for more. Allan already looks defeated, his shoulders slumped, his gaze downcast.

"Riluzole can slow down the disease's progression," the doctor continues, "but it can't reverse it, or the accompanying symptoms. So, obviously, the more symptoms you have, and the more progression that has been made..." He grimaces in apology. "It's a one-way road, and you've come down it a fair bit since I last saw you, with the slurred speech, the loss of muscle control, the trouble swallowing..." He trails off as Allan simply stares at him, abject. "There's no going back, as you know, and some studies show that the farther down the road you are, the harder it becomes to slow the progression. Most of these medications are for patients in the earliest stages of the disease."

I have to bite my lip to keep from saying something unhelpful. All the arguments Allan and I had, all the pleas and tears and *shouting*... none of it did any good, but oh, if it had. If only it had.

"But..." Allan speaks slowly, doing his best to enunciate every word, "is it still worth doing?"

"It's always worth doing, Allan." Dr. Bayler's voice is gentle. "You have a daughter, don't you?"

Wordlessly, his eyes bright, Allan nods.

"Well, then," he says, like that's the end of the argument. He looks down at his notes. "Now you'll take riluzole orally twice a day on an empty stomach, and there are side effects... nausea, dizziness, drowsiness, and sometimes numbness in the mouth."

"Okay." Allan nods again, resolute, determined.

"There are some other medications we can look at to control some of the symptoms, such as the uncontrolled laughing or crying, but I also should mention something that's relatively new to the market, which is the drug Tofersen. It was only approved by the FDA a couple of years ago, but it's had some really promising results in terms of slowing progression. We can run some tests to see if you're eligible. You need to have a certain gene mutation, which is evident in only ten to twenty percent of ALS patients, and besides that, medical insurance doesn't always cover it because it's so new, so I don't want to get your hopes up."

"Trust me," Allan says with his crooked smile, "my hopes are not up."

Dr. Bayler smiles back at that, but it's a smile tinged with sorrow, because every time we come up against this disease, it reminds us just how unrelentingly awful it is for everyone involved, and Allan most of all.

How can I think—or care—about Elise Dunnett, when this is the reality I'm facing?

And yet it's Elise I am forced to think about when I go to pick up Kyra that afternoon, grateful that it's the weekend, and I don't have to face the firing line outside school for two whole days, and Christmas vacation begins in less than two weeks.

A woman I barely recognize, with frosted blond hair and an avid expression, grabs my arm as she thrusts her face close to mine.

"You should know Elise is coming out of the hospital soon," she says, her nails digging into my wrist. "No thanks to you."

The comment is absurd, but I get the gist.

"It's thanks to her doctors and surgeons, I imagine," I reply as politely as I can. I try to remove my arm, but the woman holds on.

"Everyone knows you did it on *purpose*," she hisses, and I flush, because even though it's what Joanna said, it still feels like a shock to hear it from someone who believes it.

"Would you have rather she choked to death?" I ask shakily and, with effort, pull my arm away from her grip. What is it with these privileged women and their talons?

"So you say," she scoffs, and I shake my head. Did this woman not see Elise gasping for air and clawing at her throat?

"I'm very sorry that Elise had a stomach rupture," I tell this woman, my tone turning cold. "I don't think there's anything more to say."

"Well, *I* think there is," she spits.

I stay silent, waiting for her to reveal whatever ace she thinks she has up her sleeve, because clearly there's more.

"Elise thinks it's your fault too," she tells me triumphantly. "And that you gave her the Heimlich with intended malice." She pauses and then delivers the hammer blow. "She's planning to sue you for gross negligence, so get ready to pay up."

TWENTY-THREE
ELISE

On Thursday afternoon, my mother visits me with the boys. She took them out of school early, and she lines them up by the door like little soldiers. I'm just glad Michael texted me with a heads-up, so I don't look like death barely warmed over. I've put on clothes instead of a hospital gown, and I'm sitting in the chair by the window instead of in my bed. I'm no longer attached to an IV, and I had a shower this morning, so I should feel fairly normal, but the truth is, all this effort has completely exhausted me. I'm meant to be going home in the next day or two, but I can't imagine being ready.

"Mom…" Lewis comes in first, looking eager and then uncertain. "Granny said we can't touch you."

I imagine one of Lewis' bear hugs and I think that was probably sage—if rather cold—advice. "Why don't you squeeze my hand?" I suggest, holding one out for him. "It's so good to see you, sweetheart."

Lewis takes my hand, while Luke hangs back by the door, my mother behind him.

"Lukie." I keep my voice soft as Lewis squeezes my hand, hard enough to make me wince. I definitely couldn't have coped with a hug. "Come say hello, darling." I lift my gaze to my mother, who is looking as stiff and formal as ever, dressed in gray slacks, a navy twinset and pearls, her hair in its neat, silvery bob. She's also looking tired; taking care of my twins must not be easy for her. "Thank you," I say. "For being there for them."

"Well, what else was I to do?" she replies, and gives Luke a little nudge. "Go on, Luke."

He takes a few hesitant steps forward.

"Come on, Luke," I say, smiling. "I'm not made of glass." Even if I feel like it.

Slowly he comes forward and takes my other hand. I smile at my two boys, my heart overflowing with love for them. They mean more to me than anything, more even than Michael. I push away the nebulous fears about my marriage as I focus on my children.

"Dad said they had to operate on your stomach," Lewis says, glancing curiously at my middle. "Did your guts spill out?" He sounds like he kind of hopes they did.

"Well, a little bit, I suppose, during the surgery maybe." I try to laugh, but it sounds brittle. I'd expect an eight-year-old boy to be curious about such things, but I don't particularly like imagining it. I slip my hand from Luke's to run my fingers through his silky hair. "How's school?"

"Mrs. Ryan was cross with everyone," Lewis states matter-of-factly. "She *yelled*." Luke looks away.

"She did?" That doesn't sound like their teacher. "How come?"

Lewis shrugs, his lower lip thrust out. "Because Kyra cried in class."

"Kyra?" I really don't want to think about Kyra, or her mother, but it seems I don't have a choice. "Why was she upset?"

"I don't know," Lewis replies, and now he's looking away. "Mrs. Ryan yelled at everyone and said we had to be nice to her." He deepens his pout. "But I *am* nice to her. *She's* the one who wasn't nice to *me*."

Why, I wonder, is my sons' teacher telling their class to be nice to the daughter of the woman who landed me in here? Shouldn't she be telling them to be nice to Lewis and Luke, whose mother nearly *died*?

"Well, I'm sure what Mrs. Ryan meant was that we should all be nice to everyone," I say as diplomatically as I can. The thought creeps into my mind that suing someone isn't exactly nice. And if I do end up suing Harriet for deliberate assault, will it affect my boys? Who will need to be nice to whom *then*?

We chat for a little while longer, and then they both get bored and my mother turns on the TV to a kids' channel while the boys curl up on my bed, instantly absorbed, and my mother sits down across from me.

"You're looking better than I thought you would," she says, which, if I'm generous, is her way of giving a compliment.

"This whole thing has been..." I shake my head. "Exhausting."

"I expect so."

We are silent for a few moments, and it amazes me that it feels like there is nothing more to say. There never has been. My relationship with my mother has been defined by silence.

And then, just like with Claire, I decide I've had enough of silence. Of not speaking because it's easier simply not to say the hard or important things. I glance at the boys, who are watching the TV, utterly rapt.

"I'm considering," I tell my mother quietly, "suing Harriet Tierney."

My mother frowns as she fingers her pearl necklace. "Who?"

Has Michael not even mentioned her name? I can't decide if that's a good thing or not; did he deliberately keep Harriet out of it, or did it not matter to him?

"The woman," I tell my mother, "who caused my gastric rupture."

Her frown deepens. "You mean the one who saved you from choking?"

"She used more force than necessary." I glance again at Lewis and Luke. Are they listening? I don't think so, but I lower my voice further anyway. "And I think she had a reason."

My mother has decided to be clueless. "A *reason*?"

"Michael," I mouth soundlessly, and my mother's brows snap together.

"Are you serious?" she asks, sounding annoyed. "Are you saying what I think you are?"

For a second, I feel scolded, like the little girl I was with my dad. I did the wrong thing. *Naughty little princess*. But I *didn't*, not this time.

"Yes," I tell her defiantly. "I am."

My mother hisses between her teeth, shaking her head, seeming disapproving... of me. "And what do you suppose that will accomplish?" she demands.

Luke looks up from the TV, gazing at us searchingly, and I give him a reassuring smile. I wait until his attention has been drawn back into the luridly neon-colored world of computer animation before I answer my mother. "It's not about accomplishing something," I tell her. "It's about what's right. *Justice*."

"Justice," my mother repeats scornfully. "Elise, have you lost your mind?"

I recoil a little, because she's never spoken to me like that before. Our relationship has always been cool, stiff, but polite, scrupulously so. Now my mom almost sounds angry, and I don't understand why. Some part of me thought she'd be glad, or at least her version of that emotion, to see me so vindicated. To realize I'm not going to take it lying down, the way I always did. The way *she* always did. We have never, ever talked about my father's affairs, but considering what I know about Michael, I can't believe my mother doesn't know about them. She must at least *suspect*, even if she doesn't know that I know.

But maybe, like me, my mother prefers pretending not to know, and now I'm no longer following our silently agreed-upon script. Well, too bad.

"I have definitely not lost my mind," I tell her shortly. "In fact, I think I've gained it, or cleared it, at least. I know exactly what I'm doing."

My mother makes a snorting sound of disbelief. "Airing your dirty laundry for everyone to comb over?"

"It's not *my* dirty laundry," I inform her, and a silence, tense and laden, ensues. Neither of us is willing to break it.

Finally, my mother stirs, rising from her chair.

"On your head so be it," she says and then gestures to the boys to get off the bed. "But think about the boys, if you don't care about Michael, or yourself. Do you really want them drawn into all this?"

"Drawn into all what?" Lewis asks.

I glance at the TV and see that a commercial has come on. Luke is watching us both with a narrowed, anxious expression, and I wonder how long they've been listening.

For the first time since Claire swept in with all her ideas and accusations, I am doubting myself. Maybe this *isn't* a good idea. And yet I can't stand the thought of Harriet having everything she wants… my husband *and* getting away with hurting me. Why am I the mean one, in this scenario?

"It's time to go," my mother tells my children, and I ache to be with them, to be the one taking them home, making them dinner, cuddling with them at bedtime, their soft, warm bodies pressed against mine. It's been less than a week, but I feel I've been in the antiseptic, halogen-lit hospital forever. Alone.

"I love you both so, so much," I tell them, gesturing for a hug.

Luke embraces me gingerly, but Lewis' hug is harder, and I can't keep from wincing.

"Lewis!" my mother scolds. "Not so hard." She jerks him back, her face set into discontented lines. She's angry about what I'm thinking of doing, and she's taking it out on the boys. So much, I think wearily, is wrong about this situation. About my life. And I don't know if suing Harriet Tierney is the right answer, but I don't have any other ones.

I tell my boys I love them once more, and then I watch them go, yanked along by my mother, yearning to be out there with them, instead of stuck alone in here with my spiraling thoughts and my aching body.

On Monday afternoon, I go home. Michael picks me up, all cheerful optimism and easy charm for the nurses. He even brought flowers—not for me, for them. It's a nice touch, especially from a surgeon—surgeons are notorious for dismissing their inferiors—but it still makes me grit my teeth that he didn't bring any for me. We don't talk about Harriet. We don't talk about anything besides the mechanics of getting me into the car he hired and then home, and that is plenty hard enough.

Walking up and down the hospital corridor a few times a day, I quickly discover, was no preparation for heading out into the real world. It's been ten days since I had surgery, but it feels like an eon. A nurse pushes me in a wheelchair to the front of the hospital, but then I walk outside into the freezing air, feeling like an old woman—bent over, hobbling, my hand on my side, Michael trailing behind me, not quite touching me, maybe not quite wanting to, or maybe I'm the one who doesn't want him to.

"The boys are so excited to see you," he says once we're in the car, speeding uptown.

I nod, looking out the window. It seems like neither of us know how to be with one another anymore.

Back in the apartment, my mother has the boys dressed in button-down shirts and khakis like they're going to church. The apartment is spotless, smelling of lemon polish, and later, when I go to look, there are half a dozen upscale ready meals in the fridge. I cannot fault her.

She leaves me quickly, with one last forbidding glance, and I know she is willing me to drop the idea of a lawsuit. I thank her again for staying, and pretend I don't notice how she's glaring.

"Your mom was a real trooper," Michael tells me as the boys go back to the playroom and I head to the kitchen to make some tea. I have to close my eyes against the dull ache radiating through my middle; it's only been an hour since I had my last dose of pain meds, but I crave more already. Hopefully I won't get an addiction to Oxycontin out of this whole debacle on top of everything else. "She did everything," he continues. "Laundry, cooking, cleaning... Honestly, she was a superstar."

I do my best to ignore the slightly recriminating tone in his voice, like I wasn't grateful enough to my mother when it's taking all my energy simply to remain upright. "She's always been a hard worker," I remark in agreement. All through my school years, my uniform was perfectly pressed, my room clean, the house spotless. Like me, my mother eschewed household help and did it all herself, but I have come to realize that a well-vacuumed bedroom carpet does not take the place of a mother's affection or love.

"Let me do that," Michael says as I reach for the kettle. I let him take it, moving stiffly over to a bar stool to sit down. "It's going to take a while to get back to normal," he tells me. "You shouldn't overdo it."

I watch him fill the kettle, his back to me, his dark head bent over the kitchen sink. I know this man so well. I've loved him fiercely, devotedly, silently, for twenty years. And it's always felt like a weakness, like the worst way I can be wounded. And I've *let* myself be wounded, time and time again. Whether that is on me or Michael I don't know, but one thing this whole experience has shown me is that things need to change. But most importantly, *I* do.

"I want to talk to a lawyer," I tell Michael.

He stills, his back to me, before he slowly turns around. "What? Elise, why?" His face is pale, and he looks shaken, and for a second, feeling almost amused, I wonder if he thinks I am talking about a divorce. Then I wonder if some part of me *is* talking about a divorce.

But, no. Not yet, anyway.

"Because I have reason to believe Harriet Tierney assaulted me when she gave me the Heimlich."

Michael's jaw drops. "*What?*" He sounds completely incredulous.

"It's called intended malice," I inform him, "and I want to talk to a lawyer about suing her."

"Suing... *Elise.*" He thrusts his hands out toward me in dramatic supplication. "Come on, that's crazy."

I smile coldly. "Is it? My doctor told me that most people don't have their stomach ruptured from an abdominal thrust, Michael. She used more force than necessary, because she doesn't like me. And," I add, my tone turning even icier, "you *know* why she doesn't like me."

"She saved your *life*," Michael responds, his voice rising. "Elise—don't do this. Harriet has enough to deal with, surely, with Allan's disease... and how will this affect Kyra? Or *our* children, for that matter, when word gets out that we're pursuing a lawsuit against someone who was trying to help you?" He shakes his head helplessly, like he simply can't believe I'd be so cruel. "Elise, come on. You must see that this is a really terrible idea. Don't do it."

And even though his words have stung me like needles, putting holes in all my certainties, I find myself digging in all the more, because I'm the one who always backs down, who apologizes and tries to make everything better, and this time I'm not going to.

Still, I strive for a measured tone as I tell him, "That may be so, but I want to talk to a personal injury lawyer. Find out my options." I pause as I level him with a stare, one hand pressing my side, which aches abominably. "And if you loved me at all," I throw at him, my voice starting to shake, "you'd support me, and not *her*."

I don't wait for Michael to reply before I add my ultimatum, my voice shaking.

"And if you want to save our marriage, Michael, you *will*."

TWENTY-FOUR
HARRIET

All week, my mind seethes with anxiety about the lawsuit I'm scared Elise Dunnett is going to hit me with.

Every morning and afternoon on the school run, I brace myself for the stares and glares, the murmurs and whispers, all which never seem to abate, although maybe I'm just paranoid. I'm half-expecting Elise to march toward me and serve me some papers—or is that kind of thing only on *Law & Order?*—but she's not there, even though I've heard from Joanna that she was discharged. A Latina woman has been picking the boys up every day and hurries them away.

When Kyra is at school, I google all the terms that woman threw at me—I discovered from Joanna that her name is Claire—and try to sift through the endless information on the internet. What I find is not comforting. I can be sued for "gross negligence," which means that I did not use slight care when I was giving Elise the Heimlich. More concerningly, if she can prove I acted with "intended malice" I could be facing a criminal conviction, which could mean a prison sentence. The Good Samaritan Law in the state of New York, I am assured on the state's Department of Health website, is "to protect YOU," but the examples given are about calling 911 for drug overdoses, not potentially manhandling someone you have a personal history with, to the extent that she ended up needing emergency surgery.

It's not looking good. It's not *feeling* good, because the last thing I want to do is trouble Allan with any of this. He's finally on riluzole, although we haven't seen any positive changes, just the side effects of dizziness, drowsiness, and swelling in his hands and feet. Next week we should hear back if he's eligible to take tofersen, after they've examined the results of some genetic testing. After that, if he is, we'll have to battle the insurance company to get it covered. One thing Elise might not have realized, that if she's hoping for some payout, I barely have a dime to my name. But if she just wants my name dragged through the mud, or to see me in jail, I'm afraid she might never let this go. It feels like she has a vendetta, and there's nothing I can do about it… and that's what scares me.

I try to focus on other things, *better* things, while waiting the whole time to be slammed with the news that I'm being sued. I don't hear anything from Elise or her lawyers, thankfully, but Kyra and I buy a Christmas tree from the bodega on the corner and drag it all the way up to our apartment on the third floor. Allan watches, sleepily swathed in a blanket, as we manage to cram its trunk into a bucket of sand to keep it upright and then decorate it with a box of plastic ornaments from Target. I cut out a star from a cardboard cereal box and cover it in tin foil, and I lift Kyra up to put it on top of the tree while Allan cheers. It's all so painfully sweet and I can't bear to think what Christmas might be like next year, what Allan will be like. Whether he'll even be here with us.

I push all those fears away and try to focus on the present—the three of us together, for now, because in so many ways I don't know what the future holds… for any of us.

. . .

On Saturday, I take the train out to Morristown, New Jersey, with Kyra to see my dad. I feel a little guilty that I haven't seen him since I moved in with Allan, but my dad and I have never had a close relationship; it's not that we don't get along, just that we have absolutely nothing in common.

He's a tough-talking, salt-of-the-earth blue-collar guy. When I was in my teens, pink-haired and rebellious, he had no idea what to do with me. And when I took out huge student loans to go to art college, he was beyond baffled. This is a man who paid for his first car in cash, and who didn't take out a credit card until he was in his forties. Every choice I've made since then has confused him—moving around so much, having a baby on my own, not getting married, never holding down a "real" job. The three months I spent at home when my mom had cancer should have made us closer, but grief can have a way of pulling people apart.

After my mom died, my dad and I lost touch without even meaning to. Without trying. Beyond the occasional email or phone call, we haven't communicated with each other since the funeral two years ago, and I don't even know what's compelling me to visit now, except the fact that I'm afraid and I have no one to talk to because I can't worry Allan with this... and it's close to Christmas, which makes me think of what little family I have.

It's only an hour on the train from New York, and then Kyra and I walk the half-mile to my childhood home, a tall, narrow colonial with a front porch on Clinton Street, near the town green. In the forty years since my parents bought it, Morristown has become gentrified and the house is now in an upscale area, instead of too close to the wrong side of the tracks of my childhood, with many of the homes having been bought by millennial professionals. There are a lot of expensive bikes locked onto front porches and BMWs parked in the street. I wonder how my dad feels about it all. He's sixty-eight and still working as an electrician, and his house is the saddest-looking one, with a sagging porch and a battered, twenty-year-old Chevrolet van in the driveway.

As I mount the steps, Kyra slips her hand into mine. When we lived here for a few months two years ago, she went to the local elementary school—the same one I did—and shared a bedroom with me. I don't remember how much she got along with, or even talked to, my dad. I don't remember much about that time, besides the blur of my mother's bedside, endless brown plastic bottles of pills, and a smell of antiseptic and death.

I knock on the front door and then, after a few seconds' wait, listen to the creak of floorboards as my father comes to the door, unbolts it, and then throws it open.

"Harriet." He doesn't quite smile, but almost. "And Kyra! Haven't you grown big?" Now he does smile, and Kyra grins back uncertainly.

Kyra's grown big, but my father has grown old. His hair is now white, when I remember it as distinctly salt and pepper, and his face looks more lined and tired than it did before, with deep creases from his nose to mouth fanning out from his eyes. His shoulders are slumped, his paunch straining against the buttons of his plaid button-down shirt.

I step forward as if to give him a hug, but then I don't, and he shuffles aside to let us in. The whole encounter already feels both weird and sad, and I wonder why I came.

"So, you're living in New York now?" my father asks as we head back to the kitchen, which has the same dark green metal cabinets of my childhood. He opens the fridge and peers inside. "I've got water and beer…" he offers with a slightly shamefaced smile. "Sorry, I should have bought something. There's coffee, too."

I think of my dad's instant Folgers granules floating in a cup of barely boiled water and smile. "It's okay. Water's fine." I squeeze Kyra's hand gently, a reassurance.

My dad fills two glasses from the tap and hands them to us, and then we all head into the living room, which is as small and dark as I remember, with a sagging plaid sofa and a La-Z-Boy recliner by the window that I always think of when I picture my dad. He sinks into it now, his hands hanging loosely between his knees. Kyra and I sit on the sofa.

"We're out in Astoria," I tell my dad. "Living with Allan, Kyra's father."

My dad stiffens slightly—I know he has always found my domestic arrangements uncomfortable—but then he nods. "Well," he says, and then again, "Well, that's something."

"My dad is sick," Kyra states quietly, and both my dad and I look startled—my dad because Kyra announced it so abruptly, and me because I've never heard her call Allan her *dad* before. The fact that it slipped out now is significant, and yet I know it's not the moment to make something of it. Still, I think, Allan would be pleased. He'd be *thrilled*.

"Sick?" My father leans forward with an attempt at a smile. "Has he got the flu or something, honey?"

She shakes her head, and I put my hand on her shoulder. I didn't really want to get into Allan's diagnosis today, but I see that I'll have to.

"Allan has ALS," I tell my dad. "A motor neurone disease. Like Lou Gehrig."

For a second, my father looks confused and then understanding dawns. "Lou Geh—that one? Oh, jeez." He shakes his head as he rubs his jaw. "I'm sorry."

"Thanks." I glance at Kyra. "I think there might be some books in my bedroom," I tell her. "Some fairy tales. They all have color names—The Red Book, The Blue Book, The Green Book. Do you want to go see if you can find them?" It's a pathetic ploy and she sees right through it, but she nods without complaint, slipping off the sofa to head upstairs.

My dad watches her go. "Must be hard on her," he remarks quietly. "On all of you."

"It's not easy," I agree, and we lapse into silence, which feels far more familiar.

I can probably count the number of significant conversations I've had with my dad on one hand, but at least there was no real animosity between us. Still, I'm trying to remember why I came, what I was hoping to accomplish here. For Kyra to see her grandfather, yes, but I wanted someone to talk to, as well. How on earth did I think it could be my *dad*? And yet, I remind myself, he's always been sensible, no-nonsense, steady. These are all qualities I realize I appreciate and admire more now than I did as a rebellious sixteen- or even twenty-six-year-old. They're what I need in my current situation.

"I think I might be getting sued," I blurt, and his shaggy eyebrow rises.

"*Sued*?" he repeats. "What for?"

Haltingly, but as quickly as I can, knowing that Kyra could come downstairs at any moment, I repeat the gist of the events on the night of the gala. My father listens attentively, his arthritic fingers steepled together. As I finish, he leans back in his La-Z-Boy and it creaks in protest.

"I think you must be protected by the Good Samaritan Law," he says, frowning.

"Well, I'd hope so, but someone told me she's going to try to prove that I did it with intended malice."

His frown deepens. "But why would you?"

I sigh. "Because she thought I was having an affair with her husband. I wasn't," I add quickly, just in case my dad thinks my morals are that questionable. "He's a neurosurgeon, and we were meeting up to talk about Allan. He offered some… emotional support. But his wife became suspicious."

"And he didn't tell her what was going on?"

"I don't know," I admit. "It didn't seem like he did. Their marriage is kind of weird. They don't talk about a lot of stuff."

Probably similar to my own parents' marriage, but I feel like theirs worked, at least on some level, and maybe Michael's and Elise's doesn't. Whether my mom ever resented my dad for giving up her art school dreams I'll probably never know, but the woman I remember smiled a lot... Something else I didn't appreciate as a sullen teenager, I realize. Is it age or experience that changes—and challenges—your perspective? Probably both.

"Well." My dad scratches his jaw. "How can there be intended malice if it was all in her head?"

I shift uncomfortably in my seat, because the more I've gone over the last few months in my mind, the more I have to reluctantly accept that it wasn't entirely in Elise's head. No, Michael and I were never having an affair, but I felt something for him, as much as it shames me to admit it, even just to myself.

"We weren't exactly friends," I tell my dad. "I... annoyed her, I guess, and she annoyed me too because it was so obvious she had something against me. And pretty much everyone at Kyra's new school knew it."

"Okay, but plenty of people get annoyed by each other," my dad points out so very reasonably. "But there was never anything going on between you and her husband?"

I hesitate, only for a millisecond, because there *wasn't*, and yet... I think of that scene I made back at the hospital. The way I looked forward to our meetings, and the hurt I felt when Michael said they had to stop.

"Nothing physical," I tell my dad, hating to have to be this honest, "but I think I might have depended on him a little too much. I was lonely, and the stuff with Allan felt overwhelming. He was refusing to take any medication and..." I shake my head. "I don't know. I didn't think I was doing anything wrong, but now I'm starting to second-guess myself..."

My dad is silent for a long moment. "Do you think she has a case?" he finally asks.

"I'm afraid she might make one," I admit. "Because she hates me so much. And she's rich and well-connected, and I'm not. I feel like she could make this into a whole big thing, just because she can."

My father offers me a crooked smile. "She sounds like a peach."

I try for a laugh. "Yeah, well, when I first met her, I thought, very briefly, that we could be friends." I recall that moment back at the picnic when I saw a glimpse of Elise's wry humor, a sense that she could stand back and laugh at herself if she was given the chance. Maybe I didn't give it to her. Looking back, I recognize I was prickly from the start. And over the ensuing months, I didn't exactly go out of my way to be friendly, far from it. I just never expected it would end up like this. "Anyway," I tell my dad, "I'm just not sure what to do. I haven't been notified or served or what have you yet, but I feel like I'm just waiting for the axe to fall."

Again, my dad is silent. He nods slowly, looking down at his hands, and then he rubs his jaw once more. I feel like he's about to say something momentous, but I have no idea what it is.

"I've been thinking about selling this place," he finally tells me. "Moving into one of those retirement condos down the way."

"You... have?" I'm not sure where this is going.

He keeps nodding, not quite looking at me. "Yeah, there are some places up Route 202 that aren't so bad. Little one-bedrooms. They've got central air, at any rate." He lets out a half-hearted laugh. "And this place... well, the mortgage is paid off and it should fetch over six hundred thousand, so that's something."

"Wow..." I still don't know what he's trying to tell me.

"Enough," my dad tells me, looking me straight in the eye as a small, determined smile quirks his mouth, "to hire a damned good lawyer, should it come to that."

TWENTY-FIVE
ELISE

Michael isn't talking to me. After I gave him the ultimatum about supporting me in the lawsuit, he went very quiet, his jaw bunched, and then he turned and walked out of the kitchen without saying another word.

I rushed to the sink, leaning over it because I was genuinely afraid I might vomit, which wouldn't do my stitches any good. In the twenty years of our marriage, I had never, I realized, stood up to Michael before. Ultimatums were not part of my vocabulary or my mindset, and yet I'd just given a pretty huge one. Part of me wanted to run after him and take it all back, but I didn't, and I was proud of myself for staying strong.

I spent the rest of the afternoon in bed resting, and at some point Luke crawled in with me, and we watched something mindless on Nickelodeon for a while, my arm around his thin shoulders. Michael heated up one of the meals my mom had brought in, and I forced myself to the dining-room table, even though I wanted nothing more than the oblivion of an Oxycontin and sleep. After dinner, Michael gave the boys a bath and I conked out. I didn't hear him come to bed or get up in the morning. By the time I woke up, he was gone, and Rosita had taken the boys to school.

The next few days passed in the same way. I wanted to get stronger, but there was something so *comforting* about staying in bed and simply letting the world slip by, unnoticed. I didn't have to deal with anything, and I mostly didn't let myself think. But the idea of a lawsuit—the fact that I'd threatened it—hung over me as much as it might have hung over Harriet, had she known about it. At some point, I'd have to show Michael I was serious and act.

I also had to deal with the dozens of texts I'd received from various well-meaning friends from TGS, although many of them, I suspected, just wanted the gossip. How was I feeling? Could they order something off UberEats for me? Could they have Lewis over for a playdate? No one offered to have Luke, something that stung. I'd known he always had trouble making friends, and while it didn't seem to bother him, it bothered *me*, especially when it was made so obvious by the lack of invitations.

For the most part, I ignored the texts. I could always apologize later and say I'd been too tired to reply, but I really couldn't cope with all the questions, the relentless demand for news on how I was, when I'd be back, what I thought about "everything" —meaning *Harriet*. But by Friday, I decide I have to do something. Michael and I have been stiffly polite to each other all week, but we haven't talked about anything important, and certainly not the lawsuit. He probably hopes I'll drop it, that I only mentioned it in a fit of pique. It's time to show him I'm serious.

So, on Friday, after the boys have gone to school and Michael to work, I shower and dress—two things I've barely done all week—and sit at the kitchen island with my laptop in front of me. I don't want to involve our own lawyer, who isn't a personal injury expert and is Michael's squash buddy, and so I have to rely on Google. *Lawyer for personal injury* brings up millions of search results, the top being some major law firms in the city. I have no idea which one to choose, what even to look for. Just getting this far is scaring me a little, because it is starting to feel like a long and painfully public road to go down... and yet if I don't do it, who wins?

Michael. And Harriet. In that order, I realize, because this whole thing is far more about Michael and me than it is about Harriet, although obviously she has something to do with it.

I trawl through the results until I settle on one that I like, because it isn't one of the big offices that seem to operate like a steamroller, and it's run by a woman. I like the look of her—not the stereotypical sharp-nailed blond in a tight-fitting power suit. Instead Jennifer Stevens, P.A., is short and dumpy, dressed in a pale pink blouse and gray slacks, but her smile is assured, and I see steel in her eyes. Before I can overthink it or lose my nerve, I call the office and make an appointment for that very afternoon. It's been so easy, and yet it still feels impossible.

I dress with care, taking an age to get myself into a pair of camel-colored wool slacks and a turtleneck sweater in cream cashmere. Everything hurts; raising my arms above my head forces me to slump on the edge of my bed and simply breathe for several minutes. *Harriet Tierney did this to me*, I remind myself. *Harriet and Michael.* And so I keep going, adding jewellery, subtle makeup, styled hair. I am still pretty sure I look like death warmed up, but at least a high-end version of it.

I practically limp downstairs, curved into myself because my stomach muscles feel like they're on fire. Raul is on duty, and he hurries toward me as soon as he sees me. I must really look bad, I reflect, as he slips his arm under my elbow.

"Mrs. Dunnett! Do you need a taxi? Or your car pulled up? Let me call someone for you."

"A taxi is fine, Raul, thank you," I murmur. There's no way I can drive.

"You sit," he insists, guiding me to a cushioned chair by the doorman's desk. "Wait here while I find you a taxi."

I give him a limpidly grateful smile. "Thank you."

A few minutes later, Raul is helping me into the back of a taxi—climbing in is a real effort—and then I am speeding toward midtown, wondering what on earth I am doing. But I am still determined to do it.

Jennifer Stevens' office is on the eighth floor of a nondescript building in midtown, and I only wait a few minutes before I'm called in. Its only selling point is a window overlooking the American Girl Doll Store, but I tell myself I didn't want something glitzy. I know firsthand how quickly the shiny gilt can flake off, mine included.

"Elise Dunnett?" Jennifer Stevens' manner is no-nonsense, and she reaches across her desk to give me a firm handshake. "Nice to meet you."

"And you."

"Please sit down."

I move gingerly to a chair, wincing as I sit down, and she notices.

"You've been injured?"

"Gastric perforation. Stomach rupture." I give her a direct look, although inside I am trembling with nerves. "I'm here because I have reason to believe that the woman who gave me the Heimlich when I was choking used more force than necessary, because of our... problematic history. The so-called lifesaving maneuver is what caused the rupture."

Jennifer sits down, meeting my gaze unflinchingly. "That's quite an accusation."

I feel rebuked, but I try not to show it. "I know it is."

"The Good Samaritan Law," she continues without missing a beat, "is a robust legal protection for anyone who comes to another's aid."

Okay, now I *really* feel rebuked.

"I know that, too," I tell her. "I didn't come here on a whim, trust me."

"All right." She lays her hands flat on her desk. "Tell me what you know."

And so I do, haltingly at first and then with growing conviction. I explain about Harriet's and my history, her meetings with Michael, the texts, the coffee receipts, the way she liked to rub my nose in it all. I tell her how they met in the bar before the gala, and how I lost my temper right before I choked. I tell her how Harriet grabbed me, told me I was aggravating, how she said "*You deserve...*" and then didn't finish her sentence.

In my head, it all sounded like a strong case, but Jennifer remains expressionless, listening mostly in silence, interrupting once or twice only to clarify points. By the time I finish, I have no idea what she thinks about anything I've said. She remains silent for a long moment, long enough that I start to fidget, and my stomach starts to pulse with pain. I should have taken another Oxycontin before I came here.

"If she was the one who had the stomach rupture," she says at last, "I think I'd understand it more."

What is *that* supposed to mean? I press one hand to my side, trying not to wince from the pain. Jennifer Stevens notices.

"Look," she says. "You've obviously been through a really hard time. And, based on what you've told me, it might be that this woman acted with some malice, whether unconscious or not. But proving it in court will be difficult." She holds up a hand to forestall a potential protest, although, in truth, I don't have any. I thought personal injury lawyers took on just about every case, but it feels like she's about to let me down, and I wasn't expecting it. "I'm not saying," she continues, "that I won't take your case. Far from it." She pauses. "But jurors tend to look favorably on someone who comes to another person's rescue. They're imagining themselves in that situation, and how much courage it takes to do the right thing."

"But if she was having an affair with my husband—" I begin, hurt spiking my words. So far, *no one* has been on my side. Not my mother, not my husband, not even my lawyer. Why am I feeling like the bad guy when I'm the only person in this scenario who didn't do anything wrong?

"And that's the million-dollar question," Jennifer Stevens tells me with a nod. "*Was* she? If you can prove she was, then it's a totally different story. But if it's just a couple of coffee receipts and your suspicions..." She trails off, and I feel my cheeks heat. She is making me sound—and feel—unhinged.

"The other factor," she continues as I struggle to form a reply, "is whether you want this all aired in public. Cases like this can attract national media attention, and it won't necessarily be favorable for you." My cheeks are burning now, and stupidly, tears come to my eyes. "I'm only saying this to warn you," she tells me, gentling her tone. "I know sometimes pursuing a lawsuit can be a kneejerk reaction. You're hurting, and you want someone else to hurt as well, and I completely understand that. And if this woman did hurt you deliberately, for whatever reason, that's something that *should* be pursued. But... it can be a difficult and painful path, and you just need to make sure it's worth it." She cocks her head. "Sometimes these cases can be settled out of court, if it's just a matter of money."

I don't care about the money, and I very much doubt Harriet Tierney has much, anyway. As I stare miserably at my would-be lawyer, I realize that Jennifer Stevens is right. This was a kneejerk reaction, and it wasn't about Harriet, but Michael. This was my way of showing him that I was serious, that he couldn't keep flirting and who knows what else while I stood by and suffered and smiled.

Was I ever really thinking about going through with it? Right now I seriously doubt it, and I feel humiliated as well as relieved. I think Jennifer Stevens sees both emotions on my face because she smiles and reaches over to pat my hand.

"Why don't you think about it?" she suggests. "You know how to reach me."

I nod and murmur my thanks as I rise stiffly from my chair. All I want now is an Oxycontin and a nap. But as I walk carefully out of the law office, my hand pressed to my side, I already know how I'm going to play this. I'm not ready to give in yet, as I'm sure Michael expects me to, so he can go on his merry way, never changing, always hurting me.

I may have decided not to sue Harriet Tierney, but Michael doesn't need to know that. Not yet.

As far as *he's* concerned, it's full steam ahead... no matter what the cost.

TWENTY-SIX
HARRIET

My dad's offer to help with the lawsuit nearly brings me to tears. I wasn't expecting it, and the truth is, I know I don't deserve it. Sitting on that lumpy old sofa, looking at the earnest determination on his craggy, kindly face, I have the same strange, swirling sensation I had with Allan, when, for a few painfully poignant seconds, I imagine a what-if that would change my whole life.

What if I'd accepted my dad for who he was—and really, who he *wasn't*—and stuck around more, both before and after my mom's cancer diagnosis? What if I'd made sure Kyra got to know him, so they had an actual relationship? What if I'd realized long before now that just because my parents' lives seemed small didn't mean they were wrong?

The questions race through me as my dad continues to smile at me. "Well?" he says. "What do you say? Do you know any good lawyers?"

"Oh, Dad." I am touched, but I already know I can't take his money. "I can't let you do that. This house is your retirement fund."

He frowns. "I've got a good pension, Harriet. This house is your inheritance."

What? I'd assumed, without even thinking about it at all, that I wouldn't inherit anything from my parents. I'm so used to a hand-to-mouth existence that I can't imagine it any other way, and it's not like I was a devoted daughter.

"I want to provide for you," he continues, his voice rising with insistence. "And my granddaughter. Let me do this."

What else can I do but accept? "Thank you," I tell him humbly. "But I really hope, Dad, that it doesn't come to that."

"Well, I do too, of course," he replies gruffly. "But this woman sounds like a real piece of work."

"Yeah..." The truth is, I don't know what to think about Elise Dunnett. Yes, she was catty and rude to me all fall, but I never once tried to make things easier for her. I knew she felt threatened by my friendship with Michael, and I never bothered to explain it.

Considering she's thinking of slapping me with a lawsuit now, I don't know why I feel like maybe I was a little to blame for the way everything happened. Did I push too hard when I was doing my best to save her life? Not consciously or deliberately, but, if I'm honest, *maybe?* Because she was struggling against me even in that, and everything about her has annoyed me, so, yes, maybe I thrust upward into her ribs with a little more force than necessary. If I did, it was the same kind of instinct as slamming a door. You don't think it could *kill* somebody.

But whether I'd be willing to admit any of that while on the witness stand...? No, probably not.

"Thanks, Dad," I say again. "I really mean that."

My dad nods, almost brusquely. He never did well with emotion; when my mom was dying, he sat in that very chair and drank a beer. But I am coming to realize there are different ways to cope, and different ways to grieve.

Kyra comes back downstairs, and my dad suggests we order pizza from Coniglio's, and, all in all, we spend a pretty pleasant afternoon together. My dad asks Kyra a few questions about school, her interests, what she thinks of New York. For him, it's a lot of effort, and I appreciate it.

When we are saying goodbye, a sudden thought occurs to me. "Dad... what are you doing for Christmas?" I'm ashamed I didn't think to ask earlier.

My dad shrugs, shoving his hands into the pockets of his jeans. "I don't know. Just hang around here, I guess."

Last Christmas, Kyra and I were in Texas, and I didn't even call him.

"Why don't you spend it with us?" I suggest. "You can stay the night if you want—if you don't mind sharing a room with Kyra." I'll have to sleep on the sofa, but that's okay.

My dad looks taken aback, and for a second I think he's going to refuse, and all the strides I feel we've made today will evaporate. But then he smiles and nods.

"All right, then," he says. "Thanks."

We hug goodbye, and the familiar smell of him—Old Spice aftershave and peppermints—gives me a weird wave of nostalgia.

As we walk back toward the train station, Kyra glances up at me. "There weren't any books in your room," she says seriously.

"Weren't there?" I try for a laugh. "Maybe my dad got rid of them."

I reach for her hand, but she slips away, walking a few steps ahead of me. With a ripple of unease, I wonder if it's intentional. Is she mad about me asking her to go upstairs for a little while—or is this something deeper? Maybe she blames me for the way parents are ignoring me at school, because of the whole gala affair.

I haven't talked to her about it because I don't want to make it a bigger deal than it is, but maybe that's the wrong call, since it seems as if everyone else is making it so. I hate the thought that the petty problems between Elise and me are affecting my daughter, but what can I do about it? I feel helpless in this situation in so many ways. Maybe Kyra does, too.

On Monday, I am doing my usual trick of arriving the very second the school doors open and leaving the second after, to avoid the usual barrage of glares and whispers.

This morning, however, I have to check myself, because walking down the street toward me, an ethereal vision in white cashmere, is Elise Dunnett herself. I haven't seen her since I saved her life and she hissed at me to go away, and now I am both stunned by how effortlessly glamorous she looks—as usual—but also how wan.

Her face is pale, her cheekbones more prominent; I suppose a stomach rupture has an effect on your appetite. She's wearing a pair of off-white wool trousers with a white cashmere turtleneck sweater and a long cream trench coat that she's left open despite the freezing weather, and the effect is a little bit like looking into the sun.

As soon as she reaches the front of the school, she is swarmed by concerned admirers who flutter around her like moths to a beautiful, elegant flame. She gives them small, martyred smiles and I hear her voice carry to where I'm standing, a good twenty feet away as I clutch Kyra's hand.

"Thank you, thank you, yes... it's been really difficult, but I think I'm finally feeling better... nothing like a brush with death to give you a little perspective!" She laughs lightly, her gaze roving over the crowds, and I have an awful feeling that she's looking for me.

I take an inadvertent step back, just as that harpy Claire swoops down on Elise, kissing her extravagantly on both cheeks as she coos how wonderful it is to see her. Elise bestows a grateful smile on her, and the whole effect, from over here at least, is pretty nauseating. I glance at the school doors, willing them to open.

Then I hear a little gasp, and when I lift my gaze, unwillingly, to the crowd of mothers surrounding the angelic Elise, I see Claire glaring at me furiously, while Elise looks away, her lips trembling, clearly pained. Claire slips her arm through Elise's and walks her toward the school doors like she's an invalid, and who knows, maybe she is. I just can't take any more of the drama, the stress. Is Elise Dunnett going to sue me or not? And how come everyone here seems to have forgotten that if I hadn't given her the stupid Heimlich, she would have *died*.

"Hey." I turn and see Joanna smiling at me. "How are you holding up?"

The gossip must be truly horrendous, I think, if she needs to know how I'm *holding up*.

The school doors open, and I try to give Kyra a hug goodbye, but she squirms away and heads toward the entrance without looking back. Once again, I wonder if I should talk to her about what's going on. I will this afternoon, I decide. I will not allow this absurd drama to affect Kyra any more than it already has.

"I'm okay," I tell Joanna, and then nod toward Elise, who is entering the school, and I wonder if she's going to talk to the headmistress about how I'm such a *problem*. Maybe I'm being paranoid, but a week of glares and gossip has taken its toll, and I see accusation and aggression everywhere, even in my own daughter. "I see she's recovering, at least," I remark to Joanna.

"Yeah, I don't think I could look that good ten days after emergency stomach surgery," she replies, and then winces. "Sorry…"

So even Joanna seems to assume it's my fault.

"Her friend said she's thinking of suing me," I tell her bluntly. "Can you believe that?"

Judging from Joanna's expression, she can, and it's not a surprise.

"Does everyone here know?" I ask her. I don't know why I thought they wouldn't, considering how these parents gossip, but I guess some part of me hoped it was just Claire being nasty.

"It's been going around," she admits. "You know how this place is..."

"Yeah," I tell her grimly. "I know." And right now, I am extremely tempted to walk away from it all and never look back. For Kyra's sake, though, I'll stick it out. Although she's gone quiet again, I still think she likes The Garden School, and the last thing she needs is more disruption in her young life.

"Hey." Joanna touches my sleeve. "Do you want to go get a coffee?" Her brown eyes are warm with sympathy, and even though I know I should really get back to Allan, I find myself nodding, because I could really use a friend, or even just a friendly ear.

"Sure," I say, managing a smile, even though I feel both fragile and angry about all of this. "Thanks."

We avoid the café I went to with Elise back in September, since it's often swarming with TGS parents, and head for a Starbucks a few blocks away. I offer to buy the coffees, but Joanna demurs and insists she'll treat me. I accept, grateful for even a small kindness.

"So, what are they really saying?" I ask her once we're seated in the back with our drinks. "I'd rather know than not know, so please be honest."

"Well..." Joanna glances down at her latte. "I'm not really in the loop. I'm new this year, and I don't know... I haven't *vibed* with a lot of the other moms, unfortunately." She makes a face.

"You must have heard something," I protest.

"Well, a little on the class chat..."

I didn't even know there *were* class chats. Is there one for third grade? If so, I was never added—something that wouldn't have bothered me before but now stupidly stings. "And what are they saying on the kindergarten mom chat?" I ask with a feeble laugh, like this is funny instead of awful.

"Well..." Joanna really looks like she doesn't want to have to tell me. "Just, you know, that Elise might be... justified... in suing, because of... you know... you and Michael."

I feel my cheeks heat. "You know there's nothing between me and Michael, right?"

Joanna nods quickly. "Yeah, yeah, of course I know that."

"I mean..." I breathe out. "We were meeting up for a *medical* reason. But obviously that kind of thing is private, so..."

"Right, right." She's still nodding. "Absolutely."

If random kindergarten moms think Elise is justified, she must feel like she's got the whole school community on her side, I realize. This really isn't looking good for me.

"This is so *unfair*," I suddenly burst out, unable to keep myself from it. Joanna reaches over to pat my hand, a clumsy gesture of comfort, but one I appreciate. "If I hadn't saved her from choking, who would have? Everyone else was just standing around, staring." I shake my head. "Part of me wishes..." But, no, I can't bring myself to finish that sentence. "Elise had it in for me from the first time I met her," I tell Joanna, fury and hurt spiking my words. "Just for *talking* to Michael, when he was the one who spoke to me first."

"I guess," Joanna ventures cautiously, "she's a little bit of a control freak."

A huff bursts out of me like a gunshot. "You know she's got OCD? Like, *severe*. Michael told me he has to give the boys baths because she was scrubbing them so hard. And she has to walk around their bedroom three times every night before she goes to sleep, and she sometimes stays up all night cleaning out their cupboards, and she can only wear one color at a time, which is probably why you always see her in fricking angelic white." I break off to catch my breath. Joanna is looking both horrified and fascinated, and recklessly I continue. "She does a lot of other weird stuff, too. Michael once wanted her to have therapy for it, but she won't go." I shake my head. "She's got some serious problems, and now she's offloading them onto *me* with this ridiculous lawsuit."

I stop then, belatedly realizing that maybe I shouldn't have said all that. Over our last coffee in Starbucks, Michael seemed to have regretted telling me, and now I've blabbed his secrets, which I have a sinking feeling would absolutely appal him.

"Sorry," I finish on a sigh. "I shouldn't have said all that. It's obviously confidential. But this whole thing is driving me crazy, and there's no one else I can talk to." I give her a shamefaced smile, along with an apologetic shrug. I know I shouldn't have said anything about Elise's OCD.

Joanna smiles as she pats my hand, seeming serenely—and maybe smugly—confident. Does hearing a juicy secret naturally give someone a thrilling kind of power? I wonder as I watch her.

"Don't worry," she assures me. "I won't say a word." She leans forward, dropping her voice to a conspiratorial whisper. "You can trust me."

TWENTY-SEVEN
ELISE

My first foray back to the hallowed halls of The Garden School goes as I expected—I am both celebrated and cosseted, treated like a heroine coming back from the wars, battle-scarred but beautiful. It's satisfying to have so many hugs and heartfelt murmurs of well wishes... at least, it *would* be, if I truly believed them.

As I stood there with my saintly smile, dressed all in white like some sort of modern-day Mother Teresa, part of me wondered if, in another scenario, these smiling, sympathetic women would be tearing me apart.

What if I were in Harriet's shoes? Would all these so-called friends be gleefully throwing me to the wolves, dissecting my nefarious motives, insisting they knew all along I had it in me to be so completely diabolical as to harm someone gasping for life? These are the kinds of terrible things they've said to me about Harriet, and I know for a fact that most of my friends haven't exchanged more than two words with her since September. So how can they possibly be so sure she's evil?

All in all, these thoughts are more troubling than I want them to be. I want this to be a black-and-white situation, with absolutely no shades of gray, but already it's feeling murky. I haven't called Jennifer Stevens since I met with her, and despite my saintly act outside The Garden School's doors, I'm feeling decidedly agnostic... about everything, to my own annoyance. I keep thinking of what Jennifer said to me, so sagely.

If she was the one who had the stomach rupture, I'd understand it more.

Maybe I would, too.

Michael is still not speaking to me, except about the minutiae of life maintenance, and then only because he's had to pick up the slack while I recover. I see disappointment rather than anger in his eyes, though, and that makes me feel even more unsure. I know now that I wasn't planning on *actually* suing Harriet Tierney, but how can I explain that to Michael or anyone, when Claire has made sure to let everyone know? The frantic whispers in front of the school assure me that my imminent lawsuit has been burning up the class chats, and I never meant it to get that far.

At least... I don't think I did.

In any case, I tell myself I can reel it all back in, be the magnanimous one who graciously decides to forgive, if not quite forget.

On Wednesday, two days after I've reappeared on the TGS scene, I'm just starting to murmur something along those lines to somebody when Claire comes to me, her face wreathed in friendly concern.

"Oh, Elise... how *are* you?" she asks, grabbing my arm, and my stomach sinks because something has happened, and I don't know what it is.

"I'm... fine," I reply cautiously, and then wait for more, which Claire clearly is dying to give me.

"I was worried you might be upset about what people are saying," she explains, dropping her voice to a confidential whisper. "Honestly, I think if we were all just *real* with one another, we'd say similar things. Everyone's struggling in one way or another, aren't they? We just don't like to admit it."

"I suppose," I reply after a second's startled pause. I wish I knew what on earth she was talking about.

"And, you know, it's practically de rigueur to have a diagnosis these days, right? I mean, there's no shame in it." She nods sagely. "Honestly, I think you're brave for admitting it, Elise."

Admitting *what*? I stare at her, feeling both annoyed and, more alarmingly, scared, because she's so clearly enjoying this.

"I'm not actually sure what I've admitted," I tell her with a light laugh. "Care to clue me in?"

Claire's eyes widen theatrically; clearly she is going to enjoy giving me whatever gossip she's heard. "You mean you haven't heard?"

"Obviously not." I can't hide the edge to my voice.

"Oh… wow." She shakes her head slowly, milking the moment. "Well, people have been saying… I guess it's gotten around… that you have OCD. Like, *severely*. Michael wanted you to be institutionalized…"

Institutionalized?

For a second, I can barely breathe. She makes me sound like I've lost my mind. It's not like that at all. But how on *earth* do the parents of TGS know this?

"We all have something, right?" Claire continues, her tone syrupy with sympathy. "Like I said, there's no shame in it. I mean, most people *say* they have OCD, but I guess they're not walking around their bedrooms three times every night." She smiles to show she understands, but what she's really doing is rubbing my nose in the fact that she knows these humiliating details. But how does she know this about me? "And I didn't realize that's why you only wear one color at a time," she adds, and I stand there rigidly, gritting my teeth so hard my jaw aches. "But you always look good, so…" She shrugs.

Elise Dunnett, the mom who seems so perfect, the envy of

everyone, clearly isn't. In fact, she might be crazy, if she has to do stuff like that.

"Of course, it's a shame that it's affected the boys—" she goes on.

"Who has been saying all this?" I cut her off, my voice a rasp.

Claire's eyes widen, and I know she's gotten the reaction she hoped for. I am horrified that people are talking about the *boys*. What are they saying? What do they really know? It feels like my skin has been peeled back, my nerves exposed. My image isn't just suffering from a hairline fracture, it's shattered. Someone else admitting they had OCD, severe or not, might be no big deal. In this crowd, you might get a grimace of sympathy, a raised eyebrow. But the fact that it's affected my family, *and* that my whole persona has been based on perfection? It's devastating. Because, I know, while I've been admired, I've also been envied. And so many people at this school can't wait to see my fall from grace... my so-called friend included.

But worse than that—*far* worse—is the knowledge that the only way anyone could know this is because Michael told them. My husband is the only one who knows about my little rituals. He's been endeared and alarmed by them in turns, and yes, at various points when I was really struggling, he asked me to get help. But he's never wanted me to be *institutionalized*, although I know that's how gossip works.

With sudden certainty, I realize I know where this particular gossip came from.

Harriet.

Michael must have told her in one of their many conversations, and she told someone at school, and from there it raged like wildfire. The betrayal is as deep as it is complete. Of all the things Michael could have let slip... Except maybe it didn't slip at all. Maybe he was complaining to Harriet, while she comforted him. The prospect is enough to make bile rise in my throat.

"Elise... are you okay?" Claire asks, and I realize I am just standing there, my jaw working as I stare into space.

"I'm fine," I tell her abruptly. "Obviously, I'd rather my personal business wasn't being gossiped about by every mother in the school, but..." I turn to give her a frosty smile. "At least you're enjoying it, right?"

Claire's sympathetic smile falters. "Elise, I'm just concerned..." she begins, and I shake my head. I am so done with all this.

"No, you're not," I tell her. "You're *loving* this. You could at least be honest enough to admit that."

Claire draws herself up, indignant. "*Elise...*"

I don't bother to stick around for whatever pathetic protest she's going to make. I don't think I can stand her, or anyone at this school, for another second. I stride down the street, faster than I should be walking considering I still have stitches, trying my best to be oblivious to the whispers in my wake. When I turn the corner of the block, I fumble for my phone and then swipe to call.

"Elise?" Michael asks, sounding concerned.

"We need to talk," I say flatly, and then I disconnect the call.

By the time I make it back to our apartment, I'm feeling calmer, or at least numb.

Michael texted to say he was coming home, and I walk around the perimeter of the living room carpet three times to get my breathing under control. My OCD started when I was around eight or so; at least that's when my mother noticed it, and found it completely embarrassing, a habit I indulged in that was both ridiculous and make-believe.

Whenever she saw me lining up the food on my plate, straightening all my shoes, or refusing to wear different colors, she'd harangue me, insisting it was an affectation and that allowing it would just spoil me. I wasn't angry with her about it, because I pretty much felt that way too. I mean, even as a child, I knew it was weird. It looked weird, it *felt* weird, and yet I have never been able to stop myself from doing it. Food arranged precisely on a plate. Cabinets organized in the middle of the night. Brushing my teeth till my gums bleed. Strict routines that *cannot* be changed—coffee, then a single poached egg and half a grapefruit, followed by vitamins every morning after breakfast. If that changes, my whole day can fall apart.

Over the years, though, I've become adept at masking it all. You'd be surprised at how much you can hide if you want to. Freshman year, I did the perimeter of my room three times every night without my roommate noticing. I just pretended I was thinking, or sometimes tidying up. When I met Michael, I was going through a good period and my symptoms, always in flux, weren't so bad. But by the time we were dating six months, he started to clock it.

At first, I laughed it off, pretended it was just this little quirk I had that hopefully he could find endearing. After we were married, though, some of the behaviors were harder to ignore. It was particularly bad when I was going through IVF. I had it stuck in my head that my rituals would somehow affect the outcomes of each attempt. I'd stopped working by that point, and I spent as much as four hours a day—or even more—trying to order and control in the ways I had convinced myself were important, even though part of me knew all along that they weren't. There's a reason why they call the behaviors *compulsions*. They feel virtually impossible to stop.

A particular breaking point was when Michael came home from work to find me on my hands and knees in the shower, scrubbing the already pristine grout with a toothbrush. I was still in my pajamas and I had blisters on my hands; I'd been doing it all day. He told me he wanted me to see a therapist, and I fobbed him off by convincing him I was just going through a hard time. The truth was, I have never wanted to talk about my problems with anyone. I have never wanted anyone to know.

But now it feels like everyone does.

And it's Michael's fault.

By the time he gets home, I am sitting calmly in an armchair in the living room, my hands folded neatly in my lap.

"Elise... are you okay?" He practically runs into the room, checking himself when he sees me. "What's going on?"

"You told Harriet about my OCD." I state it as a fact, but my voice trembles.

Michael walks slowly to the armchair opposite mine and drops into it, raking a hand through his thick hair. For the first time, I notice how tired he looks, even old. There is more silver threaded through his hair than I remember seeing before. He's fifty-one, and even though he works out all the time, with a jolt, I think he looks his age.

"I didn't mean to," he says as he drops his hand from his hair, his gaze on the middle distance. "It just... slipped out."

"Really?" My voice is arctic.

Anger feels stronger than hurt, but the truth is, I'm devastated by this. Of all the things Michael could have told her about me, this is the most private and intimate, and makes me the most vulnerable—and even more painfully, he *knows* all that. I can see from the miserable look on his face that he already knows how much this has hurt me.

"Elise..." He shakes his head. "I'm sorry. But I meant it when I told you there's nothing between me and Harriet, I swear—"

"What kind of conversations," I ask, and now my voice is

shaking, "were you having with Harriet, that this kind of information could just *slip out?*"

Michael sighs and drops his head into his hands, and that feels like answer enough. "I wish," he mutters, "you could just believe me."

"I wish you could be believed!" I cry out, unable to keep my hurt from spilling out.

I want to say more, to explain that whether or not anything physical happened between Harriet and my husband, something emotional obviously did, and that hurts just as much, albeit in a different way. I want to tell him that I'm so tired of being afraid, of keeping his secrets the way I kept my father's, of being perfect even though I've always known it would never be enough and I never could be perfect, anyway.

But before I can say any of that, my phone rings. I glance down at it and see it's The Garden School. When I answer the call, I hear the words that freeze the very breath in my lungs.

"Mrs. Dunnett? You need to come to school right away. It's Luke."

TWENTY-EIGHT

HARRIET

When I get the call from the school, I am kneeling on the cold, hard tile of the bathroom, holding Allan's head as he retches into the toilet.

The side effects of the riluzole have hit hard, and he hasn't been able to keep anything down for several days. Yesterday, I picked up some anti-nausea meds for him, but they have yet to kick in and it's starting to feel like the cure is worse than the disease––and, of course, it isn't even a cure. The hopelessness of it all keeps smacking me in the face. And meanwhile, poor Allan can only retch and sob, wiping his eyes and his mouth, helpless.

In such a situation, I'm inclined to ignore the call, except *no one* calls me these days, and so while Allan slumps onto the toilet with a groan, his stomach seemingly emptied, I glance at my phone and see it's The Garden School. The foreboding kicks in right away, like a punch to the gut, but maybe that's just because it feels like everything in life lately has moved into worst-case scenario before I can even absorb what it is.

I murmur something to Allan, and I answer the call.

"Ms. Tierney? This is about Kyra. You need to come into school right away."

"Why? What's happened? Is she hurt?" The questions spit out of me like bullets.

"*She's* not hurt," Marla, the school secretary, says with curt emphasis, and my stomach curdles with dread.

What on earth has happened? What has my daughter done?

I finish the call, promising to come to school right away, although I can't leave Allan alone in this state. I do my best to clean him up, with him miserably mumbling apologies the whole time, and then I run downstairs to beg Barbara to sit with him, all the while knowing Allan won't like her to see him in the state he's in—weak, sick, his hands trembling, his words slurred, still smelling faintly of vomit. So far, I can't really see how the riluzole is helping, but that's something I have to think about later.

Right now, I need to focus on Kyra.

It takes me forty-five minutes to get to The Garden School, and as soon as I'm buzzed through the front doors, Marla instructs me to go to the headmistress' office, a place I've never been. I only met the woman once, when Kyra visited back in May, after Allan had asked us to move to New York. Now I feel like she might hold our fate in her hands. Is this serious? Is Kyra in trouble? Part of me wonders if this is the excuse to leave this school behind forever, because God knows I've had enough of it.

As I step into her office, I come up short because Michael is sitting in front of Ms. Weil, looking exhausted and anxious.

Ms. Weil's eyes narrow as she catches sight of me, and she presses her lips together. "Thank you for coming, Ms. Tierney."

I thought, in a school where all the students are called *friends*, we might be on a first-name basis with teachers and staff, but apparently not.

"It wasn't presented to me as a choice," I reply a little stiffly.

I can't look at Michael; the last time I saw him I was near tears, trying to argue that we'd shared something. The memory makes me cringe like a snail in salt, everything in me curling up in mortification.

"I'm afraid the situation is serious," Ms. Weil says gravely. "Very serious."

"Eleanor..." Michael begins, and I give him a sharp look. Okay, so *he's* on a first-name basis with the headmistress of this wretched school. Of course he is. She's probably the twins' godmother or something.

"If you could just tell me what's going on," I state in what I hope is a firm but neutral tone. I sit in the chair next to Michael's, scooting it a foot farther away from him. I wonder why Michael is here, and where Elise is. And what the hell has happened.

"This morning, Kyra *attacked* Luke," Ms. Weil states in a voice that suggests she thinks Kyra is one step up from a serial killer. I blink, trying to take in her words.

"Eleanor..." Michael says again, in a voice that is half jokey, half pleading.

"Attacked?" I repeat.

"She pushed him in the playground, and he fell and hit his head," Ms. Weil states coldly. "And then he immediately had a seizure. He's currently at Hassenfeld Children's Hospital, awaiting further treatment."

"He's stable," Michael adds quietly, to me. "They don't think there's been any damage. But they're keeping him overnight, just in case."

My mind is a blank void of shock and fear. Kyra *pushed* Luke? Why? And why is the headmistress acting like my daughter tried to *kill* him?

"I'm very sorry," I say carefully. "It sounds like... an unfortunate accident."

"From what Mrs. Ryan said," Ms. Weil replies carefully, "it

seems that Kyra pushed him intentionally. Naturally, that's a concern to us, not to mention the certain... behavioral issues Kyra has been having in class."

Behavioral issues? Until this moment, I didn't realize she had any. For a second, I can only gape at the headmistress. I feel like I'm being set up; this has Elise Dunnett's fingerprints all over it. Did she threaten the headmistress if she didn't come down hard on Kyra—or me? It might not be rational, but I could see Elise intimating she might withdraw their annual gift if "appropriate measures" weren't taken or something like that. I know Luke is hurt, but surely this had to be an accident.

"I wasn't aware she had any issues," I tell the headmistress, my voice decidedly cool. "And if she had, I would have expected the school to contact me directly and immediately, so we can work through them *together,* as a family, for Kyra's benefit." I meet her implacable gaze with a steely one of my own. I am not taking this lying down, no way. "So it's a little bit of a surprise, shall we say, to hear you talk about this like it's been an *ongoing* concern."

Ms. Weil, fortunately, has the grace to back down. "Not ongoing, necessarily," she murmurs. "But her teacher, Mrs. Ryan, has had some... concerns... in the last few weeks. Considering everything else that was going on, there wasn't the opportunity to discuss them with you, and I think Mrs. Ryan was hoping they might settle down on their own. They often do with children, don't they?" She smiles and then suggests in a friendlier tone, "Perhaps we should call her in, and she can tell you herself what happened?"

"That seems like a good idea," I reply evenly.

Ms. Weil rises from her desk, giving both Michael and me a quick, professional smile. "I'll just go find her."

She leaves the room, plunging the two of us into an awkward silence. Michael breaks it first.

"How are you?" he asks. "How is Allan?"

"He's finally on riluzole, but the side effects are tough," I reply briefly. "How is Luke? Is he okay?"

"He will be," he says in a firm doctor's voice. "Naturally, a seizure is scary, but he's had a few before. The doctor thinks he'll grow out of them eventually, but..." He shrugs. "Luke's health has always been a little compromised. We work around it."

"And Elise?" I ask finally.

Michael hesitates before answering carefully, "Recovering."

I fold my arms and look away; I can't bear to talk to him anymore, because when I do, all I can think about is how much I embarrassed myself the last time we met, in the hospital.

"Harriet..." he begins, leaning forward in his chair, "I know this isn't the best time to mention this, but... did you tell someone what I said about Elise and her OCD?"

I force myself to look at him, even though I don't want to. His expression is anxious, even haggard, and a wave of guilt crashes over me. "I... I did mention it to one person," I admit. "I didn't mean to..."

"It just slipped out?" He finishes wearily, without any real judgment, as he slumps back in his chair, shaking his head. "What a mess."

"Why..."

"It got around the whole school. Elise feels humiliated. She shouldn't," he adds quickly, "I mean, everyone's got something going on, right? Half the mothers at this school are addicted to something or other... booze, Vicodin, Xanax... And obviously that's not even the same kind of thing as... " He trails off, sighing. "I never should have told you."

And I never should have told Joanna. I know that. I'm surprised and disappointed that she gossiped about it considering how condemning she was of others' gossip, but I'm hardly in a place to point fingers. I wish I'd never said anything. I wish Michael had never told me.

"I'm sorry," I say quietly. "I was angry about her threatening a lawsuit—"

He straightens in his chair. "You know about that?"

I let out a huff of something that can't quite pass for laughter. "Michael, the whole school knows about that. It seems like everyone is talking about it, judging by all the whispers and glares I get whenever I come to school."

He presses his lips together as he shakes his head. "I didn't know that everyone was talking about it—"

"But you knew Elise was planning to sue me?" I surmise.

"I knew she was *thinking* about it," he admits. "I told her it was crazy—"

"I bet that went over well," I mutter. I don't want to think about all that right now. We need to focus on our children. "I hope Luke is going to be okay," I say.

Michael nods graciously before asking, "Do you know why Kyra might have pushed him?"

I shake my head. "I have no idea."

"She and Lewis were friends—"

"I think that might have ended after she shouted at you at your apartment," I interject dryly. "But I didn't think she had any issue with Luke, and, frankly, Kyra's never been one to stir things up. She has a lot going on, as you know," I tell Michael quietly. "With Allan..." I stop. "Maybe she just lost her temper. I don't want this to become more than it is, just because of everything else that's been going on."

I hate the thought that the drama swirling around *me* might have affected my daughter. Could Kyra pushing Luke really have something to do with what's been going on with Elise and me?

Michael nods seriously. "Agreed." He reaches over to brush my hand with his. "I'm so sorry about all this," he murmurs, his fingers resting on mine just as Ms. Weil comes in with Mrs. Ryan. Michael jerks his hand back guiltily and so do I, and both women notice. It's not a good start to whatever's coming next.

Ms. Weil sits back behind her desk, and Mrs. Ryan draws a chair up next to her, giving us a smile of unhappy apology. "Mr. Dunnett, Ms. Tierney," she murmurs as she sits down.

"Why don't you tell us what happened?" Ms. Weil suggests, her hands folded in front of her on the desk.

"Well..." Mrs. Ryan frowns, her kindly round face crinkling up in concern. "Kyra's been such a lovely addition to our class. Quiet but diligent, and you can always tell she's listening." She's smiling at me, and I feel myself relax just a little bit, because this is the Kyra I recognize. "But a few weeks ago, maybe sometime in November, I noticed a change. She seemed less quiet and more withdrawn, if that makes sense. And she'd been friends with Lewis, but that friendship seemed to have faded..."

Michael and I exchange uneasy glances. It seems pretty clear that friendship ended the day Kyra came over to Lewis' apartment... because of *us*.

"And then, one day last week she burst into tears all of a sudden," Mrs. Ryan continues. "I would have called you, but you know how kids can be, and she recovered pretty quickly." Mrs. Ryan grimaces. "I was going to bring this all up at the parent/teacher conference next month. Sometimes it takes a little while for children to settle in, and I've never wanted to go to the parents with every little thing and distress them." She glances at the headmistress. "I'm sorry if I was negligent."

"No, no," I say quickly. "I completely agree with everything you're saying. In any case, Kyra has had a lot to adjust to... including her having recently learned that her father has a terminal illness. It's been very hard on her."

"Oh." Mrs. Ryan's eyes widen and Ms. Weil's jaw drops.

Belatedly, I realize that I should have had this conversation earlier, gotten Mrs. Ryan on board so she could be supportive of Kyra. With all the stress around Elise, I didn't think of it.

"I'm so sorry," Mrs. Ryan murmurs.

I nod, lowering my gaze. "Thank you."

For a moment, a respectful silence ensues, and it feels like the mood has shifted in my favor. Suddenly, Kyra pushing a child in the playground might not seem like such a big deal.

And yet the question remains, why did she do it? And what is she hiding that I don't know about?

TWENTY-NINE
ELISE

I sit by Luke's bed, his hand lying limply in mine. He's sleeping now, his eyes closed, his dark lashes fanning across his pale cheeks. When I think of what could have happened to him…

When Marla from school called me, I could have never imagined this. My little boy, *attacked*, suffering a seizure, and now staying overnight in the hospital. Luke has suffered in so many small ways, yet this feels like something bigger. Michael was, in his I'm-a-medical-professional way, somewhat dismissive of it all.

"Luke has had seizures before," he told me calmly. "This is not that unusual for him."

"Yes, when he was a baby with a fever," I had snapped. "Not when he hit his head after he'd been *attacked*!"

"We don't know yet why Kyra pushed him," Michael had pointed out, like that mattered. "It could have been an accident—"

I had shaken my head so violently he fell silent. "Michael, *don't*." My voice had been low and lethal. "Don't make this about Kyra or her mother. We need to focus on *our* child. On *Luke*."

Seeming chastened, Michael had nodded his assent. "Okay," he had agreed quietly. We both fell silent, the tension in the room palpable.

"They'll run some tests and keep him overnight just in case," Michael said, his voice gentling. "But, Elise, I really do think he's going to be fine."

And even though I knew he was trying to be comforting, his words infuriated me. It was like he considered this whole thing to be no big deal, thought I was making a fuss over nothing. He was acting as if defending Kyra was more important than worrying about his own son.

And that suspicion was sealed when, after Luke had woken groggily, smiled at me, and then been moved to a room on the pediatric ward, Michael suggested he head back to the school. "I think I should be there, to find out what happened," he said. "Eleanor's asked Harriet to come in as well."

And somehow I just knew he wasn't going back to school to make sure we—and Luke—knew the whole story. He was going to make sure *Harriet* was okay.

"Fine," I told him as I sat down next to our son. "Go."

"Elise..."

"*Go*," I said again, savagely, my head turned away from him, and with a sigh, he did.

That was three hours ago, and he hasn't returned or called or even texted. The silence from him feels damning. The school called before either of us had been able to say anything about what was going on between us, and the truth is, I don't know what I'd been going to say. Never mind what Michael would have said... or what the state of our marriage is now.

But right now I have to think about Luke. I called Rosita to pick up Lewis from school; she can stay till dinnertime, but after that Michael will need to be home for our other son. I've already decided to stay the night with Luke, even though sleeping on a recliner is not going to be easy with my stomach still hurting. I can't leave my little boy alone overnight in the hospital.

It isn't until eight o'clock, when the ward has settled down for the night and everything is dimly lit and quiet, that Michael returns.

"How is he?" he asks in a whisper as he comes into the room, looking a little haggard.

"Where have you been?" I demand in a low hiss. "You didn't even *call*."

He grimaces. "I'm sorry... I was at school, and then with Lewis—"

"Where *is* Lewis?"

"He's asleep. Helen is watching him."

Helen is a widow in her seventies who lives on the same floor as us. Occasionally, we've asked her to babysit, but she isn't the best with children and she's usually reluctant anyway.

I turn back to Luke as Michael comes to stand at the foot of his bed.

"How is he?" he asks again.

"He woke up a little while ago and managed to drink some juice," I say woodenly. I am angry at Michael, but I don't want to give in to that now.

"Did you talk to him about what happened?" he presses.

"No, he doesn't need that right now," I reply, unable to keep from sounding sharp. "Did *you* find out what happened from the school?"

"Not really. Kyra's been unhappy at school, apparently—"

"I don't want to hear about Kyra," I snap. I cannot believe Michael is making this all about Harriet and her daughter, rather than his own family.

"She's part of the bigger picture, Elise," Michael replies, and now his voice is rising.

Luke stirs, and we both fall guiltily silent. We should not be arguing in here.

"All I'm saying," he continues in a quieter voice, "is that there's more going on than maybe we realize. Did you know Kyra burst into tears at school?"

I recall Luke telling me that, although I didn't feel it was my concern, and I still don't. "Lewis was crying at school, too," I tell Michael. "Maybe you should be thinking about that."

"*Lewis* was?" Michael asks in surprise, and I realize I'd never told him. Our relationship was already in breakdown mode then.

"Children get upset and cry sometimes," I tell him. "I'm more concerned about the fact that our child was *attacked*."

"And you don't think the two might be related?" Michael demands, his voice still low.

"What are you saying? That *Luke* upset Lewis? Or Kyra?" I can't help but scoff; Luke is the gentlest child either of us have ever known.

"Oh, I don't know." Michael sits down in a chair with a sigh, running his hand through his hair.

For a few minutes, we are both quiet, the weight of all we haven't said heavy between us. What do I even want out of this moment, out of my marriage? Part of me just wants to punish Michael, and yet what purpose does that really serve? Don't I want to be a bigger person than one who pursues some kind of twisted revenge?

Then I think about how my stomach still throbs, and how Michael has chosen Harriet over me time and time again, and how everyone at school is now gossiping about the most vulnerable and private part of my life, and my heart hardens. This isn't revenge. This is justice.

"I'm going to go forward with the lawsuit," I tell Michael abruptly, my gaze firmly fixed on our son.

"Elise—"

"I wasn't going to," I continue. "I met with a lawyer, and it made me think that maybe I just wanted you to think I was, to wake you up—"

"Wake me up to *what*?" Michael demands. "Seriously, Elise, if this lawsuit is about me more than it is about Harriet, or the fact that you got hurt..." He trails off, shaking his head.

"Don't these things matter?" I reply quietly. "Doesn't your *marriage* matter?"

"You don't have to bring Harriet into—"

"Yes, I do."

"I told you," he says, his voice rising again, "nothing happened between us, *ever—*"

"Nothing *physical*," I correct, and he falls silent, staring at me wordlessly for a moment before he shakes his head.

"What are you implying?" he finally asks.

"Emotionally, there was something going on," I state. "There had to have been, for you to have told her about—about *me* in that way..." I find I can't continue. I draw a ragged breath as Michael remains silent in a way that is starting to feel ominous. Can he not see it? *Feel* it?

Finally he speaks. "Maybe there was," he says tonelessly, and somehow that feels even worse than if he'd denied it.

Tears blur my vision and I have to wipe my eyes.

"Elise, sometimes you can be... closed off," he tells me.

"Oh, so this is my fault?" A ragged laugh escapes me.

"No. *No*." He leans forward, earnest now. "It's just... talking to Harriet made me realize how little *we* talk. I mean, *really* talk. I feel like there's so much we never say, we never tell each other—"

"Like about Helene Dubois?" I interject, my voice touched with acid. "Or Grayson Wells? Or Miss James?"

Michael stares at me, looking flummoxed. "Who...? What?"

"Was nothing going on there, either?" I fill in sarcastically.

"*What?*" He looks so surprised, I feel a sudden wave of doubt, like the ground is shifting under my feet.

"Come on, Michael. I saw you with Grayson at last year's gala, your arms around her—"

His expression clears before his brows snap together. "I was *comforting* her, because she was getting divorced—"

"And Miss James, at the parent/teacher conference? All the flirting? She kept *touching* you."

"I wasn't..." He rubs his hands over his face. "Elise, I have *never* been unfaithful to you. I swear my life on it, our *boys'* lives. What you've seen as flirting... I guess that's just how I am."

I let out a hard-edged laugh. "Oh, trust me, Michael, I *know* that's how you are."

"And isn't it what attracted you to me when we first met?" he presses. "At least partly?" He shakes his head slowly. "I wish we'd talked about this sooner, Elise. I wish I'd known how you felt—"

"Are you saying you didn't?" I demand. "Michael, it takes two people to *not* talk. You never once started a conversation. Don't make this all about me."

"And don't make this all about me," Michael replies quietly.

"Who, then?" I ask with a huff of disbelief.

He stares at me for a long moment, looking like he's weighing up whether to answer. "Come on," he says quietly, like I should know what he's talking about, and something in his face makes everything in me tense.

"You're going to have to spell it out for me," I tell him shortly, doing my best to hold onto my sense of outrage.

"Elise..." Michael's voice is gentle. "I've suspected for a while that you know this, but..." He blows out a breath. "I'm talking about your father."

I jerk back, startled. Michael doesn't know about my dad. I never told him. "*What?*"

"Right after we first got married," he explains, and now he sounds sad, "I saw your dad with another woman at a hotel here in the city. They were having drinks, and there was clearly something going on. Your dad saw me, and he came over, introduced the woman, and then gave me a wink. When she'd gone to the ladies', he said in this jovial way, 'what goes on in the city stays in the city, right, Michael?' and then laughed like we were sharing this big joke. I didn't know what to do about it. I didn't want to tell you back then because I know how you idolized him, and I thought it would break you."

I stiffen at that. *Idolize* is a very strong word.

"But then," Michael continues slowly, "over the years... I started to suspect that you already knew. Something about the way you talked about him, looked at him even... Am I wrong?" He holds my gaze and I have to look away first. I find I can't speak. "I realized," he says heavily, "that you were keeping his secrets for him, which seemed... strange, and frankly seriously messed up. And that felt like something that was even harder to talk about, and so I didn't. Maybe I should have, though. This isn't blaming you, it's more just about realizing there's some emotional baggage here."

I still can't speak. I never expected this.

Michael pins me with a gaze that is more sorrowful than accusing. "Am I right?" he asks quietly.

I hate that he's diagnosed me, that he's made this all about me and my *emotional baggage* rather than his own. Why can't he take responsibility for his own actions? Consider that maybe he doesn't need to flirt with every woman that crosses his vision, that he doesn't have to be so admired all the time, and acknowledge that it's just as much about his arrogance as my insecurity?

But of course Michael will never acknowledge any of that. He won't even think it. He's made this all about me and what I've done wrong. Right now, the weight of all the things we never said over the course of our marriage is far heavier than those we did... and it's a weight I can't bear any longer.

It feels like there's no going back from this, for either of us.

Maybe too much has been said—or, in our case, hasn't been said. What I do know, I realize, is that I can't live the way I have been any longer. Trying to be perfect. Pretending not to notice Michael's flirtations, and even more painfully, not to care.

"I'm going to get a coffee," he says tiredly, rising from his chair. "Do you want one?"

I shake my head. It's only after he's gone, and I check that Luke is still asleep, that I think to check my phone. And then I see the rambling text message from Harriet Tierney that fills me with fury—and fear.

> *Hi Elise, this is Harriet. I'm so sorry that Kyra pushed Luke today, and I really hope he's recovering well. When I talked to her, I found out some things...*

What things, that could possibly justify her daughter attacking my son? The gall of the woman is unbelievable.

First thing tomorrow morning, I'm calling Jennifer Stevens.

THIRTY

HARRIET

I still don't know why Kyra pushed Luke when I leave Ms. Weil's office. She seems to have softened to me since I told her about Allan, which is something.

I go to pick up Kyra. I'm dreading another afternoon outside the school doors on this cold December day, doing my best to ignore the glares and whispers, although today they don't seem to be so bad.

Maybe these mothers finally have something else to talk about—the Christmas concert for the fourth through sixth grade tomorrow night, or the fact that school ends for the holidays next Friday and everyone is planning their trips to Aspen or Aruba, or the round of holiday cocktail parties and charity events that seem to fill the two weeks off school, judging from the snatches of conversation I overhear.

Whatever it is, no one seems to pay me much attention, which is a relief. I'm already worried about how I'm going to approach this whole situation with Kyra. She is close-mouthed at the best times, and I have to find out why she pushed Luke. I'm pretty sure she's not going to want to tell me.

I stand by myself as I always do, trying not to look anyone in the eye, wondering how long this is going to go on, when I feel a light touch on my shoulder. I turn and see Joanna, and even before either of us has said a word, I see guilt written all over her face.

"Harriet... I'm so sorry..."

I cock my head, waiting for more. Is she sorry that Kyra is in trouble, that Allan is sick, or that I'm about to be sued? Or, I wonder, is she sorry that she let Elise's OCD slip? Will she even admit she was the one who spilled the secret?

"I shouldn't have said anything," she continues wretchedly, and my esteem for her goes up a notch. So she *is* going to be honest. "I didn't mean to. I was just talking to another mom, and she mentioned having OCD, like a joke, and I said something about Elise..." She shakes her head. "I kind of get the gossip thing now," she admits in a low voice. "I mean, for a few seconds there, I felt important, because I had some dirt. It was awful." She closes her eyes, and I realize she is near tears.

"Joanna, it's okay." I pat her shoulder awkwardly. "I shouldn't have told you in the first place."

"I know, but..." She opens her eyes, blinking hard. "I thought I was better than that, you know? I've been standing here in judgment over all these gossipy moms and then I just do the exact same thing." A shuddery sigh escapes her. "I think we really need to get out of this place."

I'm not sure it would be much better elsewhere. It's tempting to think it's this particular cohort of parents that's so toxic, but I'm just not sure that's true. Gossip and malice are everywhere, but so are discretion and kindness. I think of Mrs. Ryan, who is trying her best for all her young charges, and my ever-patient neighbor, Barbara, who is always willing to be with Allan, no questions asked. My dad who, in his silent, stoic way, supported me more than anyone else has.

"I just wanted to ask your forgiveness," Joanna says humbly. "I hope it didn't cause any problems for you."

"I forgive you, of course," I reply immediately. As for problems? Well, I already had a few to begin with. What's one more? "I'm not sure it's made much difference to me," I tell Joanna, and then add, the words aimed as much at myself as my friend, "I think it's Elise we both need to apologize to, if word is getting around."

Joanna cringes. "But she scares me a little... She always seems so *perfect*."

"Well, obviously she's not," I tell Joanna with a small smile. For the first time in a long while, I feel a stirring of sympathy for Elise. Maybe if I talk to her, she'll drop this lawsuit idea. Maybe we just need to speak honestly to each other...

I can't help but feel it's a vain hope, but right now it's the only hope I've got. I can't think about it too much more, though, because the doors to the school open and children start coming out, some running, some slouching, parents holding out their arms, nannies tugging them along.

Kyra is one of the last third graders to come out. Out of the corner of my eye, I see the Dunnetts' babysitter collect Lewis. He doesn't look upset that his brother is currently in the hospital; children really are resilient, Kyra, I hope, included.

Kyra trudges out toward me, shoulders slumped, not meeting my eye, and immediately I know she knows I was summoned to school.

"Shall we get a hot chocolate?" I suggest. "On the way home?"

Kyra glances up at me suspiciously. "Am I in trouble?"

"Does a hot chocolate sound like you're in trouble?"

She shrugs in reply.

"Come on." I put my arm around her shoulder. "Let's get a hot chocolate and talk about what happened."

To my surprise, Kyra presses her head against my shoulder. "I don't want to talk about what happened," she mumbles, and when I glance down at her, I see that she is crying.

"Kyra..." I cup her cheek as she wipes her eyes. "Honey... can't you tell me what's wrong?"

She shakes her head and then shrugs off my arm and keeps walking. This is going to take some patience, but already I'm feeling anxious, desperate to know what is going on in my daughter's mind.

I don't try to get anything out of her until we're seated in Starbucks, with two hot chocolates topped with whipped cream and chocolate sprinkles. I know I need to get back to Allan, but right now this feels more important.

"Okay, so," I try to take a matter-of-fact voice, "Ms. Weil said you pushed Luke, and he fell and hit his head. Is that what happened?"

No reply as Kyra dips her finger into the swirl of whipped cream topping her mug and then licks it off.

"Kyra." I strive to keep my voice gentle. "I'll settle for yes or no answers for now, but I need to know what happened. Did you push Luke?"

With her gaze lowered on her mug, she nods.

I let out a small, soft sigh. I knew that already, of course, but at least she's being honest with me.

"Was it an accident?" I ask. "Were you two playing or something?"

A shake of her head, vigorous enough for me to realize this might really be serious.

"Okay." I rack my brains, trying to think of another softball question she might answer. "Did you push Luke because he made you mad?" I suggest.

She hesitates, her gaze still on her mug, and then slowly shakes her head. I feel as if I'm groping through the dark. What on earth happened?

"Did he do something to you first?" I ask, a little desperately. I can't imagine slight, shy Luke, with his thick glasses and his air of anxiety, doing something to Kyra, but who knows?

At this question, Kyra stills, and then she carefully reaches for her hot chocolate and takes a sip. Her lack of response is enough to solidify my suspicion into certainty.

"Kyra." It's hard to keep my voice gentle, because I so want to get to the bottom of this, but I do my best. "Is that what happened?"

Still no response.

"*Kyra.*" I reach for her hand, drawing it down so she has to put her mug back on the table. "Please. This is important. Did Luke do something to you?"

Reluctantly, she lifts her gaze to mine. Her eyes are filled with tears and her lips tremble.

"Kyra…" I whisper. "What happened, honey?"

She shakes her head, the tears spilling over, and I glance down, frowning when I see what looks like reddened, angry skin peeking out from beneath her sweatshirt. Before she can stop me, I grab hold of her arm and pull up the sleeve of her sweatshirt.

"Don't," she protests, trying to pull away, but it's too late. I've already seen the fingernail marks in her skin, causing painful-looking welts, along with the bruises, each the shape and size of a small fingerprint. There are five of them.

"Kyra," I whisper, appalled. Even staring at the evidence in front of me, I can't believe it. "Did… did *Luke* do this?"

Slowly, sniffing, her eyes still full of tears, she nods.

I am still shaken by the sight of Kyra's bruised arm as we head back to the apartment. She has begged me not to tell anyone, which mystifies me all the more.

"Kyra, if someone is hurting you, it needs to stop. A teacher needs to be told." I was trying to sound reasonable, but my voice was shaking. I was angry at Luke, and the whole Dunnett family by this point, but I was also afraid. Why on earth would Luke be doing this? Did I want to find out?

"Don't, Mom," Kyra begged. "Please, don't tell anyone."

We didn't get to discuss it much beyond that, because as soon as we get home, I find Allan in the bathroom being sick, and Barbara wringing her hands in the living room.

"I'm so sorry," she says, sounding wretched. "He wanted to be alone. I offered to help, but…"

"It's okay, Barbara." I pat her shoulder, and then, because she looks so upset, I pull her into a quick hug.

"I've been Allan's neighbor for twenty years," she whispers against my shoulder. "I'm so sorry…"

"Thanks. And I'm sorry, too." I ease back, trying for a compassionate smile, although I feel decidedly shaky—about everything. Allan's illness, Kyra losing her father just as she's gained him… it all feels like too much. I want one thing in my life to be, if not easy, then bearable, and right now it feels like nothing is.

Somehow, we get through the evening. I clean Allan up, settle him on the sofa, and then Kyra brings a book to read, and they spend the whole evening curled up together, which is painfully sweet… and yet I can't help but wonder if she's just trying to avoid me.

I consider texting Michael to tell him what I've learned and then end up deleting his number from my phone. He can't be my go-to, not now, not ever again. Then I think about texting Elise. Maybe I should tell her what's going on? If I frame it in a way that isn't too accusatory, maybe we can meet in the middle somehow?

I need to do *something*, I decide, and so I type out a text.

Hi Elise, this is Harriet. I'm so sorry that Kyra pushed Luke today, and I really hope he's recovering well. When I talked to her, I found out some things that might shed light on the situation. I think we need to all talk together about this in order to get to the bottom of it and realize it's a little more complicated than maybe any of us thought.

It's vague and too wordy, but it's the only way I can think of to keep from antagonizing her too much. I push send and then wait, staring at my phone, but there's no reply.

There's still no reply when I tuck Kyra in bed. I don't ask about the bruises again because I can tell she's bracing herself for me to, and maybe we both need a break.

I will get to the bottom of it, I tell myself, with or without Elise Dunnett's help.

The next morning, I leave Allan asleep as I take Kyra to school. Barbara popped her head out of her door as we headed downstairs and offered to sit with him. I felt guilty for accepting, but I didn't like leaving him alone anymore. Soon enough, I realized, we were going to need extra help, more than just a kindly neighbor. It was a thought that filled me with heaviness. This was all happening so much faster than Allan or I ever thought it would. When he first called me, he said he'd be stable for years. Maybe I should have recognized wishful thinking when I heard it, but I wanted to believe him so much.

"I want you to have a *great* day today," I tell Kyra firmly, holding her gently by her shoulders as I gaze down into her wide-eyed face, as we stand in front of the school doors. I want to imbue her with all my love and strength and certainty; I wish it could be absorbed through my touch, through my words, through my very breath. "Luke won't be at school today," I continue in a low voice. "And we can talk about the bruises on your arm later, okay? But for now... just have a good day. Because you have a great teacher and some good friends and... and I love you." I'm not great with emotion or displays of affection—I guess I get that from my dad—but now my voice trembles and I pull her close for a hug she returns.

"Thanks, Mom," she says softly, and then she's heading for the doors.

She's just disappeared through them when I feel a tap on my shoulder. I turn, already smiling because I assume it's Joanna, but then I see a stranger standing in front of me, holding out an envelope, her expression flatly professional.

"Are you Harriet Tierney?" she asks.

"Yes—"

"I am officially serving you with these legal documents," she states, and it takes me a second to realize what is happening.

Elise Dunnett is suing me.

The woman walks away before I can say anything, leaving me standing with an envelope and everyone around me whispering.

From behind me, Joanna whispers, "Is that..." She trails off as she stares at the envelope.

I swallow hard. "I think so."

I stuff the envelope in my pocket, because I am not about to open it with an audience, and then I start striding down the street, because I just need to get away from everybody and everything. Part of me wants to start sprinting, just run and run until I've left all of this behind me—the gossipy school, the envelope in my pocket, Kyra's misery, Allan's illness. All of it is happening, all the time, and I just want a moment's *break*.

In my pocket, my phone buzzes. I come abruptly to a halt, out of breath just from walking fast, and reach for my phone. It's Barbara, and part of me already knows what she's going to say before I've swiped to answer.

"Harriet? I'm so sorry. It's Allan. He just got out of bed and he's... he's collapsed."

THIRTY-ONE
ELISE

The Monday after Harriet gets served with the lawsuit, Luke is back in school, and I am driving to Connecticut to visit my father. I haven't seen him since before the gala, and even though I'm not meant to drive for another two weeks, I decide to go. I need to get away from New York, from the gossip and the tension and the fact that Michael is furious I went ahead with the lawsuit. I didn't even tell him; he found out from another parent.

"I told you I was thinking about it," I replied when he mentioned it, and he shook his head, seeming caught between despair and fury.

"What is *wrong* with you, Elise?"

"What's wrong with *me*?" I shot back, doing my best to ignore the needling of guilt his words caused. When I'd called Jennifer Stevens, she'd agreed to pursue the case, but I'd felt a tacit disapproval that I was doing it at all, even though I'd pulled back from pursuing a criminal lawsuit. "What's wrong with *you*?" I flung at Michael. "Someone injured me intentionally—"

"You don't know that."

"I'm pretty sure." I've gone over those few, frightening

seconds in my mind time and again, and I am more convinced than ever that Harriet *did* use excessive force. I remember the feel of her fist in my stomach, her voice in my ear.

"You deserve... you are so aggravating!"

What if she'd finished that sentence? What was she going to say?

I don't want to think of any of that now as I head across the Tappan Zee Bridge, the water glittering wintry-white below me. I wonder at what age my dad will freeze me today, and I realize I am looking forward to play-acting anything but who, and what, I am now. Let me be ten again, or eighteen, or thirty. Any of those will feel like an escape.

"Princess!" His voice is filled with delight as I walk into his room, and my heart lightens. I stoop to kiss his cheek, wincing slightly at the pain pulling at my stomach.

"Hey, Dad." I sit gingerly in the chair across from him. My dad has no book or notepad today; he's just sitting in his chair, staring into space. His hair, I notice, is a little mussed, and his shirt is buttoned wrong. These details cause me a lurch of something like panic, because even though I know my dad has a disease that will eventually kill him, it's surprisingly easy to let myself forget that when I'm with him, and he looks just as he ever did.

And as much pain as my father has caused me with his affairs and his insistence that I keep his secrets, I still love him. I've loved, I realize, being his secret-keeper, because it made me feel special and important in a way I know I never truly was to my father. The realization is both sad and humbling. That's not what love is, I think, or at least, it's not what it's supposed to be. Earning someone's approval is *not* the same as being loved. How has it taken me so long to realize that?

Maybe Michael is right, and what's happening between us does have to do with my father, more than I've wanted to

THE SECRET BETWEEN US 255

acknowledge, anyway. Maybe I can finally learn to be different, right here and now. With my husband, and also with my father.

It feels like a frail hope, considering that, as of this morning, Michael still isn't speaking to me.

"So how are you, Elise?" my dad asks seriously, and I realize for once he has not pinned me at a certain age, allowing me to escape back into the past with him. He's staring at me with an honest—and even somber—expression, and I think right now he sees me exactly as I am...

I don't know how to reply.

"I'm..." I shake my head helplessly. "I've been better, Dad, honestly."

"Oh, honey." He puts his hand over mine, and it is intensely comforting, large and dry and strong. "Life can be so tough, can't it?" he murmurs, commiserating with me in a way he never did before the Alzheimer's took hold.

"It can," I whisper.

I have to blink back tears. I know this is only a fleeting moment of lucidity, that in mere minutes, or maybe even seconds, my dad will sink back into whatever surreal world he lives in, pigeonholing me at six or seventeen or thirty-three. But for now, while his mind is clear, while he knows me as I am *now*, I decide to break the silence once more.

"Dad..." My hand tenses under his as he smiles at me, waiting for more. "Dad, did you ever think... how it would feel, for me to keep your secrets?" I ask him in staccato bursts, the words so difficult to say, while he simply stares at me, frowning.

"Honey...?"

He has no idea what I'm talking about, but maybe that doesn't even matter. He'll forget this conversation soon enough, anyway. Maybe I just need to say it out loud, for once, for *me*.

"The *affairs*, Dad!" I tell him, my voice rising with years of buried frustration. "All the affairs you had that I knew about, because I caught you sneaking in or with lipstick on your collar or a strange woman answering your phone. All the affairs you told me not to tell Mom about, because what she didn't know wouldn't hurt her and I knew you loved her, right?" My voice rings out, jagged with pent-up pain, as my dad stares at me in wordless confusion.

The silence stretches on, and I realize in his current state, he has no idea what I'm talking about.

"Do you *know* how much that messed me up?" I demand finally. A tear trickles down my cheek, but I don't care. I didn't come here expecting to say all this, but I know now that I need to, even if my father can't fully understand. It's like a bloodletting, an emptying of the most wounded part of myself, the part that has affected so much of my life. "How impossible I found it?" I continue. "I started with OCD tendencies when I was *eight*, because it was the only place I could feel in control of my life. I was terrified of letting something slip... of not being your princess anymore... Even as a kid, I think I knew you were using me, but I let you because it was better than being ignored."

The words tumble out in a torrent, and my father continues to just stare.

"And I kept doing it in my own marriage," I continue raggedly, "which I know is even more messed up. Keeping the secrets, because somehow that made me feel important. Thinking if I was just good enough, I could make someone love me, or at least seem like they loved me. If it looked like love, it was, right?" I shake my head wearily as I finally let the words die away. My father is still staring at me, looking nothing more than confused.

"Do you know when lunch is?" he asks after a moment, and a ragged laugh escapes me. That moment of lucidity? It's already over. I don't know if I feel any better for all the things I said.

"Lunch is in a few minutes, Luke," my mother says as she strolls into the room, her face expressionless, and with a horrified jolt, I realize she must have heard every word I said. I stare at her, as gormless as my father, utterly shocked. The secrets are finally well and truly out.

My mother bends to kiss my father's cheek as he beams at her, my tearful tirade completely forgotten. I sink back into my chair, overwhelmed and defeated. I don't even know how to feel about anything right now, my mother overhearing everything included. As I sit there, inwardly reeling, my mother doesn't even look at me.

It isn't until my father has had his lunch and is back in his room, seated in front of some legal show, that my mother speaks to me.

I've been dreading talking to her. All through lunch, we were basically both avoiding the other, but now as the TV drones in the background, there's nothing to keep one of us from speaking. She goes first.

"Elise," she says, and her voice is strangely, surprisingly gentle, "I always knew you knew."

It is the very last thing I ever expected her to say. For a few seconds, I can only stare. "What..."

"I knew you knew," she states again, tiredly. "From the beginning. That phone call at your friend's house, when you were five or so? That night, you were talking to yourself in the mirror about it, reminding yourself not to say anything to me. I overheard you... It was heartbreaking." She pauses. "And humiliating, which is why I never told you I knew. I could see how you liked keeping the secrets, how important your father made you feel. And I didn't want to burst that bubble, but... I also didn't want to admit that I knew you'd chosen your father over me, time and time again." She holds up a hand to forestall any protest I might make, although, in truth, I have no idea what to say. This has completely floored me.

"I know I wasn't the most affectionate mother," she continues. "Your father took up all my energy and air, and... it was also partly because there was always this thing between us. I suppose," her voice turns ragged in a way it never has before, "I was hurt. I've always been hurt, and I've never wanted to let you know it." A sigh escapes her, and she dabs at her eyes. "I'm telling you this now because I see the same cycle has happened with you and Michael. I saw it from the beginning, and I didn't want for you what I had... to love a man who will never love you back in the same way."

Ouch. I wince, because the truth certainly does hurt.

"But, Elise..." My mother leans forward. "I've come to realize that Michael *isn't* like your father. I thought he was, the way he's so charming, and how women of every stripe and shape flock to him, but... I'm ashamed to admit, I think I've misjudged him. When you were in the hospital..." She shakes her head slowly. "He was so worried about you, Elise. Genuinely... it was obvious to me how much he cared for you. And this woman? This Harriet?" Her tone turns scoffing, her lips pinching together in a way I recognize. "I think that was just Michael going into doctor mode. Yes, her neediness might have attracted him a little. What man doesn't like feeling like the big protector? But you shouldn't read too much in to it. Trust me, I know when a man loves you... and when he doesn't."

For a few seconds, I can't speak. There's so much to unpack there, to absorb and accept.

"I'm sorry," my mother says into the silence. "I should have been the bigger person, the adult, the *mother*, and said something before now. Sometimes..." A small sigh escapes her as she shakes her head. "Sometimes I wish everything had been different."

She lapses into silence, and I find I still can't speak. I have no idea what to say. Yes, I wish things had been different, too. I wish my mother had been different, that my father had, that *I* had. As for what she said about Michael? I don't know what to believe, or even to feel.

From in front of the TV, having been oblivious to our whole exchange, my dad stirs. "Hey, Laura," he calls to my mother. "You should come and watch this."

She gives me a small, sad smile, and then goes to join him.

I still have no idea what to think about any of it as I drive back to the city to pick up the boys from school. I feel like I'm too full, my emotions bubbling over, so I could either burst into laughter or tears at any given moment. All the secrets I kept were worthless. I feel stupid, but I also feel free.

I don't have to keep any secrets anymore. Not my father's, not Michael's, and not even my own. My secrets are out there already, after all, with half of the school parents gossiping about how crazy I am. There's a humiliation in that, absolutely, but there's also a surprising freedom.

With no more secrets to keep, I don't have to be perfect any longer. I don't have to pretend. And if I don't pretend... then who am I?

The question reverberates through me as I walk to school from the parking garage around the corner. My phone buzzes with a call, and I almost don't answer, but then I see it's the office of my gastroenterologist.

"Elise Dunnett?" the secretary asks, and I confirm. "Dr. Allers would like you to come in to discuss the results of the tests you underwent a few weeks ago. Could tomorrow work?"

For a second, I feel blank. *What tests?* Then I remember one of the doctors in the hospital telling me they'd run some tests right after my surgery. I was so out of it then, I'd completely forgotten about them.

"Okay..." I transfer the phone to my other ear as panic starts to flutter within me. "Do you know what the results were?"

"Dr. Allers will talk you through them," the secretary replies smoothly. "Are you free tomorrow morning?"

"Yes..." Fear clenches my insides. Are these results *urgent*? Why do I have to talk to the doctor so soon?

I make an appointment for tomorrow morning, my mind whirling. I feel like I've learned so many things today, and something more is coming.

What on earth is Dr. Allers going to tell me?

THIRTY-TWO

HARRIET

Several days after Allan collapsed, he's still in the hospital under observation. There isn't, we've been informed, anything that can actually be *done* for him, but they need to get his breathing and swallowing under control before he can be released, and that might take some time.

I didn't even think to look at the papers I was served with that have remained crumpled in my pocket until the next morning, after I'd taken Kyra to school. I thought she might not want to go, with Luke most likely back in school, but she didn't put up a fuss, which was just as well, because I was going to be at the hospital all day with Allan, and that was no place for an eight-year-old girl.

I kept things matter-of-fact and no big deal when I told her that Allan was in the hospital for some checks, not wanting her to worry, and although she went very quiet, she seemed to take it, as she has so much, in her stride. She was more upset, in fact, when I told her I intended to talk to Mrs. Ryan about what had happened with Luke.

"Kyra, he *hurt* you—" I protested.

"And I pushed him back! *Don't*, Mom." She looked both

furious and adamant, her eyes wild as she stamped her foot. "It will just make everything worse."

"What *everything*?" I asked, desperate to find a way into this whole debacle. If my drama with Elise and Michael had somehow spilled over to my children. "What's going on with you two, Kyra?" I practically begged. "Please, just tell me. I want to help—"

She went red then, and even more furious as she stamped her foot again. "I don't want to talk about it!" she cried, and, considering how upset she was getting, I felt I had no choice but to let the matter drop… for now. I didn't talk to Mrs. Ryan, but I told Kyra I would if things continued.

It felt more like a threat than a reassurance.

Back at the hospital, with Allan asleep, I took out the legal-sized envelope with a feeling of dread as well as a weird sort of curiosity.

Part of me couldn't believe Elise had really gone through with it. I slipped the yellow legal documents out of the envelope and studied the words emblazoned on the official-looking paper. I couldn't understand all the legalese, but the heavy black print at the top was plain enough, detailing that Elise Anne Dunnett was the plaintiff, I was the defendant, and I was being sued for gross negligence. I had twenty days to file my response to the court.

Staring at those words on the page, all of it stated so bleakly in black and white, stirred something in me. For a second, I could imagine myself back at the gala, Elise in my arms, a sense of frustration firing through me that she was resisting my help, as well as the residual anger that she had made such a scene. In the heat of the moment, I'd said something to her, I can't remember what, but I do remember feeling angry.

Fortunately, I didn't have to think about what to do about it all just then. I had twenty days to respond, which felt like a long time when every day since the summons so far has been spent in a halogen-lit hospital room, wondering if—not when—Allan was going to get better.

On Sunday morning, the doctor talked to me about discharging him. I had Kyra in the hospital with me all day, reading to him or coloring quietly. She insisted she come, even though Barbara offered to watch her at home. I was worried about exposing her to too much, but this is our life now, and she had the right to choose to be a part of it.

In the end, I felt I'd made the right choice because Allan was so delighted to see her. It perked him up, which is why the doctor was talking about discharging him, and then on Saturday he developed a cough and by the evening they were talking about how it might develop into pneumonia.

"It's very common with ALS patients," the neurologist explained to me, "as they lose their respiratory function. Often the common cold becomes anything but."

Which was hardly cheering news. It looked like Allan was going to be in the hospital for a while, maybe even for Christmas if things took a downturn, and meanwhile I had the summons to respond to, and Luke Dunnett to deal with, as well as presents to buy for Kyra so she could have something approaching a normal Christmas. Besides that, there was my own complicated grief to work through, which felt like a tidal wave ready to crash over me at any moment. It all felt like way too much to deal with on my own; I wanted to be strong, but for the first time I recognized that maybe I wasn't. That I couldn't be.

And so, on Monday afternoon, I ended up calling my dad.

"I got served the papers," I tell him while standing in the hallway outside Allan's room. Kyra is sitting with him, after I picked her up from school, and the ward is decorated in red and green tinsel.

"We'll talk to a lawyer," my dad replies, his voice low and gravelly and sure. "Together."

The *together* is enough to make my eyes sting. I've been alone for most of my life, have *chosen* to be alone, but right now I realize just how tired I am of that solitary existence. Independence, I'm discovering, is overrated.

"I can't do anything about it right now," I tell my dad, my voice wavering with emotion and exhaustion, and then I explain about Allan being in the hospital, the chance that his cough might develop into pneumonia.

"Oh, honey." I can't recall the last time, if ever, my dad called me honey. "Why didn't you say?"

"I don't know." A laugh escapes me, wobbly and uncertain. It didn't even *occur* to me to say anything. "I mean, you've never even met Allan."

"He's the father of my granddaughter," my dad replies, as if it's all there is to it, and maybe to him it really is that simple. Maybe it can be that simple for me, too? A pause, and then, with a thrum of vulnerability in his voice, he asks, "Do you want me to come?"

In that moment, I realize just how much I do. I really don't want to be alone anymore. I need someone else to be strong, if just for a little while. "If... if it's not too much trouble," I whisper. "That would be great, Dad."

"I'll leave right now," my dad says in his gruff way, and a sudden rush of love and gratitude almost overwhelms me. It feels so *good* to have someone strong on my side, to know I don't have to keep battling by myself. I give him the hospital details, filled with relief.

Back in the hospital room, Allan is asleep, and Kyra is sitting quietly by his bed.

"Grandpa's coming," I tell her with a smile. "He wants to help out. Won't it be nice to see him?"

Kyra blinks at me. "Will he stay for Christmas?"

"Maybe," I reply, although I can't see my dad staying with us in Allan's little apartment in Astoria for the next few weeks.

"Or..." I am filled with a sudden reckless sense of possibilities opening up, for both of us. If Kyra's not happy at The Garden School anymore... "Maybe we'll go and stay with him," I tell her. The idea just occurred to me, but now I wonder why not. My dad has the space, and it would be so nice to get away from everything here, for Kyra too. "Maybe we'll live with him again," I add, and Kyra's eyes widen.

"You mean move? *Again*?" she demands.

I hesitate, not quite expecting the anger in her response. "Well, it was just a thought," I quickly backtrack, and she shakes her head violently.

"I don't want to move again," she states. "I *like* it here. I like living with Allan. I like going to The Garden School." She thrusts her chin out as she glares at me.

I am not about to point out to her that Allan won't always be with us, or that things at school have seemed fraught. The notion to move in with my dad leaves me almost as quickly as it came. Moving again, I realize, will just be running away, and I wonder if that's what I've always done. Has my restlessness really just hidden a fear of facing things? Of staying and walking *through* something, rather than leaving it behind?

"It was just an idea," I tell her. "Of course we don't have to move again if you don't want to." I hesitate, then gently press, "You are still liking school, though? Because with Luke—"

"I don't want to talk about that," Kyra interrupts. She turns her face away from me. "I told you that already."

"I know, but... I still want to know why Luke was hurting you, Kyra. I need to know." She doesn't reply and I press hesitantly, "Was it... was it because of me? And the stuff going on with Luke's mom? I'm guessing some of the kids are talking about that."

"I don't want to talk about it," Kyra says again, her voice stifled. "*Please*, Mom."

I feel like I have no choice but to let it go, *again*. One day we'll get to the bottom of this, I tell myself, and in the meantime, at least Kyra is safe here with me.

An hour later, my dad walks into Allan's room, looking both out of place and wonderfully welcome in his flannel jacket and work pants, so much the burly blue-collar guy. I rise from my chair and before I've even got my arms out, he envelops me in a big bear hug, which I return, curling into him like a little child, craving the sense of being protected. Safe.

"I've called a lawyer," he tells me. "We can talk to him as soon as tomorrow, if you want. We'll find a way through this, Harriet. It's going to be okay, I promise."

Standing wrapped in his arms, I let myself believe him. I *need* to believe that things might be okay, that I'll get through this, that we will. *Together*.

From behind me, I hear a rasping cough, and I turn to see Allan is awake, smiling weakly at us.

"I think..." he manages to rasp, "I'm feeling a little better."

"*Dad!*" Kyra exclaims, and a look of shock at the endearment—one she's never called him to his face before—flashes across Allan's face before he beams at her, shyly and deeply pleased. He reaches out one hand and gently Kyra puts her arms around him.

I let out a trembling laugh, so grateful for this moment, even in the midst of so much uncertainty. Maybe this is all we can do—find the happiness and the peace within the sorrow and the brokenness, and let it be enough.

A tap sounds at the door, and then Dr. Bayler steps in the room, smiling to see Allan awake. "I have some good news," he tells us, "Which I imagine will be pretty welcome."

"I could definitely use some good news," Allan replies with a small smile as I step out of my dad's embrace.

"You've been approved for tofersen," Dr. Bayler states

without preamble. "Which is lucky, because only about ten percent of ALS patients have the mutated gene that tofersen targets. As soon as your lungs are clear, we'll start you on it. It's administered by spinal tap every twenty-eight days and has been proven to be pretty effective in slowing or even stopping symptoms."

"Wow." Allan's voice and smile are shaky. "That's really good news."

"I don't want to get your hopes up too much," Dr. Bayler continues seriously, even though mine are already ballooning at this possibility. "It's not a magic pill or a miracle cure. But it can help."

"I'll take it," Allan jokes, and I let out a shaky laugh as Dr. Bayler places a gentle hand on his shoulder.

"I'm glad to hear it."

After Dr. Bayler has gone, my dad offers to take Kyra to the hospital café for some lunch, and I realize, with a rush of tenderness, that he wants to spend some time with her. This is all new, and so strange, and yet so wonderful.

When they've gone, I blow out a breath, overwhelmed by the emotional roller coaster we've been on. I know there's more to come, but right now it feels like a little bit of a rest. I turn to smile at Allan, but he still looks serious.

"When I asked you to move here," he says, "I didn't think it would be as hard on you and Kyra as it's been."

Slowly, I straighten and turn. "Oh, Allan..."

"I should have, obviously," he continues with a wry smile, the words coming slowly and slurred, although he's doing his best to enunciate. "I mean, I knew what the prognosis was. It was never going to be pretty. But when you feel more or less well in yourself, it's so hard to imagine that you'll get worse. And I thought I'd have more time... I told myself, when it starts to get bad, when I'm not in control anymore, I'll just take myself off. Disappear into the night. Let you and Kyra have the apartment, she can keep going to school, and you could both be happy here."

"And where would you have gone?" I ask quietly.

"Does it matter?" Allan replies with a sigh. "I didn't do it. I couldn't. Because I wanted to be with you both so much. Even like this."

I swallow the lump in my throat before I can speak. "We want to be with you, too," I reply as I come to sit next to him and take his thin hand. I smile down at his dear face, weathered by age and pain. The whole left side of his face droops, both his eye and mouth pulled down in a permanent grimace, and he looks far older than his years, far older than he did even just a few months ago. "Even like this," I echo quietly.

He holds my hand, turns it over in his. "I don't expect you to love me," he says, the words coming slowly and still slurred. "But I want you to know... I love you, Harriet. The *you* you are now, just to be clear, and not who you were back then."

I let out a rueful laugh at that bit of honesty. "Have I changed so much?"

"Maybe I'm the one who's changed, and not just because of this rotten disease," he answers with a smile that pulls at the right side of his mouth. "Or maybe we both have. Whatever it is... I love you."

"I love you, too, Allan." I never expected to find love when I came to live with him—and it's not the dizzying, head-over-heels kind of love I might have once longed for, but still something deep and true. I don't know what kind of future Allan and I can have as a couple, if we can even be a couple in that way, but I know I want to be with him, and I want Kyra to have him as her father.

I wasn't sure I was making the right choice by coming here, or whether Kyra would be able to have any kind of relationship with him, or whether Allan would even want one, no matter what he'd said. Back when I was pregnant, I could have never imagined that he would.

Yet everything has changed now, and despite what feels like a very uncertain future, I am grateful that I got to this place at all. That we all did.

There's another tap on the door, and I turn, expecting a nurse or maybe my dad and Kyra back already, but isn't any of them.

It's Michael.

THIRTY-THREE
ELISE

On Tuesday morning, I am sitting in Dr. Allers' office waiting for her to tell me about my test results, whatever those are.

I would feel nervous except, after yesterday, I am completely numb. I can't dredge up any emotion about what these ominous test results might be, because, yesterday afternoon, while the boys were in the playroom and I was cleaning the kitchen, Michael told me he was leaving me.

"I know this sounds clichéd," he said tiredly, a long, low sigh escaping him as he stood in the doorway of the kitchen, "but I need some space."

I stared at him, a dripping sponge in my hand, shocked to the core. I realized that, in all my endless, nebulous fears, I never considered *Michael* would leave *me*. I anticipated thoughtlessness, deceit, *infidelity*, but not this. Maybe because my father never left my mother. Or maybe because I couldn't bear to think about such a possibility, the reality that I'd failed as a wife. Whatever it was, when he said it as bluntly as I that, I felt as if I'd been punched in the gut, which, considering the state of my stomach, was devastating.

"You want a divorce?" I whispered.

"Not a *divorce*," Michael replied in that same weary tone. "Just... a break."

"From me?" I had to state the obvious.

"You're hard work, Elise," he told me, an edge entering his voice. "The way we never talk about things, and how you always watch me, the OCD..." He shook his head. "I'm *tired*."

I was hard work? For a second, I couldn't speak. I, the perfect wife who graced his arm, who cleaned the kitchen, who birthed his children, who never complained or was too tired for sex... *I* was the one who was hard work in this marriage?

It seemed inconceivable. I'd been the one who had made his life *easy*, and the first time I stopped and said *no more*, suddenly I was hard work. Suddenly, my OCD, something I'd always managed, was too much. The injustice of it burned.

I took a deep breath, let it out slowly. "Is this about Harriet?" I asked. "And the fact that I'm going ahead with the lawsuit? Are you punishing me for that?"

"Are you punishing *me*?" Michael returned. "Because I really don't think slapping her with a lawsuit is about her at all, frankly."

"Maybe it *is* about you," I admitted recklessly. "But if you'd stood beside me in this, if you *believed* me and were as concerned for me as you were for *that woman*, always running to her..."

"*That woman*?" Michael shook his head. "Elise, take Harriet out of this for once. Take out all the women you've been threatened by over the years, and all the women your dad was with, and all that complicated *history* that has completely skewed your thinking." I recoiled, because he made me sound so... *broken*. "And make this just about us." He met my gaze directly, unflinchingly. "You and me. Have we *ever* been honest with each other? Have we ever truly talked? For twenty years, you've been showing me this airbrushed version of yourself, believing I buy it, and the truth is, I never did."

He held up a hand and I fell silent, reeling too much to say anything. "I should have told you that before. Long before. I know I should have. I was happy enough to go along with the status quo, because it felt easy, and it seemed to work. But just because something looks like it works on the surface doesn't mean it really does, and I don't think either of us have been happy for a long time."

"That old chestnut," I scoffed hoarsely. "Such an excuse. Marriage is hard work, Michael, anyone honest will tell you that. And I have worked *so hard*." My voice rose on something like a cry, and I shook my head, angry with myself for sounding so weak. Already I felt like I was begging him to stay.

"I know you have," Michael said, and now his tone had turned gentle, which felt so much worse. "But I don't know that it should be *that* kind of work, Elise. You proving something rather than us in it together, striving for a common goal."

Had I ever felt like Michael and I were working together? I wasn't sure I had. I wasn't sure I'd even know what that would look like. But did that mean we stopped trying? The funny, or really the painfully ironic thing, was, when I'd come home from my dad's, I'd been thinking about dropping the lawsuit. I'd felt free in a way I never had before, free from who I'd felt I needed to be and all the secrets I'd been compelled to keep... and I'd wanted to share that with Michael. I'd wanted a fresh start, but he'd already decided we were over.

"I think it's better this way," Michael stated. "For now."

"And what does that mean?" I asked, a wobble in my voice.

"I'll move out for a little while." He sounded resolute. "We can see how things go."

"We can hardly try to work together if you're not even here," I flung at him, but it was half-hearted. It felt as if I'd lost my husband, which was, I supposed, something I should have considered might happen all along.

THE SECRET BETWEEN US 273

"I'll get some stuff together," Michael said then, already turning away.

"What will you tell the boys?" I had called after him. Had he even thought about them?

He hesitated, then turned slowly around. "There's no need to tell them anything yet. You can just say I'm at work. I have to go to the hospital, anyway."

"You do?"

Another hesitation, and somehow I already knew, just by the guilty yet resolute look on his face.

"Please don't tell me—" I begin.

"Yes, I'm going to see Harriet," he cut across me. "Allan collapsed a few days ago and apparently his condition has deteriorated. He's been in the hospital since Thursday. This is in a professional capacity, Elise."

I shook my head slowly. "But he's not your patient."

"I still feel a responsibility. I'll text you when I know where I'm staying." And then he walked out of our life without another word, leaving me feeling sucker-punched all over again.

Somehow I got through the evening, placating the boys, feeling numb. And now I'm here, sitting in a doctor's office, wondering what on earth she's going to tell me. What if the stomach rupture caused even more problems than I knew about? Nearly three weeks on, and I still ache abominably. Maybe that's not normal. Maybe there's something seriously wrong with me.

"Elise." Dr. Allers enters the room with a brisk smile as she closes the door behind her. "How are you?"

That's not a question I can answer easily, but I force a small, tight smile. "Well, I've been better, actually," I reply. Maybe honesty will be my policy from now on, no matter what. Faking it so clearly didn't work, with anyone.

Dr. Allers gives me a sympathetic grimace. "Recovery can

be hard. And harder still, because the tests we did caught a condition that would have made everything all the worse."

"What...?"

She pulls a file toward her on the desk. "You have peptic ulcer disease. Really, it should have been caught earlier, and certainly during surgery. But the trouble is when you come through ER, there are a number of surgeons and gastroenterologists involved, and they don't always communicate well with one another." She gives me an apologetic smile before moving swiftly on. "Anyway, the important thing is, it's been caught now and can be treated."

"What is peptic ulcer disease?" I ask.

I can't believe I have a *disease* and didn't know it.

"It's just a fancy name for being prone to open sores in the lining of your stomach or small intestine. You know what an ulcer is, right?" Numbly, I nod. "Well, PUD just means you get them a lot. There are a number of treatments—we can look at histamine blockers to reduce stomach acid, or cytoprotective agents to coat and protect your digestive tract. There are several ways to help the situation." She gives me the brisk smile of someone who wants to move on.

"How did I not have any symptoms?" I ask, still trying to get my head around this news. "And how did I get it?"

"Symptoms vary, and as many as seventy percent of people with PUD don't have any symptoms at all," she explains. "They don't know they have it until something happens like a gastric perforation."

"Wait..." I stare at her in dawning suspicion. "You mean my stomach rupture might have been caused by this disease and not by being given the Heimlich?"

"Well... the Heimlich obviously brought something on," Dr. Allers allows. "But the truth is, you were a walking time bomb. It would have happened one way or another, without treatment, and judging by the state of your small intestine, I'm amazed it didn't happen before. Really, having it come to a head in this way is a blessing, albeit a mixed one."

I can't believe it. All this time I might have had a stomach rupture anyway? It might not have even been Harriet's fault? I can practically hear Michael crowing *I told you so*. Except he wouldn't be crowing, he'd be shaking his head sadly and lamenting how vindictive I've become.

"As for how you got it," Dr. Allers continues, "it's hard to say. A stomach infection or an overuse of painkillers like ibuprofen are sometimes the cause, or even just stress. It's a lot more common than you think."

Stress. Well, I've certainly had plenty of that.

"Right," I murmur.

I am barely listening as she tells me what medications we'll get started on, and then hands me a prescription, suggesting I make a follow-up appointment in four weeks.

I walk out of her office in a daze, having no idea what to do now.

Drop the lawsuit? Call my husband? Apologize to Harriet? Try to mend all the broken pieces of my life, but I don't know how. I don't know what to do. I don't know who to *be*.

My phone buzzes, and I grope in my bag for it, hoping it might be Michael. That he might be rethinking everything the way I am. Maybe there's a way back from this after all, especially with what I've just learned.

"Is this Elise Dunnett, wife of Michael Dunnett?"

The serious, official-sounding voice makes my stomach, aching as it already is, drop toward my toes. "Yes..." Has Michael already called a divorce lawyer? Am I about to be served papers? Suddenly, I can imagine how Harriet felt when she was handed such papers, that swirling sense of disbelief and dread. *This can't be happening...*

"Michael Dunnett is in the intensive care unit of New York Presbyterian Hospital," the voice tells me. "With a traumatic brain injury. You should come right away."

THIRTY-FOUR

HARRIET

On Monday morning, the doctor tells us that Allan's lungs look clear and he can be released.

He's having his first shot of tofersen before they discharge him this afternoon. Kyra practically skipped into school today, joined by a little girl I didn't recognize, and for once things feel hopeful. Even my conversation with Michael last night, painful as it was, ended on what I believe was a positive note.

I was shocked to see him there, since I hadn't told him or anyone besides my dad that Allan was in the hospital. Our roles had been reversed; I was the one wanting to hurry out of a hospital room, hide his presence from my loved one, but that wasn't possible.

"Michael." Allan had brightened at the sight of him, not suspecting anything but a doctor's concern, while I sensed something more. "We just had the good news that I can take tofersen."

"That's *great* news, Allan." Michael came over and shook his hand, then smiled at me. I smiled back before looking away quickly; I still wasn't comfortable being around him. The loneliness and isolation I'd felt just a few weeks ago, when those coffees we had together were the highlight of my week, already felt like a long time ago. My life had changed. *I'd* changed. But why was Michael here?

He chatted with Allan for a few minutes, but it was obvious Allan was getting tired, just as it was obvious Michael had something to say privately to me. And so, after he shook Allan's hand again and said goodbye, I walked him to the door.

"Can I talk to you for a second?" he asked in a low voice, just as I suspected he would, and I slipped outside into the hallway.

"What is it?"

"I just want to say how sorry I am about the lawsuit. Elise..." He blew out a breath. "I feel like I don't even know her. For her to do something as vindictive as this... I've left her, actually." He grimaced as I stared at him in shock.

"You *left* her?" I couldn't believe it. "Why?"

"This whole thing has brought up too much. I don't think I ever really knew her—"

"*Michael*." I held up a hand to stop him. "Don't say anything more. I... I have to tell you something."

He frowned. "Harriet..."

I took a deep breath before forcing myself to go on. I knew this might change everything, and just when things were finally turning a corner with Allan, with my whole life. Did I really want to put all our happiness at risk? Yet I knew I had to be honest. For my own sake as much as Elise's.

"That night at the gala..." I began haltingly. "When I was giving Elise the Heimlich... I think I *did* use too much force."

I closed my eyes briefly as I remembered the moment. My hands on her stomach. My voice in her ear. The sudden wave of frustration and fury that had risen in me, overwhelming all rational thought. For a second, I'd wanted to punish her. Hurt her, even...

It hadn't hit me until I'd seen the legal papers. Somehow,

seeing it in black and white had brought it all back, and I'd recalled exactly how I'd felt in that split second. That blaze of anger that had fired through me, the feel of my fist driving into her stomach. All this time, I hadn't wanted to second-guess myself; I'd been determined to believe I'd done the right thing, because, at the end of the day, I *had* saved her life.

But when I was holding those papers, I'd been forced to acknowledge that maybe the situation was more complicated than I'd let myself believe. Maybe Elise had had a point.

"Harriet..." Michael shook his head. "You don't mean that—"

"I do. It took me a while to realize and accept it, but... Elise has a case, Michael. I mean, I did go to her to help her. I was trying to save her from choking. But in that moment? When she was struggling and I was so frustrated with her, and with all the history we had? I think I did push too hard. And I'm sorry—so sorry—for that."

He stared at me for a long moment. "If you admit that in court, you could be liable for damages."

A sigh escaped me, long and heavy. "I know." The thought of a court battle right now was so exhausting and overwhelming, I could barely get my head around it. "I don't have any money, though," I pointed out with an attempt at wryness, "so if Elise wants a payout..."

Michael let out a huff of breath. "I don't know what she wants."

And yet I thought I might have the glimmering of an idea.

"I think she wants her *husband* back," I told him quietly. "Michael, please don't leave her. Not because of what happened then. Whatever went wrong between you... it can be worked out. At least, you can try." Michael and Elise might have had problems I didn't know about, but I knew I did not want to be considered the cause of their divorce. I might have appreciated his company at a vulnerable point in my life, and maybe even made it into more in my mind for a little while, but that's as far as it went, or as I ever wanted it to go. And really, I felt sorry for Elise. I'd made her into a villain in my mind and I was starting to accept that she wasn't one. I wasn't, either, and that was something she might need to accept one day, too. "Please, at least try," I told him.

Just then, my dad and Kyra came down the hallway. They didn't see us, and I wanted to keep it that way.

"I have to go," I told Michael, my tone firm. "And so, I think, do you."

I gave him a quick smile of goodbye and then I turned to my family. And by the time Kyra told me her smoothie flavor and gave me a sip, Michael had disappeared.

And now it's Monday afternoon, and Allan and I are heading home in a taxi.

He's had one shot of tofersen and maybe it's just wishful thinking, but he seems a little more with it already. We hold hands in the taxi and I help him up the stairs; Barbara has left two casseroles and a loaf of banana bread in front of our door.

"I can't believe it's almost Christmas," I tell him as I settle him on the sofa with his blanket and his book. "I guess we'll have a quiet one."

"I'm just happy to have it with you and Kyra."

"And my dad," I remind him, and he smiles and catches my hand.

"Thank you, Harriet," he says, his voice a low thrum of sincerity. "For everything."

I shake my head as I squeeze his hand. "You don't have to thank me, Allan. This is our life now. Our life *together*." I smile as I let go of his hand and lean over to plump his pillow. "I'm happy."

And amazingly I am, even if I still have a lawsuit hanging

over me. Admitting that I might have been guilty to Michael was weirdly freeing. It was a secret I'd been keeping, even from myself, but I'm glad to have it out... no matter what the results might be. Hopefully I'll still be feeling that way when I'm standing in court.

I'm still holding onto my good mood when I head to TGS to pick up Kyra. I glance around for Elise, mainly to avoid her, but then I recognize her babysitter standing by the front doors. I'm relieved not to see her, but also strangely disappointed, too. If there's some way to reconcile with her, I'd like to find it. I just don't know if there is.

The school doors open, and when the third grade comes out, I see, to my shock, that Kyra is walking with Luke and Lewis, and they're all smiling. Mrs. Ryan is behind them, and she makes a beeline for me.

"I just wanted to reassure you that everything seems to have settled down with Kyra and Luke," she tells me in a low voice as Luke and Lewis peel off toward their babysitter, and Kyra comes toward me. "I haven't gotten to the bottom of it, but I guess they had some kind of argument, but it seems to have been resolved. I just didn't want you to worry."

"I..." I shake my head as I start to smile. I have no idea what to think. "Thank you," I finally tell her, and Mrs. Ryan smiles back.

"So often these little things resolve themselves. I always appreciate it when parents don't kick up a huge fuss, you know? It often just makes it worse." She lowers her voice conspiratorially. "But then, I know a lot of parents wouldn't necessarily agree with me on that one."

"No, probably not," I reply wryly. I feel like I've found an unexpected kindred spirit.

"I also wanted to say I saw the backdrops you painted for the silent auction. I'm in charge of our class play, and I was wondering if you'd come in and lead the set-making? Only if you have time, of course…"

Startled, I nod. "Yeah, sure, I'd be glad to." Everything about this conversation is so unexpected… and so welcome. I'd fallen into the mode of feeling like worst-case scenarios were the only possibilities. It's refreshing to remember that some things in life can in fact be easy and even good.

"So, are you finally going to tell me what all that was about with Luke?" I ask Kyra as we walk toward the subway, swinging hands. "Since it seems like you and Luke and Lewis are all friends again?" I still can't quite believe it. After all that drama and fear on my part… can things really be that simple?

"Ugh." She makes a face, before looking away "*Fine*. I was mad at Lewis because he said he was going to *marry* me." She groans theatrically while I stifle a surprised laugh.

"He did?"

"Yes!" Kyra sounds genuinely outraged. "And I said I wouldn't be friends with him anymore if he kept saying that, and then he got upset."

I still have to piece it together. "So, you didn't stop being friends with him," I say carefully, "because… because you were angry with his… *dad*?"

Kyra turns to look at me, her face screwed up in confusion. "No, why would I do that?"

I shake my head, bemused. After all, why should she think that? "No reason," I reply lightly. "So then what happened?"

She sighs. "Then Luke got mad at me for making Lewis sad, and that made *me* sad." Her lips tremble. "He wasn't very nice to me…"

I rest my hand on her shoulder. "I'm sorry, Kyra." I pause. "And so what happened, when you got those bruises on your arm?" They still seemed serious to me.

A shuddery sigh escapes her. "Luke and I were fighting. He told me I should be friends with Lewis again. And he grabbed me, and so I pushed him. I didn't mean to make him hit his head."

"I know you didn't, honey." I squeeze her shoulder.

Accidents happen, I think with an ache in my chest. *And sometimes no one is to blame, and sometimes both people are.*

"I was sad about it," Kyra continues quietly, "and I didn't want to tell you because..." Her face goes pink as she thrusts her lower lip out. "It was *embarrassing*. Everyone was teasing about Lewis wanting to marry me, and I *hated* that."

"Oh, Kyra." I put my arm around her, because even if this seems like no more than a childish escapade, it obviously hurt. And I can certainly relate to how seemingly small things can take over our lives. "But no one's teasing you now?" I clarify.

"No," she tells me with relief, "because Lewis likes Chloe now."

I laugh at that, passing a hand over my forehead. "Phew."

"Yeah." She nods seriously. "*Phew.*"

It's all so innocent and sweet, and yet it feels like there is a lesson in it for me, and maybe for Elise. I was so sure all the drama between the adults had affected the children. I was ready to blame both myself and Elise and Michael for what ended up being just a normal, if painful, part of childhood.

Maybe, I reflect, in this whole tangled situation, we shouldn't have blamed anyone at all. Or, conversely, we could have blamed everyone. We all had a part to play, and maybe that's how it so often is in life. We look for heroes and villains, winners and losers, and the truth is often a lot more complicated than that.

I wonder if I'll be able to tell Elise that one day. If she'll let me.

That thought is still pinging around in my mind when I drop Kyra off at school the next morning—and find out from Joanna that Michael Dunnett is in a coma with a traumatic brain injury, and they don't know if he'll recover.

"What...?" I stare at her in dazed shock. "How? When?"

"Apparently he was mugged on Sunday night," she tells me gravely. "Whoever it was took his wallet and phone, so he wasn't identified for a while. Poor Elise must have been beside herself. I feel so sorry for her." She gives me a guilty look, and I know she still feels bad for gossiping.

"I can't believe it," I say numbly.

"It was right outside a hospital," she continues. "And no one saw him for hours."

I freeze at that, because if it was right outside a hospital, it was right after when he'd been visiting *me*. I don't feel guilty, not exactly, but I still feel responsible.

And I realize, after everything that has happened, I need to talk to Elise.

THIRTY-FIVE
ELISE

I am sitting by Michael's bedside when I hear someone at the door. Before I turn, I already know who it is.

I'm not sure how; maybe it's just an instinct, or a suspicion, or a fear. But when I see Harriet standing uncertainly in the doorway, I am not surprised.

For a second, we simply stare at each other, not so much a stand-off as an acknowledgment.

"Elise... I'm so sorry," Harriet finally says, twisting her fingers together in front of her as she takes a hesitant step into Michael's room. "How is he?"

"He was in an induced coma for twenty-four hours, to reduce the swelling on his brain," I tell her, my voice even. I've been surprisingly calm ever since I arrived at the hospital, but maybe that's just the shock. After all the fears I had, all the pain and grief at Michael leaving me, having something like this come out of nowhere has left me feeling more lost than ever. You think you prepare for life's possibilities, and then something comes that scatters every certainty you clung to. "They started bringing him out of it this morning," I tell Harriet, "but so far he hasn't responded. They're still hopeful, though."

"I'm so sorry," she says again, her voice choking a little. She looks as shocked as I felt when I got that call. When I realized, *again*, that life can change in an instant.

"You don't need to be sorry," I tell her, managing a wry smile even though I'm exhausted and emotionally as fragile as I've ever been. "This one... well, it isn't your fault."

I hope she realizes I'm joking, sort of, anyway, and then she lets out a shaky laugh of acknowledgement and I know that she does.

"Look, I know we have a complicated relationship," she begins, "but... there was never anything between Michael and me. I'm guessing he's told you that—at least I hope he has—but I felt like I needed to tell you, too."

"All right." My voice is toneless, giving nothing away, because I don't know how I feel about her telling me that, and whether it matters. I have too much to deal with now to worry about whether Harriet and Michael were a little overly friendly.

Harriet continues stiltedly, "I mean, full disclosure, there might have been something on my side. Emotionally. You must know how charming Michael can be, and I felt so lonely..." She sighs. "I'm not proud of it, but I probably put more importance on our coffees and meetups together than he ever did."

"There was something on Michael's side, too," I tell her. Maybe she needs that reassurance, that it wasn't all in her head. "I've known that for a while." I pause and then state baldly, "He never would have told you about my OCD if there hadn't been."

She flinches. "Honestly, that just slipped out—"

"From you or from him?" I wave a hand, not wanting to dissect it any more than we already have. "It doesn't matter. Everyone knows. In some ways, it's a relief. No more keeping secrets. No more pretending to be *perfect*."

I look away, because while I've been honest, which is how I

want to be from now on, I don't necessarily want to see what I suspect will be pity on her face.

"No, no more secrets." She's silent for a moment. "I get that, actually. I've... I've been keeping a secret from you," she admits, and now there is a tremor of fear in her voice that makes me curious. "I told Michael on Sunday—when he came to see Allan, I don't know if you knew—"

"Yes," I reply calmly. "I did." Which was how he came to be outside the hospital, getting mugged. Not that I'm looking to blame Harriet for that. I'm done with assigning guilt, to anyone, for things that just happen.

She nods jerkily. "I told him that I'd been thinking about everything a lot and... and I think you were right, Elise." Her words come thickly now, and painfully. "I think I did hurt you on purpose. On a subconscious level, I mean I wasn't... Oh, I don't even know." She lets out a ragged laugh while I simply stare. "Maybe it was on a conscious level, too. Some part of me, anyway... but what I'm trying to say is, you weren't that off base there. I was angry, and I pushed too hard. I don't know what that means for the lawsuit, admitting any guilt is probably not a good idea on my part, but—"

I laugh with genuine humor, surprising her. It's freeing to have her admit what I think I knew all along, but I also know it doesn't really matter anymore. "Harriet," I tell her, "I'm dropping the lawsuit."

She stares at me dumbly. "What...?"

"I haven't gotten around to calling my lawyer, because of all this..." I nod toward Michael. "But I'd already decided to drop it. It was never about you, anyway. You may have been angry, but you still saved my life. I am truly grateful for that, even if I never acted like it." I try for a wry smile as Harriet stares at me, shocked. "And, really," I continue painfully, "it was more about me being hurt by Michael. And..." A sigh escapes me. "I discovered yesterday I have a condition, some kind of ulcer thing, that meant my stomach would have most likely ruptured at some point anyway."

Now she looks completely stunned. "*What—*"

"You having given me the Heimlich still caused it," I tell her, just in case she thinks I'm absolving her completely. "And administering it harder than you should have undoubtedly didn't help matters. But... the whole thing was a lot more complicated than I wanted it to be." I turn back to look at Michael, his eyes still closed. I'm trying to be optimistic, but when will he wake up? What will our future look like? "I suppose," I tell Harriet as I gaze at my husband, "that's how most of life is."

"I was just thinking the same thing myself." We are both silent, acknowledging this truth, and then she glances at Michael. "Have they said anything about his recovery?"

"It all depends on how he comes out of the coma. Like I said, they're hopeful." I sit up straighter as I glance at my husband, whom I love. "*I'm* hopeful," I tell her firmly. Even if Michael was planning on leaving me. Surely this changes things. I so desperately want to believe that, that we can find a way through this, that we *will*.

"I'm hopeful, too," Harriet says quietly, and I glance back at her, noticing how tired she looks. Her hair is a mess of different dyed colors, and she's wearing an old, holey fisherman knit sweater and a pair of baggy jeans. More than any of that, though, I see the sorrow and even grief etched onto the lines of her face, and I remember just what she's dealing with—a diagnosis for Kyra's dad that is almost certainly worse than whatever I'm facing with Michael.

"How is Allan?" I ask, and she looks surprised that I thought to ask. To care.

"He's... okay," she says after a moment. "For now. We're both learning to live in the present, because, frankly, the future is very uncertain."

"That's a lesson we could all learn, I'm sure," I tell her, and we both fall silent in a way that doesn't feel companionable, but almost. I'm not angry with her anymore, and she doesn't seem so dismissive of me. Maybe that's enough.

"I found out what was going on with Kyra and your boys," she tells me after a moment, and she sounds amused, which has me stiffening instinctively before she explains the whole thing.

So Lewis had a little boy crush on Kyra, and Luke, dear Luke, was protective of him, and it escalated from there? I feel relieved that it was nothing more serious, and yet some part of me also feels sad. How swiftly small things can become the ones that change our lives. I'm relieved our children have resolved their drama, and I'm also glad that maybe Harriet and I have resolved ours.

"Thank you for telling me," I say, and Harriet nods and takes a step back.

"I should go. But... when you can, will you let me know how he is? And how *you* are," she emphasizes, and I smile.

I don't think Harriet and I will ever be friends, but maybe we could have been, once upon a time. And maybe that is enough, too.

"I will," I tell her, and with a little smile and wave that seem to hold both apology and acknowledgment for everything that has happened, she slips out of the room.

I turn to my husband and see that his eyes are open.

It's not until Saturday, when Michael has been out of his coma for several days, that we actually get a chance to talk.

It's been a long few days, with cognitive tests and brain scans and talk about moving to a rehab facility. The good news is, they think Michael will make a good, if not full, recovery. He's likely to have long-term problems with concentration and memory, as well as some balance issues and the potential for seizures, but all those effects will hopefully lessen with time. The doctor explained how difficult it is to predict how things will go with a traumatic brain injury, which Michael could have explained himself, since he's a neurosurgeon.

At least, he *was* a neurosurgeon.

One thing that has become clear is he will not be able to operate again. Like Harriet and Allan's, our future is looking very uncertain.

"Christmas is in just three days," I tell him cheerfully as I come into his room on Saturday morning with a poinsettia for the windowsill. The boys got out of school for the holidays yesterday; my mom came a few days ago to take care of them, and it's been surprisingly pleasant. She'll stay through New Year's, at the very least. "I was thinking I could bring the boys in to see you, and they could give you their presents." They've been a few times already, but I've kept the visits short for everyone's sakes.

Michael smiles wearily; everything exhausts him these days.

I sit down next to him, touch his hand. "Would you like that?"

"Yes, that would be nice." He glances away, out the window. Along with my poinsettia, the windowsill is filled with vases of flowers from former patients and friends, the many, many people who know how wonderful Michael is.

"You're going to get better, Michael," I say softly.

"But I won't operate again." He sighs, shaking his head as if to stop me from talking even though I haven't said anything. "Please don't deny it. I wouldn't want someone who has had a TBI operating on me. As a surgeon myself, I wouldn't allow it on anyone."

"I wasn't going to deny it," I reply quietly. "But you can still get better, and one day you can practice as a neurologist again." Even if surgery has been the thing he's loved most. "And..." I pause, because in the five days since I've been sitting by my husband's bedside, the fact that he left me before this all happened has not come up. "I'll be with you, every step of the way," I tell him, and then hold my breath, because there are gaps in Michael's memory and I am wondering—hoping, even—that he's forgotten what he'd said he was going to do. That he felt our marriage was more or less over. And that if it is, we can move past it like it never happened, and keep on living our lives.

"Is this really what you want?" Michael asks, sounding dispirited.

"Well, a traumatic brain injury isn't what either of us want," I reply, "but this is what marriage is about, right? In sickness and in health, for better or for worse."

He turns to me, and I can't tell from his expression whether he remembers leaving me or not. But then I realize it doesn't matter if he does, or, more to the point, if he doesn't.

I'm not keeping secrets anymore, even if I am so very tempted to keep this one.

"You might not remember, but before this happened," I confess quietly, "you told me you were going to *leave* me. You said you wanted a break, but it felt like our marriage was over."

His eyes widen, and I can't tell if it's because he didn't remember, or he didn't think I would remind him.

"Things hadn't been great between us for a while," I continue. "We'd both been... less than honest with each other. And I know you were right when you told me that neither of us had been happy."

"And now?" Michael asks curiously, when I've lapsed into silence, uncertain where to go from here. How much to risk.

"Now I want to try again, *together*," I tell him, my heart beating hard as I force myself to lay it all out there—no secrets, no striving to be perfect, just this painful, raw honesty. "Not just to get through this, but to make our marriage stronger. I know I need help for—for some of the things I've gone through." I've already decided I need to see a therapist, both for the OCD and the trauma I experienced, keeping my father's secrets. "I want to be better, for you as well as for me," I explain. "We both made a lot of mistakes before, but we can do things differently now. Who knows, maybe really differently." Suddenly, I feel reckless, heady. "We could leave the city. Buy a big farmhouse upstate and—and raise chickens. Live a slower, quieter kind of life." Weirdly, I realize that the thought appeals. "Get out of the rat race and the gossip mill and everything about our lives that I've come to realize we hated. This can be an opportunity, Michael, and one most people don't get."

"Well," he says wryly, leaning his head back against the pillow, "most people don't get a TBI."

I manage a shaky laugh. "True."

We are silent for a long time, and I feel like my future, my *marriage*, hangs in the balance. Then Michael takes my hand, threads his fingers through mine. It's a moment before he speaks.

"I remembered," he says quietly. "And I want to do things differently, too." He squeezes my hand. "With you."

EPILOGUE
HARRIET

Nine months later, I'm standing in front of the school steps on a sunny September morning, watching Kyra mount them, her TGS backpack slung over her shoulder as she walks in with her best friend Chloe. It's the first day of fourth grade, and I can hardly believe how much she's grown. How much has changed.

In February, after Michael came out of rehab, he and Elise ended up selling their apartment and taking the twins out of TGS. They bought a rambling old farmhouse up on the Hudson River, near Kingston, and in May, Michael started back to work part-time as a neurologist, at the aptly named Good Samaritan Hospital. The boys are in public school and Elise is in therapy. I know all this because I follow her blog, where she details the reality of living with severe OCD in a wry and compassionate way. She's already got twenty-five thousand followers and, just like Grayson, who still swans about the school, she's been on cable TV, talking about her struggles, sounding warm, honest and assured.

It seems strange to me that Elise left The Garden School, while I was the one who stayed. If I'd had to predict it, it would have been the other way around. But then, after Michael's accident and the whole lawsuit was dropped, people started coming out of the proverbial woodwork, telling me how they'd been thinking of me. I realized that the toxic, gossipy atmosphere I'd experienced by the school steps really was down to just a few women whom I now know to avoid.

Chloe's mother Kim, who was meant to be my new-school buddy back in September, texted me in January, apologizing profusely that she hadn't been in touch sooner. We go to the gym together once a week now. And Rachel, who was on the gala committee but barely said boo because she was so intimidated by Elise and Grayson, now gets a coffee with me at Bellissimo, with a few other moms who are genuinely kind and like the school for what it is, rather than the only place their kid got in. It's a nice group.

"Hey, Harriet." Joanna strolls up to me, holding Polly by the hand. In the end, she decided not to leave TGS. Like me, she learned that moving on can sometimes be running away, and it's better to face your problems... whatever they are. "Are you nervous?" she asks, nodding to the messenger bag slung over my shoulder. "You look prepared."

"I am nervous," I admit. "But I'm excited, too." After doing the sets for the Class Three play, Ms. Weil surprised me by offering me a part-time job teaching art. I'm going to go in two mornings a week, while Barbara sits with Allan.

It's just the right amount of work, because while the tofersen has certainly helped Allan, Dr. Bayler was right when he said it wasn't a miracle cure. Allan's degeneration has slowed, but he still struggles. He uses a mobility scooter now, and talking is hard. But we're together and we're happy, choosing to live in the present like I told Elise, and be thankful for what we have.

Kyra is blossoming, and my dad sold his house in Morristown and moved into a retirement condo closer to the city. We see him every few weeks and he's taken up golf, which amuses me, since he's such a blue-collar guy. But then, people can change... in all sorts of ways. Even me. Even Elise.

Maybe even anyone.

It's a thought that buoys me as I mount the steps to The Garden School. Halfway up, I catch Claire's eye. I haven't spoken to her since the whole gala debacle when she was so vicious to me, but now I notice how tired and thin she looks, her face pinched, her arm folded across her middle, and I give her a little smile and a wave.

Who knows what might happen, I think, as her jaw drops and she stares at me, startled, maybe a little suspicious, by my greeting. I keep her eye and widen my smile, and after a few tense seconds, she smiles uncertainly back.

I keep smiling as I head into the school.

A LETTER FROM KATE

Dear Reader,

I want to say a huge thank you for choosing to read *The Secret Between Us*. If you enjoyed it, and would like to keep up to date with all my latest releases, just sign up at the following link. Your email address will never be shared, and you can unsubscribe at any time.

Having sent my children to a small private school in Manhattan (although nothing like The Garden School!), I've always felt it would be a great setting for an intriguing drama around the perils of the PTA. I always enjoy tackling difficult issues from both sides, and I hope you've been able to see and relate to both Harriet's and Elise's perspectives in this story.

www.bookouture.com/kate-hewitt

I hope you loved *The Secret Between Us* and if you did, I would be very grateful if you could write a review. I'd love to hear what you think, and it makes such a difference helping new readers to discover one of my books for the first time.

I love hearing from my readers—you can get in touch on my Facebook group for readers, through Substack, Goodreads or my website.

Thanks again for reading!

Kate

katehewittbooks.com

facebook.com/groups/KatesReads
goodreads.com/author/show/1269244.Kate_Hewitt
substack.com/@katehewitt

ACKNOWLEDGMENTS

As ever, there are so many people who are part of bringing a book to see the light of day! Thank you to the whole amazing team at Bookouture who have helped with this process, from editing, copyediting, and proofreading, to designing and marketing. In particular, I'd like to thank my editor, Jess Whitlum-Cooper, as well as Imogen Allport, Laura Deacon, Mandy Kullar, and Sarah Hardy, Melanie Price in marketing, and Kim Nash in publicity, Richard King and Saidah Graham in foreign rights, and Sinead O'Connor in audio. I have really appreciated everyone's positivity and proactiveness! Thank you also to my family, who brainstormed with me some of the twists and turns in this story. In particular, my husband Cliff had a great suggestion. It's something of a joke between us that I usually dismiss his ideas when it comes to my novels, but I took this one! Thank you, and I love you!

PUBLISHING TEAM

Turning a manuscript into a book requires the efforts of many people. The publishing team at Bookouture would like to acknowledge everyone who contributed to this publication.

Audio
Alba Proko
Melissa Tran
Sinead O'Connor

Commercial
Lauren Morrissette
Hannah Richmond
Imogen Allport

Cover design
Alice Moore

Data and analysis
Mark Alder
Mohamed Bussuri

Editorial
Jess Whitlum-Cooper
Imogen Allport

Copyeditor
Jade Craddock

Proofreader
Tom Feltham

Marketing
Alex Crow
Melanie Price
Occy Carr
Cíara Rosney
Martyna Młynarska

Operations and distribution
Marina Valles
Stephanie Straub
Joe Morris

Production
Hannah Snetsinger
Mandy Kullar
Ria Clare
Nadia Michael

Publicity
Kim Nash
Noelle Holten
Jess Readett
Sarah Hardy

Rights and contracts
Peta Nightingale
Richard King
Saidah Graham

RAISING READERS
Books Build Bright Futures

Dear Reader,

We'd love your attention for one more page to tell you about the crisis in children's reading, and what we can all do.

Studies have shown that reading for fun is the **single biggest predictor of a child's future success** – more than family circumstance, parents' educational background or income. It improves academic results, mental health, wealth, communication skills, and ambition.

The number of children reading for fun is in rapid decline. Young people have a lot of competition for their time, and a worryingly high number do not have a single book at home.

Our business works extensively with schools, libraries and literacy charities, but here are some ways we can all raise more readers:

- Reading to children for just 10 minutes a day makes a difference
- Don't give up if children aren't regular readers – there will be books for them!

- Visit bookshops and libraries to get recommendations
- Encourage them to listen to audiobooks
- Support school libraries
- Give books as gifts

Thank you for reading: there's a lot more information about how to encourage children to read on our website.

www.JoinRaisingReaders.com

Printed in Dunstable, United Kingdom